THE LUC

AIMEE BROWN is a writer of romantic comedies set in Portland, Oregon, and an avid reader. She spends much of her time writing, raising three teenagers, binge-watching shows on Netflix and obsessively cleaning and redecorating her house. She's fluent in sarcasm and has been known to utter profanities like she's competing for a medal.

Aimee grew up in Oregon, but is now a transplant living in cold Montana with her husband of twenty years, three teenage children, and far too many pets. She is a lot older than she looks and yes, that is a tattoo across her chest. (In the Portlandia spirit, yes, I lived many years in PDX and I do indeed have a bird tattooed on me (2!))

Aimee is very active on social media. Stop by and say hello!

THE LUCKY DRESS

Aimee Brown

First published in the United Kingdom in 2018 by Aria, an imprint of Head of Zeus Ltd

Copyright © Aimee Brown, 2018

The moral right of Aimee Brown to be identified as the author of this work has been asserted in accordance with the Copyright, Designs and Patents Act of 1988.

All rights reserved. No part of this publication may be reproduced, stored in a retrieval system, or transmitted, in any form or by any means, electronic, mechanical, photocopying, recording, or otherwise, without the prior permission of both the copyright owner and the above publisher of this book.

This is a work of fiction. All characters, organizations, and events portrayed in this novel are either products of the author's imagination or are used fictitiously.

9 7 5 3 1 2 4 6 8

A CIP catalogue record for this book is available from the British Library.

ISBN 9781788547253

Aria
an imprint of Head of Zeus
First Floor East
5–8 Hardwick Street
London EC1R 4RG

About *The Lucky Dress*

We all have our lucky dress…

Emi Harrison hasn't been feeling particularly lucky lately. Ever since her ex-fiancée, Jack Cabot, successfully shattered her heart into a million pieces. She's managed to avoid him for a whole year, but all that's about to change at her brother Evan's wedding…

She will have to face Jack, Jack's sister, Jack's parents, and Jack's new girlfriend: a mean girl that just won't quit. What could possibly go wrong?

With her lucky dress on, all bets are off, and maybe Emi will find her happily-ever-after at last?

To Corey, my husband, who
never doubted for a second that
I was a writer.
Though, it did take fourteen years to
finally prove it to him.

<u>One</u>

A Bad Dress

Present Day

Dallas, Texas

I peer over my shoulder in an attempt to see my back in the mirror behind me. This zipper has to zip. *Has to.*

The seamstress pulls open the curtain and peeks in.

"Oh…" She taps her lips with her forefinger.

"It'll never zip," I say with a defeated sigh. And here I thought the actual wedding would be the worst part. The possibility of walking down the aisle in a dress that clearly doesn't fit would definitely make things a tad more awkward than they are already bound to be.

"Maybe a corset will help?" the seamstress smiles.

"A corset? Like, what they used to wear in the 1800's?" I ask, worried that instead of just looking like

I've put on a few pounds I'll end up with crushed ribs as well.

"Luckily they aren't quite as excruciating as they were back then. I'll just go grab one and you get undressed before I get back."

I'd collapse in the chair sitting in the corner of this dressing room but I'm afraid if I did the seams would also pop out, creating only more of an embarrassment when I finally do walk out and show Lily the disaster this thing is.

"A corset, Lily!" I yell through the curtain at my best friend. "Did you hear that? I've gained so much weight that I need to cinch it all in with a freaking corset!" I peek my face out of the edge of the curtain, only to see Lily's nod.

"I don't know what you're complaining about? I wear Spanx every day of my life," she rolls her eyes at me with a smile.

Spanx isn't even an option for me; I need the big guns of underwear to make this dress even the tiniest bit presentable.

I peel the dress off and drape it over the small chair. This bridesmaid dress reminds me of those episodes of *Say Yes to the Dress* where the Bride's entourage starts shopping for the most expensive and over the top gowns they can find but as soon as the bride slips on the dress that was beautiful on the mannequin, it turns out, the dress was made *only* for that specific mannequin.

The dress is beautiful, it's just *not* beautiful on me. It might be if I was six inches taller, thirty pounds lighter, and still had my early twenty something perky chest.

"Here we go!" The seamstress holds up a white corset in one hand and a handful of undergarments she didn't mention in the other hand. "We'll just get you tied into these and we should be good to move onto alterations."

I wish tying me into the garments was truly as easy as the seamstress had made it sound. Ten minutes of pulling, pushing, sucking it in, and adjusting, is what it took. If I breathe shallowly, the agonizingly uncomfortable corset nearly does the trick. But, since there are still a few uh, lumpy areas, I slide on the high waisted Spanx-like underwear that hit me just below the breast and just over the corset. The seamstress then insists I step into a slip that flares at the bottom, obviously to help the dress that does the same look a little more… the way it should.

I do a spin in front of the mirror in the dressing room. It's not the most graceful spin but it does show off the areas I normally try to hide.

"I might have to wear this stuff under everything." If only my ass could look this good in my favorite pair of jeans.

"Ha!" the seamstress laughs. "Let's try the dress again."

Since I can no longer lift my legs to step into the dress she pulls it over my head and this time it doesn't get caught up anywhere, sliding effortlessly from my chest to the floor.

"See, much improvement. Now to just alter the length and any last minute fixes."

"Wow, I do look a little more hourglass shaped, don't I?"

"A good seamstress can work miracles."

She isn't kidding. If only I could bring her with me to the wedding to make sure all the miracles I need can be worked out, like a fairy godmother of sorts.

"How's it look?" Lily calls from her seat near the dressing room and display pedestal.

"Like it's painted on..." I sigh.

"That's something, come on out."

The seamstress pulls the curtain open and takes my hand, helping me waddle out into the room before pointing me to the pedestal I'm to stand on for alterations.

"Wow," Lily says, reaching out to take both my hands and force me onto it. "You're a little stiff."

"A little stiff? I'm wrapped like a freaking mummy under this thing." I gain my balance on the pedestal, three mirrors staring back at me almost illuminating all the things I hoped the ancient underwear would hide.

"How will you ever walk like a normal human being in this?"

"No idea."

"Is it even the right size?" Lily is now walking around me, looking me up and down from every angle.

"It is now, after crushing my internal organs into everything I'm wearing underneath it. It should have fit to my measurements I sent Hannah a few months ago, though."

When I finally tried this dress on this morning at my apartment I couldn't get it up over my waist. I knew if I pulled any further I'd have ended up in tears, with a shredded dress and Hannah would hate me for years to come. That's when I started to panic and gave up, deciding that I would cross my fingers, call the alterations lady and hope she could work some serious magic.

"It's a beautiful dress, but it's just so—"

"Tight?" I finish the sentence for her.

Lily and I have known each other a long time so finishing each other's sentences, even unintentionally, is something we just do.

Lily nods, her face scrunched into an awkward smile. "Sure, tight is one word," she makes her way to the pink velvet couch facing the pedestal I'm standing on, her arms crossed over her chest. "Can you even sit? Or walk without looking knock-kneed?"

I glance down at the dress. It is pretty, and on anyone a size two and under it'd probably be va-va-voom gorgeous without any extra unseen help. The medieval underwear I'm referring to does appear to be helping fake that look though. My boobs look fantastic too. I'm not sure they've sat this high on my chest since I was in my early twenties. The rest of me... well, it pretty much fits like a glove. The latex kind. Or like one of those nude statues that have got the clothing painted on and you can hardly tell. That'll be me, *miss, the dress didn't fit so we've hired a professional body painter to fake it.*

The dress is made of a gray shimmery material that fits like a second skin all the way to the knees, where it then flares out and is covered in black and gray feathers that are seemingly dipped in gold glitter. I'd preferred it to be strapless but no, it's got these droopy sequined off the shoulder straps that allow me to lift my arms just inches from my body.

I glance over at the shoes sitting peacefully on the sofa next to Lily. They're strappy, glittery, platform, and at least ten inches high. Well, OK, maybe not *ten* inches, but it feels that way. The fact that I can't take full steps in this skirt anyway will prove either helpful or hurtful with said shoes. I'm that girl who has fallen in the middle of the sidewalk wearing no heels at all, so these ones aren't giving me much hope for grace and poise when walking down an aisle in front of everyone I know.

"I'm not sure I can walk at all with the combo of layers; cinched up underwear, a skin tight dress and stripper shoes..." I chew on my bottom lip as I stare into the tri-fold full length mirrors in front of me. I wonder if this is one of those deceptively flattering mirrors Elaine is always going on about in *Seinfeld*? Probably instead of me looking lovely, I look more like an overstuffed sausage.

"It doesn't look completely terrible now," Lily reassures me with a small grin. That's what best friends do, they're honest until you can't take it and then they just find the best honest quality and talk up that angle. She was also unlucky enough to witness my panic of the dress not fitting at my apartment this morning. "The underwear does help. You just look stiff."

"I'm a little worried that if I take a full breath something will pop, the dress will explode and the impending underwear malfunction will be the center of some viral video before the wedding is even over." The last thing I need is an internet worthy video surfacing to prove that I was not at all ready for this week.

I force myself to look away from the mirror and watch the seamstress, who is kneeling at my feet and already working on the necessary alterations. Swiftly pinning the hem, just above the feathers, so I don't drag it across the floor.

I'm not exactly tall, standing at only five foot three, and since Hannah didn't think of how a dress like this fits a short girl, this poor woman has a long night of hemming ahead of her I'm afraid.

Seamstress Lady, whose name I still don't know, isn't all that exciting looking considering she works in a bridal shop that looks like you've just stepped into a giant, sparkly, tulle cloud. Her gray hair is piled high on her head and her dress is a plain black version of Mrs Doubtfire's dresses, including the drabby cardigans. She's kind of depressing looking. I can imagine the bridezilla's she's had to work with over the years have drilled her down into what she is today.

"I have to ask," Lily breaks the silence. "What's with the shiny gray material anyway?"

I've wondered this myself. Gray, I can see, it's one of my favorite colors. But the muted sheen of the fabric is not helping to hide imperfections.

"Her official wedding colors are black, gray, and pink."

"It's so depressing, Emi. It kind of makes me sad just looking at it. I mean seriously, it's the color of gray skies or an impending tornado and you know as well as I do that isn't a color that brings out anything but dread."

Lily taps her phone, taking a photo so I can remember this disastrous moment for a lifetime. "I've just never seen anything like it in a bridesmaid dress. She may as well have wrapped you in foil. I mean seriously, you look like a foil wrapped burrito from Del Taco."

Great.

"Thanks," I mumble.

Only a best friend could be as blunt as Lily and add to my list of clothing styles not to wear. I already do a fine job of that myself. When you're a short girl and wear what clothing companies consider plus size, you might as well just have a seamstress on call for alterations to anything you purchase. For some reason, clothing designers seem to think that if you're not a sample size that you're unreasonably tall. My boobs are big, my legs are short, my hips are the tiniest bit wider than I'd like, and my thighs shudder at the phrase *thigh gap*. I am thankful for that last part as my lack of thigh gap has prevented me from accidentally dropping my phone into the toilet a time or three.

"Can you let it out at all?" Lily is talking to the seamstress who's still knelt at my feet.

"No," she shakes her head. "You don't let a dress like this out. You take it in," she says in a sharp irritated voice. "Did she order you two sizes above your actual size? Formal dresses always run small. Someone should have told her to order up." She doesn't stop pinning while she talks, and can somehow speak with a mouth full of pins. If it was me, I'd be on my way to the nearest Emergency Room, because I'd have swallowed at least one of them.

"That's likely the problem. She didn't order it from a store. She designed it and was supposed to make it fit my measurements." I glance down at Alteration Lady, who rolls her eyes without speaking and goes back to pinning. She must have dealt with designers before.

"News flash," Lily flashes jazz hands into the air. "Yours doesn't fit. Maybe you gained some weight since you sent her your measurements?" she suggests.

"Lil, I've gained nearly thirty pounds in the last year. I threw out my scale a while ago, so I have no doubt that my ass has only got bigger since measurement day six months ago."

It's not completely my fault that I've gained some weight. It happens when you own a coffee shop and you love everything you serve. It wouldn't be right to set out pastries that I hadn't tested. I mean, what if they were bad? When I test one I know they are the quality that I want to serve. Plus, who doesn't drink five lattes a day? Opening a business on your own, two thousand miles from the life you never thought you'd leave, is stressful.

Why didn't I think of faking my measurements and adding an inch, maybe three, to all of them in the first place? Probably because I had planned to start going to the gym, I bought a membership for, so I could actually lose the thirty pounds before having to go face a room full of people, I never thought I'd see again. Those gym salesmen really have a way with all the right words, making you as excited about joining the gym as if it was your own stupid idea.

I should have known that this dress would be as sexy as possible, though. Hannah has always been a bit on the sexy side. Her parents sent her on a trip around the world after she graduated college so she could find out what she wanted to do with her life. None of us were shocked when she settled on fashion. Now that she's well on her way to planning her new fashion lines she's only really been working on the wedding and her clothing label, *Hannah*. That's it. No last name, no cutesy *Miss Me* title, just *Hannah*. She said she wanted her brand to exude simple, classy, and elegant. If I'm honest, I can see almost all of that in this bridesmaid gown, except for the fact that I'm the one wearing it. I guess it's time for me to finally admit that I'll never be a fashion model. I haven't seen the wedding gown yet but after seeing this dress, I'm a little nervous just how sexy or over the top it will be?

"I think you should call her and show her every flawed inch of this thing, *without* the underwear assistance, unless you actually think you can survive a full day of being in it?" Lily is now pacing the floor, her irritation starting to bubble over. "If she plans to run a business doing custom designs, she needs to pay more attention to her clients' body types," her lips are pinched together and her eyebrows raised. "I know if I ordered this from her and it fit the way this one does, I'd refuse to pay her and go somewhere else. It's appalling."

Lily may or may not be the bitchier one in our relationship. She doesn't hold back. If you don't want to know what she thinks, don't ask. I have an unspoken appreciation for it. Her bitchiness is handy in a variety of situations and she's somehow become successful because of it.

She is head of English at a small private college here in Dallas. Let's just say, she's the professor about whom students use the phrase "Oh... you got *McConnell*? Sucky." She knows it and she loves it. The fear of the kids as they walk into her class is better than a cup of coffee for Lily.

"Grab my phone and FaceTime her," I say. "Let's see what she thinks. Maybe I'll get lucky and look so terrible that she'll decide I don't even have to go."

"You know that won't happen, she's marrying your brother." Lily taps at my phone before turning it to me making sure it's a full body shot.

"OH! Emi!" Hannah's face fills the screen without me even hearing the phone ring. "Wow! What do you think?"

"I think I can barely breathe, I definitely can't sit, and I'm pretty sure it's way too small?" I ask it as a question, hoping to God I'm right and she'll offer to whip up a new one in the next three days.

"No, it's not too small. It's supposed to be very Marilyn Monroe vintage. I think you look gorgeous! It's exactly how I pictured it!"

Lily's eyebrows rise again behind the phone, a smirk creeping up on her face. She's probably glad Hannah can't see it because it would give away her disapproval. Obviously, Hannah and I have different ideas of 'gorgeous.'

"Um, it's exactly as you pictured because underneath it all I'm tied in as tight as possible! Without the helpfulness of the torturous underwear, I definitely would not look this... curvy," I opt for a word that is kind of code for fat. I slide my hands down my sides, enjoying the feeling of fake perfection while I can. "I can't wear this for more than a few hours, Hannah, I'll crush my insides!"

"Shut up! No one thinks you're fat!" She immediately cracks my code word. "You look totally hot. And I, for one, know for a fact that even Jack will be smitten."

I force away an irritated sigh. "I don't *want* him to be smitten, Hannah." I snap at her into the phone. She knows as well as I do that any conversation topic that starts with the words *Jack*, or *My brother*, is off limits. "I want him to be miserable." He deserves at least that.

I already know that this is going to be a mess of a week. Jack and I have been separated for one year. Not a single day goes by that I don't relive everything that happened. Part of me is going to this wedding to support my brother Evan, and his now fiancée Hannah while they take the path that Jack and I never quite got to. Part of me is going just to prove to myself that Jack is exactly the guy I witnessed the day we broke up. But, I'll be the first to admit, a tiny part of me, a part that I keep buried as far down as possible, somehow keeps finding its way to the surface and wants to know if I'm over Jack, or if he's over me. Or if the getting over part is even conceivable?

Two

The Break Up

Nine months ago.

Portland, Oregon

"I'm doing a final alteration because I've lost another five pounds, Lil. If you're free today do you want to come with me?" I ask her before she can even say hello into the phone. That's our relationship, we start conversations in the middle and expect the other to keep up.

"Sure. My classes today were canceled due to some flooding issue at the school, so if you promise to let me drink the champagne this time, I'll come."

"You might have a problem, ya know?" If only she could hear my eye roll through the phone. "It's a fitting. I don't think they serve champagne at the fittings. We're not in Beverly Hills. They likely save the champagne for the initial dress consultation when you need a little buttering up to spend thousands of dollars on a dress you'll only wear for one day."

"It's Friday, I have an unexpected day off, and if I want to drink at 9:30 in the morning I'm gonna," she laughs into the phone. "I'll meet you there in twenty.'

Thirty minutes later and I'm walking into the bridal salon. Lily is reclined on the couch waiting for me.

"Sorry, I'm late. I planned on being early but you know me."

She nods her head in agreement. "What was it this time? A pair of shoes you couldn't leave behind?" she glances at my worn old vintage Doc Martin boots. "A coffee shop you hadn't been to before, then?" She waves her hand in the air as if there is a never ending list of excuses I use when I'm late.

The list isn't exactly never ending because I'm not always lying. At times it does take me a while to come up with a believable story for why I'm late. That is not the case this time.

"Neither. Lara's husband just called and she fell on her way into work this morning and shattered her ankle. She's on her way into surgery now and he wanted to let me know that she can't be a bridesmaid," I heave a sigh, trying to hold back the tears hesitating just behind it. These kinds of things are not supposed to happen two days before your wedding. "How in one day am I going to find someone who can fit into her tiny dress to replace her?"

I went to college with Lara and she is quite possibly the sweetest woman I've ever met. She works as an editor in a small publishing company based here in Portland, and she is one of those girls who refuses to use a red pen on her clients' work because she doesn't want to seem too harsh. Having to drop out of the wedding via a phone call from her husband is probably killing her.

"Ugh, Em, I don't know. That's not good news on such short notice," Lily frowns, her irritated that I'm late attitude melting away into something a tad less harsh.

"Emi!" Glenda (the woman who's done all my fittings) excitedly pulls me in for a hug. "It's almost here, are you excited?"

"Sure," I try to hide the disappointment in finding out I now have only a Maid of Honor and no bridesmaid which throws off the total balance of the entire wedding party.

"Uh-oh... What happened? I'm sure there's a fix."

"My bridesmaid, Lara, just dropped out at the eleventh hour." I wipe away an escaped tear rolling down my cheek. I don't know what it is about planning weddings but they seem to bring out a woman's emotional side, even when she didn't exactly know she had one.

"She didn't *drop out*," Lily corrects me. "The girl is injured and in surgery. That's hardly dropping out."

"Oh no. The tiny one?" Glenda suddenly side eyes Lily with a forced smile. Lily glares over at us for basically just calling her the big one, even though she's still smaller than me.

"Yes! Who could possibly fit into that dress?"

"Hmm..." Glenda taps her foot on the ground. "What about the young woman that was here for your fitting? The gorgeous blonde one?"

"Hannah?" Lily scrunches her face in disapproval. She's never loved Hannah quite the way I do, even though they spend a lot of time together.

In Lily's defense, Hannah was kind of an add on to our friend circle mostly because I was dating her brother Jack. We are all close to the same age and Hannah was always the girl to invite herself to anything Lily and I, or Jack and I for that matter, were doing. After a while, you just start to assume that she'll be anywhere you are. The only thing is, Hannah always seems to be trying to pinch Lily's BFF title. It'll never happen, but that doesn't mean Hannah won't continue to try.

"You think?" I ask Lily, who's still shaking her head.

"No way. She's the most annoying woman on the planet. Nothing is ever up to her standards. Plus, she'll probably try to squeeze me out of Maid of Honor spot since now she'll 'officially' be family."

The quotes Lily is using around officially are the exact air quotes that Hannah uses when she compares being family to being my BFF.

Having two best friends never works, and this is exactly why. There are just too many opportunities for jealousy, talking about someone behind their back, and someone feeling left out. I've tried to make it very clear to Hannah that she's going to be my sister-in-law, and that is just as important as Lily being my best friend, but she's not buying it.

But sisters should be best friends, she whined to me one day while I was planning the bridal party.

"She might be my only option," I look to Lily whose frown is still lingering on her face. "She was pretty disappointed when I told her I was only having two bridesmaids and she wasn't one of them."

Jack had asked a friend from high school and a friend from college to be his groomsmen, and I figured I would do the same. Even though he and Evan are really close, he didn't ask Evan to be one of the groomsmen, just another reason why I didn't ask Hannah. I might look pathetic if I could only get a friend from high school and a future family member to stand at my side during the wedding as if I had no other friends.

"See if she can stop by today and I'll make any necessary alterations before you pick up the dresses tomorrow." Glenda smiles sweetly. "Now come, let's try on this dress and see just how much you've shrunk!"

Five pounds is not as much as I hoped it was. It was only a few pins for Glenda. No wonder she said she could get it done and move my pick up time from tomorrow morning to tonight. The alteration will probably take her ten minutes tops.

"You look beautiful," Lily grins, as I walk out to model, her approval clear on her face. "I can't believe Amelia let you get this one and not her top pick."

Amelia is Jack's mom and since my mom passed a while back, she's been the one helping me plan this over the top wedding that I never even knew I wanted. Our theme is something along the lines of Old Hollywood, so the gold sequined art deco fitted, yet flowing, dress she chose, was beautiful, it just was not me.

"How could she have said no? I love this one."

It truly is the most beautiful dress I've ever seen. I'm not a flashy girl so there isn't a lot of pizzazz in this dress. It's off-white, alternating matte and glossy charmeuse panels that create a subtle chevron pattern making me look much slimmer than I am. A trail of buttons runs from the plunging back all the way to the hem. I decided to stay with the Old Hollywood theme and wear the small headpiece veil as opposed to the long dramatic one. It's just more me to stay simple. It's vintage but without all the glitter and glam that I so wanted to avoid.

"It's going to be a gorgeous wedding." Glenda beams at her previous work of fitting me into a dress that was a size too big when I bought it.

"It will. OK, as much as I'd love to wear this dress all day, I need to get going. I'm meeting Jack for lunch and we're picking up the tuxedos and then we have to meet with Megan for a quick run through of everything to be done over the next twenty-four hours."

"Why does she need your help with that? Aren't you paying her to plan the wedding? I'd think the decisions would've been set in stone by now."

"Of course, they are," I say through the dressing room curtain. "She just likes to make sure we know everything that's happening so problems don't arise. It's why she costs so much," I explain.

I glance around the curtain to see Lily shrug her shoulders. Lily didn't have the big formal wedding. She decided to bring a few of her closest friends and family to Mexico where she eloped in a flowing dress on the beach. It was gorgeous, quick, and very Lily. No wedding planner needed.

"What are you doing the rest of the day, Lil?" I ask through the curtain as Glenda helps me get out of the dress without poking a needle through my skin. A bloodstain is the last thing I need on a wedding dress right now.

"I'll probably go home and watch talk shows all day."

"Perfect," I say sarcastically, knowing Lily lives for talk shows and has since we were tweens. Not that they are anything like they were back then. Sally Jesse Raphael, Jenny Jones, and Montel were all the rage back in those days. Nothing like a little night time news murder coverage to go with a storyline you first learned about on the daytime talk shows. Now the shows are so boring, you have *The View, The Talk*, and not as much family drama makes it to the shows unless you're a politician or celebrity, and let's face it, those stories are at times yawn worthy.

I give Glenda Hannah's number as I leave the shop and make my way to the Max station to grab a train downtown to Jack's office. His office makes me wish I'd become a lawyer instead of playing it safe and studying business management. I guess all those years of student loans make for a great office space. Granted it's only on the third floor level of a building right downtown, but he's got a corner office facing a busy street and it's really great for people watching. The best part, though, is that I helped him decorate it *Mad Men* style, so it's got a retro-cool feel to it that just screams you need a martini the second you walk through the door.

"Hey, Andy" I greet the head of the firm as I walk past his opened office door and he waves me in.

Andy Morgan is the top dog at *Morgan, Steller & Cabot*. He's been in the business longer than I've been alive and according to Jack, he's the best of the best. He's won cases that nobody thought possible, and he's taken Jack in like the son he's never had. He may be a little creepy at times, although, according to Jack that's only because he's on his fourth marriage and just can't seem to keep his hands to himself when it comes to random women. It's safe to say I keep my distance.

"So, you're stealing our boy away for three weeks after today, huh?"

"That's right, and if I need to I'll throw his phone into the ocean too."

We both laugh, even though I know it might actually happen. I swear I never knew lawyers were on the clock 24/7 until I got involved with one. He seems to always be needed to answer a question or update someone on a case they are looking into.

"I supposed that'll be OK. Hey, I wanted to give you this before the wedding." Andy grabs an envelope off his desk and walks over to me, dropping it into my opened hand. "I truly hope this wedding will be the only marriage you'll ever need." He winks as he walks back to his desk chair, settling in to watch me open his surprise. "Go on, open it."

I hate opening gifts in front of people. I'm totally that girl who since her teens has requested no gifts at my parties. What if what they gave you is embarrassing or horrible? How do you keep your face from going with your feelings as opposed to the *thank you* coming out of your mouth? Normally that's what gives me away. Despite my best efforts, my face doesn't always match my words.

When I open the card a check glides to the floor, landing at my feet. I reach down and grab it, stunned for a moment over the amount it's made out for.

"Five thousand dollars? What? Andy... we can't—"

"Yes, you can," he demands from his desk with a stern look on his face. "Now, I never had kids and you two are special to me. I want to make sure you get the best start."

"Wow, well…Thank you." Thank you seems nowhere near the appropriate response, but it's all I know how to do.

"Now go, find that fiancé of yours."

"Thank you again, Andy." I back out of his office safely shoving the card and check into my bag before heading down the hall towards Jack's office.

"Hey, Mad—" I start to say hello to Jack's assistant Madison when I realize she's not sitting at her desk. She was hired about a month ago, so I don't know her well, but she always seems like the sweetest woman whenever I'm here. She's just out of school as a legal assistant and she really has helped Jack with organizing his cases and information.

"Are you ready?" I open Jack's office door and hear a startled squeal to my left. I turn towards Madison, who is nearly completely naked, and straddling Jack face to face on the couch. She has a hand in his hair, and another on his shoulder.

For a second my head spins until I finally pull myself together. She nonchalantly grabs an article of clothing from the arm of the couch, a haughty smile on her face.

"Emi!" Jack pushes her aside and jumps up while trying to straighten his rumpled shirt and tie. "It's not what you think."

For a moment I don't even know what I think or even why I'm here. As I glance around the room to see if what's happening is actually happening, it feels as if my feet are suddenly giant cement blocks attached to the floor preventing me from just getting the hell out.

"Ems," Jack is kneeling on the floor grabbing my purse that has fallen there and picking up the things that have rolled out. I stare down at him, unable to speak. "I was not having sex with her. I know it looked bad but that's not what happened."

Have you ever actually truly experienced the moment your heart breaks into a million pieces? I swear there is an audible sound. Like a shatter that turns into heart wrenching silent sobs which only you can feel.

I shove away the silent sobbing and allow the rage to quickly take over.

"Why are you even in here?" I yell at Madison, who is taking her sweet time walking around the room picking up her stray pieces of clothing.

"What does it look like I was doing?" She smirks before disappearing into Jack's private bathroom.

"Please, let me explain," Jack begs, his hand resting on my arm and his face as pale as if he had just seen a ghost. His dark hair is disheveled and unruly, and all I can picture is her hands running through it.

"What. The. Fuck. Jack? How could you do this to me?"

"I didn't. I... uh... I..." He stumbles over his words, kicks Madison's shoes out of his way and takes a few steps towards me as I back away from him.

"Give me that!" I jerk my bag from his hands and turn to the hallway to make my escape.

"Emi, stop." He grabs my arm gently, pulling me back into his office and shutting the door. "Please, Em, let me explain." He's leaning over me, my back against the door, his words echoing directly into my ear.

But, the sobbing from within is more than I can think through. The words my mom once said after I had a break up in high school suddenly swirl through my head. *There is no excuse for cheating, none. Find someone who will love you the way you deserve.*

The pain from my heart breaking rushes up to my throat, pushing the tears close to flooding down my cheeks but I somehow choke them back.

"I can't. There is nothing to explain. I saw what I saw, now please, Jack, just let me leave with a little bit of grace," my voice cracks and for a moment I don't think he's going to let me out of his office but he takes a step back, the pain on his face is obvious, though it can't even compare to what I'm feeling inside.

I jerk the door open, slamming it against the bookcase behind it and speed walk down the hall, stopping momentarily in front of Andy's office, who is now out of his chair and nearly in his own doorway, trying to see what the commotion is about.

"Please, Emi, just talk to me," Jack begs behind me.

I turn to face him, just a few feet between us, Andy watching the scene play out. I can't even pretend that what I saw was right on any level. He allowed Madison to be nearly naked, and *on* him, touching him. If he truly loved me it should have stopped long before it reached that point.

I take a deep breath, pushing down the feelings that are starting to suffocate me.

"She can have you." I pull the three carat diamond off my finger and for a moment I stare at it. I'm supposed to marry Jack in two days. When I hear him take a step towards me, I wipe away the tears so he maybe won't notice them. "Don't follow me. I've got nothing to say to you." I pitch the ring at his head and watch him duck before scrambling to pick it up off the floor.

While he's preoccupied with finding the irreplaceable family heirloom I run to the stairwell. When I hear the heavy door boom behind me a flight up I know I might make a getaway without him. I continue to run three blocks before dodging into a parking garage.

"Are you OK?" I hear a voice behind me and realize I'm leaning on this man's car, sobbing. "Can I get you some help?"

I shake my head and wander in a daze to the garage stairwell. I collapse onto one of the stairs and start sobbing into my own knees. Jack is the one guy who I thought would never ever do this to me. I fell in love with him almost the first moment we met and now he throws it all away for some receptionist. How humiliating will it be to have to tell people the wedding is off and why? I mean, Jack can move on with his new piece of ass but *I'm* the one who didn't measure up. *I'm* the one who didn't deserve to know that things weren't going well. *I'm* the one who Jack apparently didn't really want to marry and he chose to tell me like this? Yet again, *I'm* the one who wasn't wanted. I can't face him. I can't face any of them.

I pull my phone from my bag and tap Lily's name.

"Can I come over?" the sobs I've tried to hold back pour into the phone.

"Of course, are you crying?! What happened?"

"Crying? Yeah. It's a long story. I'll be there in a few."

How do I explain over the phone that I just caught my fiancé, the man I loved more than anything in the world, underneath his nearly nude receptionist two days before our wedding? How could this happen? How could I have not seen this coming? I thought there were always signs of a cheating boyfriend, but I sure didn't see any. He can't possibly be that good a liar, can he?

"What happened?" Lily ushers me into her apartment an hour or so later, wearing a look of worry I haven't seen since my mother died.

I've had a lot of time to think about what I saw on my way over and I don't feel good about it, but at least I found out before I was standing in front of a church full of people that would silently judge me.

"He's cheating," my voice cracks again as I try to hold back the seemingly never ending sobbing. I walk across the room, throwing myself face first onto her couch. "I caught him with Madison in his office."

"You what? No way, Ems, Jack would nev⌐

"He did!" I jerk up off the couch and yell it at poison. "It's been replaying in my head for the last I saw it! I'm not just imagining things. She was on h⌐ ON him, Lily." I exaggerate the words so she understands just how serious this is. Life altering, really.

"It doesn't make sense? Jack adores you."

"Apparently not enough to keep his hands off his receptionist." I lie back on the couch and cover my face with a blanket draped over the back. "Maybe I wasn't enough. Maybe he got in too deep and didn't know how to tell me he wanted out? It's not like we're from the same worlds. Let's face it, Lil, we both know Jack is way out of my league. He could have anyone he wanted. Madison, Claudia Schiffer, Kendall Kardashian, even you! I just don't know how I didn't see it coming? Am I really that unlovable…"

*

I'm not sure what happened; one minute I'm sobbing and rambling to Lily about Jack, and the next I hear a door shutting and Lily is walking in with a pizza, her husband Josh behind her carrying two bottles of wine.

"What's going on?" I ask.

"Um, you stopped making sense about five minutes into your story so I may or may not have slipped you a Xanax." Lily attempts a guilty smile. "After that, you cried yourself to sleep, and I have been declining Jack's calls all afternoon."

"And I heard about all the crying and thought some booze was in order," Josh says, not wasting any time filling his plate with a pile of pizza and shoving my legs off the couch so he can sit in his usual spot in front of the TV.

"He called?" I pull the blanket off and make my way across the room to the wine.

"Yeah, he called you, he called me, he called Josh, he even called Evan. I finally answered and agreed I'd try to convince you to go talk to him later."

"No way." I pour wine into the biggest milk glass I can find, all the way to the top, with Lily side eyeing me from the opposite side of the table.

"That's a lot of wine."

"Not yet it isn't."

"Can I give you some advice?" Josh talks in between pizza bites. Putting down a plate of food, no matter how serious the situation may be, has never been Josh's strong point.

"Do you have to?" I ask, more than irritated, having no patience for stupid ideas right now.

"Go and talk to him. This isn't like Jack. I'm sure there's more to the story." He bites off the end of a piece of pizza. "I'm not saying go over there and forgive him and take him back, but at least hear him out."

I down half the glass of wine and set it on the table. "He doesn't deserve to be heard. I saw what I saw and even if Madison somehow accidentally fell on top of him, how did her clothes accidentally get strewn across the room?"

"True enough, still, doesn't seem like something Jack, of all people, would do."

As Josh speaks, I drink down the other half of the glass of wine and set it on the table.

"Fine. He gets five minutes. Drive me?" I ask Lily who nods, grabbing her purse and keys from the chair next to her.

*

Jack and I live in a high-rise building on the river downtown. We are on the fifteenth floor and our apartment was originally overlooking the river and city beyond it, but after we moved in they started construction on a building next to ours and now our view is the living room of the elderly couple next door. Thankfully, they keep their curtains closed most of the time and when they don't they spend a lot of time waving every single time we walk into the room.

I make my way to the elevator, glancing in both directions before sliding my key card and choosing my floor. When the elevator doors slide open on the fifteenth floor, I hear it, Jack's voice.

Our apartment is only a door away from the elevator so we often hear loud conversations as people make their way down the hall to their apartments. I make my way to the edge of the elevator, peering around the wall, hoping not to be seen.

"What are you doing here?" Jack asks a woman standing at our door. She's tall, lanky, wearing shorts that could cross over as lingerie and a hooded jacket that is covering just enough of her that I can only see long blonde hair draped down her chest.

"I heard you're newly single and thought you might need someone to talk to?" She runs her perfectly manicured finger down the front of his t-shirt before standing on her tiptoes and planting her lips on his cheek. "I'm a great listener."

Ugh! I'd know her fake woe-is-me voice anywhere. Greta. The girl who's been flirting with Jack since the day she met him, despite knowing that he's with me.

I can almost audibly hear my heart burst in my chest for the second time today, and rain down through my insides, crushing any hopeful feelings that were still hanging on.

Jack says nothing, only opens the door for her to enter and steps aside as she does, closing the door behind her.

"What in the holy fuck?" I say in a near whisper as I step back into the elevator. I can barely breathe or even think about what to do next. All I can see is my wedding day and me standing at the front of the church, watching Jack try and decide if I'm the right choice out of the three girls it appears he's got lined up.

He knows I hate Greta. She's made my life miserable because she thinks I'm not good enough for Jack, and now not only is she in my apartment but him letting her in there pretty much shows me what choice he's made.

I slide my card through the elevator keycard reader and click the button for the lobby. As I walk through it I don't even know what I feel. I want to say rage but it's not, it's more numbness than anything else. I'm humiliated.

"What happened?" Lily asks as I slide into her car silently.

"Is Josh still considering the transfer to Dallas?"

Josh is from Dallas, he went to medical school in Portland and was recently offered an opportunity to work at the same hospital his father works at. I was devastated when I heard my best friend would probably be moving thousands of miles away but maybe this is how things were meant to be.

"Yeah..."

"How do you feel about taking me with you?" Sometimes, life throws something at you that you have escaped. Sometimes, you just need a new life.

"Emi, what happened up there?"

"He let Greta into our apartment. She kissed him. He didn't turn her away." I glance over at Lily, a single tear sliding down my cheek before I can wipe it away. "I can't stay here, Lil. I'm mortified. I can't face all those people expecting to see us get married this weekend."

"Oh my God, Emi. I'm so sorry. Yes. I won't say a word, it'll be a fresh new start," Lily rubs my back for a moment before finally putting the car in drive and leaving behind what I thought was my perfect life.

Three

Working Up The Nerve

Present Day

Dallas, Texas

"Today is the day, huh? Are you nervous?" Alisha, the assistant manager at The Coffee Bean, my coffee shop, knows good and well that I'm nervous.

I'm pretty sure it's all I've talked about for the last three months. I've searched high and low for reasons to not go to this wedding but Evan, my twin brother, and also the groom, won't approve of any of them.

"I think you owe it to yourself really. It'll be a chance to prove that you really are over him."

"You can stop making sense now," I say as I sit at my desk staring at the email. Normally I would delete it as soon as it came in but for some reason, I just couldn't delete this one without reading it. He wasn't mean, or rude, or anything really. Just to the point. *We need to talk, please give me at least that.*

The second it appeared I sent Lily an SOS text and she's now on her way over at the speed of light to talk me off the cliff I'm edging towards.

Alisha throws her hands in the air with an audible huff as she makes her way back to the counter. Hearing the business of people at the counter is a tad relieving because it means Alisha can go back to work and I can talk this through with Lily when she gets here. Don't get me wrong, I love Alisha, but it's hard to explain the feelings I've had over the last few months to a woman who's only seen the after effects of things.

"What happened!?" Lily says as she races through the office door.

"He wants to talk," I point to the opened email.

Lily leans over me, a single eyebrow raised before she finally rolls her eyes and takes a seat in the corner.

"I think it's time for the speech."

I nod. I know she's right. It's actually something she came up with not long after I opened the shop. Sometimes, a girl just needs a little reassurance that she's doing the right thing. Something she can hear herself say out loud until it becomes reality.

"I do not need Jack Cabot. I've moved on, I'm happy, and my life is exactly what I wanted it to be, here, in Dallas, thousands of miles from where I once had the worst day of my life." I recite.

"Good… and…" she prompts.

"I am over Jack Cabot. I don't love him anymore and that feels great." I *almost* believe myself when I say this.

Lily nods with a smile. "See, don't you feel better?"

I raise a single eyebrow. "I guess so." I don't. In fact, it feels different this time because I know that in just a matter of days, I'll have to finally face Jack in person. It's easy to believe a lie when you never have to actually encounter the truth.

"Can I get some help out here?" Alisha yells across the room. Sending Lily and I both into the crowded room. The door dings as someone leaves and when I look in that direction I swear I see the back of Jack walking away, but there's no way. Is there? I shake my head, hoping to bring myself back to reality. He doesn't even know I run this place. I've made sure of that.

"Didn't you tell me when we first met that the whole reason you came down here and opened this shop was to prove to yourself that someone else didn't define you? You could be anything you wanted. You could create your own happiness. What happened to that girl?" Alisha asks, knowing that my little speech in my office didn't exactly up my self esteem the way I'd hoped it would.

"She sometimes temporarily flees." I sigh as I wipe down the counters after our crowd finally dies down. "I looked him up on Facebook last night, something I promised I'd never do and despite my best wishes, he's not fat, he's not poor, and he's not ugly. If anything, he looks better."

"Then what's the problem?"

"Look at me!" I throw my hands out. "I had to be sculpted with medieval underwear to even present this bridesmaid dress at all. And he's all suave and lady killer as usual."

And he had the nerve to send me the email asking for a chat making sure I would indeed be at the wedding because he had some things to get off his chest and needed to do it in person. A final farewell to make himself feel better and free himself of any lingering guilt.

Although, I've been staring at this email for twenty-four hours now and it has a different ring to the ones he'd sent before. The ones where he begged me to please just see him so he could explain things. The more stubborn I was, the angrier he got. He deserved to feel what I felt.

I don't blame him. I mean sure, I had every right to be mad, hurt, even heartbroken but, I did leave him with having to deal with his family and the canceling of the wedding. The only people who know what happened that day are me, Lily, Jack, Josh, Madison, Greta, and Alisha. I didn't even have the nerve to tell Evan or Hannah what actually went down because I have never been so embarrassed in all my life. I spent so many amazing years with the man of my dreams only for him to yank them away just days before our wedding.

The Coffee Bean has helped me dump all that frustration and anger into something that's been really good for me. Without it, I'd probably still be wallowing around Lily's apartment watching sappy romance movies all day, eating daily cartons of Ben & Jerry's. With the shop I'm earning a living, making some friends, and actually, having a lot of fun.

"Do you have everything? Josh will be by to pick you up in the next ten minutes. Dress? Suitcases? Makeup? Toiletries?" she glances over my many hot pink bags sitting near the front door. She raises on eyebrow and says, "The Lucky Dress?"

"Shhh..." I say glancing around for wherever Lily has disappeared to. "Lily and Josh can't know about that. It's just um... just in case."

"Right..." Alisha laughs, holding both hands in the air with her fingers crossed. "Just in case."

I don't know what just in case means but it can't hurt to bring it.

The honk of the cab outside startles me out of my daydream. I start grabbing bags as the front door pulls open, Josh on his way in and Lily following me out.

"Remember, you're just closing the door to the past and moving on, for good. Jack Cabot does not own you, does not deserve you, and you are over him."

I nod, "Got it."

"Is this something we're going to have to chant the whole way there?" Josh asks with a roll of his eyes.

"Maybe..." Lily says, grabbing one of the bags and wheeling it to the back of the cab.

"This is it! Your brother and Hannah's wedding. Are you even a little bit excited?" Lily asks, attempting to change the subject from Jack to Evan.

"Of course, I'm excited. Evan is my only brother. I can't help the fact that he fell in love with my ex-fiancé's only sister, can I?"

"Completely out of your control," Lily says as she pats my back with a smile.

"Also, out of your control, whether it ends up as one big episode of Jerry Springer," Josh laughs to himself until he notices that neither Lily, Alisha, or I are amused.

"It was a joke." He protests.

"Call me if you have any problems, Alisha! OK, promise me?" It's my first time leaving my newly opened coffee shop in the hands of my assistant manager and even though I know she knows everything I do, it's hard to leave something you've poured your heart and soul into while avoiding the exact thing you're leaving it for.

"You know I will. Have fun! Lay off the stubborn thing."

"Yeah, yeah," I roll my eyes at Lily as I slide into the cab next to her as Josh secures our bags in the trunk.

"She's right, you know. Technically, whether you like it or not, Jack will be kind of family now, so you might as well take this time to learn how to let that happen without constantly needing to hate him."

"I don't hate him."

"Really? And before Alisha convinced you to not respond to his most recent email, what would your response have been?"

"To call you over and panic, exactly like I did. I have nothing to say anyway so Jack can just go away."

Josh slides in, closing the door beside him and letting out an already irritated groan. "If that was true we wouldn't still be sitting here talking about him almost one year later like it just happened yesterday."

"I have an idea. Let's just not talk about him at all!"

"Avoidance... yes, that's actually my favorite Jack game. I'm in." Josh says as he snaps his seatbelt.

"I'm in too, actually. This week isn't about Jack or you, it's about Evan and Hannah and I think we owe it to our friends to make sure they have the best wedding possible, without throwing in our own issues." Lily glares through a smile.

"Exactly. It's like we're one mind." I turn my attention to the drive to the airport we're flying out of.

Everything will be just fine. I haven't really spoken to Jack since just after everything happened and we agreed that a break would be best. I've learned a lot with him gone actually. I opened my own coffee shop, which, if you've never run your own business before, is a great way to spend every second thinking about something besides the thing you're trying to avoid. Really therapeutic in leaving the right people behind when you need to. It also showed me that I really could do anything I wanted. I didn't need a man from a rich family to be my family when I didn't have one any longer. I've got great friends, both old and new, a great apartment, and I don't really long for anything. I'm happy, by my own doing.

Of course, there are those times where I wish I could just call someone up for a movie and a cuddle, but those moments usually pass pretty quickly and are a lot less messy than if it had actually happened the way my fantasies allow it to play out.

*

"Two glasses of wine, Em?" Lily lectures me as the stewardess collects our empty containers in preparation for landing. "You should have stopped at one."

"I think at three I would have been able to tune this out better…"

"Ha, ha. I just don't think you should be going into this drunk." Lily scolds me.

I laugh as I walk down the hall leading between the plane and airport departure gate. "I'm far from drunk, miles actually."

"Don't listen to her," Josh winks at me before grabbing Lily's hand with a sympathetic look on his face.

No matter how much I've prepared myself, this could possibly be one of the most stressful weeks I've had in a while. So, I had a minuscule glass of wine or two, it's not like I'm suddenly going to be ready to deal with my past after all the bad luck I've had. I really just don't want to face Jack for the first time in a year in front of a room full of people who were also invited to our wedding. Actually, if I had a choice I'd rather not face Jack at all.

"I'm just saying that this week might be miserable enough already, I just don't think she should start it off with two glasses of wine."

I stare down at the ugly green patterned carpet that is somehow famously known as the Portland Airport. They actually sell souvenirs of this ugly carpet.

I finally stop and turn towards Lily, "Two plastic, tiny glasses of wine, Lil, not bottles, not a case, not even hard liquor that I considered smuggling in my bag. Two tiny airport size glasses of wine. I'm pretty sure I'm well below the legal limit."

"Fine, just please, don't overdo it?"

"Do I ever?"

Lily raises a single eyebrow. So, everyone has overdone something at some point. So, kill me.

"There he is." Josh nods in the direction of my brother.

I couldn't miss him if I wanted to. Despite the fact that we are paternal boy and girl twins, we do still look alike. We both have dark ash-brown hair, blue-gray eyes, and pasty white skin. He stands a good head taller than me, and there are the obvious boy and girl differences but besides that, he's like looking in the mirror.

He's standing in front of the schedule boards with a homemade sign that says Esmeralda the Great like I'm some sort of palm reader coming to read him his fortune. I still don't know why our mother chose names straight from a circus sideshow act, but she did.

I am the two minute younger twin sister of my brother Evan. We were adopted at birth and given names that, I hate even to admit, are legal. Emi and Evan are just covers for the much worse names that show on our birth certificates. We've never known anything about our birth parents so maybe our real parents did and that's where the weird names come from. My full name is Esmeralda Erin Harrison, and my brother is Evangelo Eron Harrison. The different versions of Erin are because we are twins and our mom thought we needed twinning names.

For as long as I can remember we insisted people call us Emi and Evan but our parents never would cave in and use them.

"You know I hate it when you call me that," I say as I approach him.

He wraps his arms around me, lifting me off the floor in a giant bear hug. "Exactly why I do it. It's what brothers do."

Every time I see Evan, I realize how much I miss him and I wonder if running from the situation was the right thing to do. He's really just about my only family left.

"Fine then, Evangelo," I say in the most annoying sisterly tone available, watching his face scrunch into a disgusted look.

"Whoa now, OK, I won't call you Esmeralda anymore if you're gonna use Evangelo."

"Good. Now, let's go grab my bags." I point to the sign over the down escalator reading Baggage Area and lead the way downstairs.

Evan gives me a disapproving look as he drags my bag onto the escalator. "You checked bags, *plural*, and brought this?" He pretends he can hardly lift it when he exits the escalator to follow me to the baggage claim.

I look back at him, irritated, "It's a wedding. I had to get the dress here and it takes a lot to maintain and dress this figure up." I point to myself in case he doesn't know what I'm talking about.

"High maintenance, huh?" Evan directs his comment towards Lily and Josh, who both silently nod their heads.

"I am not high maintenance. This is just—"

What is it?

It's a wedding that my ex will be at. That's what it is. If I didn't come prepared for anything even I would wonder what was wrong with me.

"Got it," Evan nods with an unspoken understanding as if he's just read my mind. Sometimes having a twin is a good thing. Like those times where you need them to spontaneously read your mind, or call when you're having a bad day and you don't want to call first. We do those weird things.

Evan jogs over to the baggage carousel that is on the point of sending my two extra large hot pink luggage bags and dress bag back through the hole in the wall to wherever they go if no one claims them. I was kind of hoping the dress bag would end up on its way to Brazil, or anywhere else for that matter. But there it is, taunting me by being draped over both my other bags, impossible to not see and accidentally leave behind.

"Is he there?" I ask Evan, not really even wanting to know if he's there or not. But if he is, I should at least be given the chance to prepare myself.

"Who?" He gives a joking smile over his shoulder at me. "No, he's not there. He doesn't live with us, Em."

I glance back at Josh and Lily who shrug their shoulders with a smile.

"I know that." Thank God. If he did I'd be heading to a hotel right now, instead of my brother's mini-mansion.

"I doubt you'll see much of him anyway, besides at the wedding. He's... uh... preoccupied."

"With work, right?" Lily suddenly appears at my side, leaving her luggage with Josh to pull to the car. "He's a *lawyer*," she narrows her eyes at Evan, "So, I'm sure he's busy on a case, or whatever."

"Right. You know, Jack, always working." Evan is obviously following her lead on something.

"What's going on?" I stop when Evan's SUV beeps at us approaching, triggering the back door to automatically open.

"Nothing is going on, Em," he grabs my bags and stacks them in the back, arranging them like a Jenga game so that Josh and Lily can maybe fit theirs in as well. "Let's head home."

We all pile into Evan's SUV quietly. A little too quietly. Like someone is hiding a secret quietly.

"Seriously guys, what is up? What do you all know that I don't?"

Evan backs out of the parking spot silently, only the hum of the engine in the background, avoiding even looking in my direction, obviously ignoring me.

I glance to the back seat, where Josh and Lily exchange a look I know all too well. The *we can't tell Emi yet* look. I know this look because it's the same one they gave me when I asked what happened to my wedding dress after the move to Dallas. I still don't know the answer to that one.

"*What* are you not telling me?"

"It's nothing, Ems." Lily is a horrible liar. Even though her mouth says *nothing*, her face is saying *please forgive me*.

"What did *nothing* do?"

"He's uh… seeing someone." Evan finally blurts it out, never looking at me for my reaction.

"Like a girlfriend?"

"Maybe it's a boyfri—" Josh stops midsentence with Lily's elbow in his ribs.

"Stop it, yes, it's like a girlfriend. I was gonna tell you, but I didn't want to chance you refusing to get on the plane. It's really a rather new relationship too I'm told, so nothing to worry about."

The words hang in the air like a storm cloud. I hear them, but I can't wrap my head around them.

I have to say this would be a lot easier if it *was* a boyfriend because that would mean that I wasn't just not good enough for him after all. I was just the wrong sex. But it's *not* a boyfriend, it's a woman. Jack has a girlfriend. As wrong as this is, I wanted him to be alone and lonely. Alone and miserable. To have gained fifty pounds and be balding and to eat his dinner alone in front of his TV every single night. That would make me happy: his misery. He deserves at least that. Even though I know it's not true because I stalked him on Facebook, I'm still going to pretend it's somehow possible.

"I'm fine with it," I lie, and stare out the window watching the buildings whizzing past us. "It's not like I haven't moved on too." Another lie, but one that Lily knows I tell myself hoping I'll eventually believe it. Why am I trying to lie to the people who know me best, though?

"Really?" Lily asks.

"Yes, *really*. I mean, come on, I refused to talk to him for three months even though he begged daily, and then I moved over two thousand miles away when you guys got transferred. So yes, *obviously*, I've moved on."

Behind me, Lily clears her throat. "Moving on physically isn't the same as letting go, Ems. We've talked about this."

"It's true, though. In this case, it means exactly that. I moved to Texas, I started my dream business, I'm happy, and I am well over Jack. We just went through all this earlier, remember? I'm just a little surprised to hear that he's moved on, that's all."

"Good, because this week isn't about Jack and Emi for once. It's about Hannah," Evan finally adds his two cents.

"And you," I say back to him with a forced smile.

"Exactly. So, we're going to have fun, and things will go smoothly. Hannah deserves that."

"Yes," I nod my head as we pull into Evan's driveway.

My heart sinks into my chest a little when he parks next to the 1952 Corvette that our father bought when Evan turned eighteen so they could fix it up together. It still looks as good as it did the day they finished it. It's cherry red, picture perfect, and belongs in a museum somewhere. Despite the fact that Dad had wanted Evan to keep it, he insisted that it was more fitting for our dad. The last time I saw Dad driving it was on the way to the country club for his weekly game of tennis. That was his last game. He died of a major heart attack right there on the court. My heart hurts as I stare at the car from my seat and all the memories that go with it.

"Kind of sad they can't be here for the wedding, isn't it?" Evan says, still sitting in the driver's seat next to me.

"Yeah. It is. I just never imagined that they'd be gone for all the big moments in life. Do you think they knew when they brought us home from the hospital that we'd have to do all this stuff without them?"

Evan shakes his head, a smile on his face. "Nah, they never felt their age as it was, so I doubt it even crossed their minds. I'm sure they're around us somewhere. Dad's probably super-impressed with my more responsible venture into adulthood, and Mom is probably still wondering when her sweet dizzy Emi will finally grow up?"

Evan laughs until I make a swing for his arm, then jumps out of the car before I can make impact.

"Not even funny! I am grown up, by the way. I run my very own business, have my own apartment, and I'm perfectly happy." I say loudly as I get out, heading to the back of the SUV to grab my many bags.

"EMI!" Hannah comes squealing out of the house and engulfs me in a huge hug. Which is a little more than awkward, considering she's a good nine inches taller than me.

I can't say that Hannah and I are the best of friends in life, but I think we are just about as close as we'll ever be. There may always be some lingering jealousy on Hannah's side that Lily is my best friend and not her. But what can I do about that? Her marrying my brother won't change the fact that I've known Lily since I was six years old. There is also the fact that I've always had a feeling that Hannah can change her opinion of someone, in a split second, over goodness knows what or why. I don't want to chance being on that side of the spectrum at some point.

"Hi, Hannah!" I hug her back and pretend my cheek isn't smashed up against her perfect plastic boobs.

"I'm so glad you're finally here!" She sets me free and hugs both Lily and Josh. "Come in, come in! I'll show you to your rooms. I'm so excited to show you everything for the wedding in person!"

Evan gives a raised eyebrow smirk. He's finally escaped the world of weddings that Hannah has become since their engagement. She's now got a new audience in Lily and me. The upcoming wedding is all that she talks about. *My wedding this* and *my wedding that* is the topic of literally every phone call we've had for the last year. I honestly don't know what she'll talk about when this is over, but I imagine her post wedding depression will be best for me when I'm two thousand miles away and can ignore the call.

"I have seriously shopped myself out this week getting your rooms ready, but since I knew you'd all be here a full week I wanted to make sure you had everything you'd have back home."

I find it hard to believe she is ever seriously done with shopping, as I gawk at her fancy house while we follow her up the grandest staircase since *Gone with the Wind* and into a bedroom more luxurious than I've always imagined a room at *The Plaza*.

"Josh and Lily, this is your room. There are robes for each of you in the bathroom, toiletries that I know you all use, and a snack basket on the dresser. If I've left anything out just let me know and I'll send Evan to grab it."

"Wow, Hannah, you've really done too much. The room is beautiful." Lily beams over at her. "And here I thought this wedding wouldn't be a vacation."

"Exactly why I did this! I know you two work so hard and I wanted this to be *like* a vacation."

Hannah and Lily always get along in a *'we have to for Emi's sake'* kind of way. Not that they don't like each other; they do, mostly. But right now, it's a little over the top. I'd guess by tomorrow night they'll be slyly at each other's throats like a scene from *The Real Housewives*.

"Now to Emi's room."

I follow Hannah out, grabbing some of my bags that Evan dumped at the top of the stair landing, and into the next room on the right.

"Same for you, but I also left a bridesmaid survival kit in here. Everything you might need for your bridesmaid duties or emergencies are in it. It's so exciting, in a few days we'll be sisters!" She's talking much quieter in here as if she's trying to keep what we're saying away from Lily's ears.

When Hannah first asked me to be a bridesmaid I was afraid to tell Lily. Not because I thought Lily would be mad, but because Hannah didn't ask her to be one too. She had some other friends she's closer to and thought it would be weird to ask my best friend, who doesn't always love her, to be in the bridal party. But of course, she invited Lily and Josh as guests and moral support for me.

"Thank you, Hannah. You truly have thought of everything."

"Grab your dress bag; we'll put that in here with the rest of the wedding stuff." She motions to the room across the hall from us. When she opens the door, my jaw drops open. The room is piled high full of boxes, gift bags, linens, decorations, and dress bags.

"Whoa. This is like a bridal shop. Why is it all here? I thought you hired a wedding planner?"

"I did, but I needed a place to store everything and we have plenty of room. Isn't it amazing?" She glances around before hanging my dress on the dress rack full of gown bags.

"How many bridesmaids *are* there?" I count the bags quickly, worried that this wedding might end up like the last scene of the movie *27 Dresses*.

"There are six bridesmaids, two flower girls, and two ring bearers."

"Why the twelve dress bags then?" I can't help but wonder.

"Did I not tell you?" She pulls a bag out and hangs it on a hook at the end of the rack. "I designed two wedding dresses; a ceremony dress and a reception dress."

"Two? Wow. That's uh—"

What do you say to the woman who probably spent twenty thousand dollars on material for these dresses?

You want to say that you hope they never run into financial hard times and drop down to middle income. But you don't dare say anything.

"It's amazing. Here, look, this one is my ceremony dress." Hannah slowly unzips the first bag which is easily the biggest dress bag I've ever seen. Inside is a dress with so much tulle and sparkle it's hard to see anything else as it all spills out.

"I know you can't tell in the bag but it's so beautiful. The bodice stops at my waist and it has a full out ball gown skirt but it's cut in layers draped offset in a handkerchief cut. Look at all this lace!" She pulls out a layer of the skirt with an intricate lace detail along the hem. "I designed this lace."

I can tell she's proud of it too, as she should be; it's gorgeous.

"There is also a layer of tulle in the middle of the skirt that is hot pink so there is a hint of pink showing through in the full skirt. The beading on the bodice took me two months to complete. Can you imagine? I thought my fingers were going to fall off," she laughs as she gently touches the intricate beading sparkling in the light.

Ever since the day I met her, Hannah has truly always reminded me of Barbie, with her perfect blonde hair, her always perfect makeup, and her obsession with all things pink.

"It sparkles, that's for sure. I'm sure you'll look beautiful in it." I'm picturing this pink tinted ball gown resembling the Barbie birthday cake I had when I turned eight years old.

She puts the ball gown back onto the crowded dress rack and pulls out a smaller bag next to it.

"This one is where I got the inspiration for you girls' bridesmaids' dresses." The feathers spill out before I can notice anything else: pastel pink, gray, and white feathers from just above her knees all the way to the bottom. If there was a giant feathered headpiece with it I'd think she was performing on Broadway or with the Rockettes. "Isn't it gorgeous?"

I nod, "It's feathery. This one is for the reception?"

Boy is it ever feathery, like a Las Vegas showgirl. I can't even picture what a row of bridesmaids will look like, all of us being feathered from the knees down. I would think she would want something unique, not more feathers for her reception. But then again, Hannah has always been full of unexpected decisions.

"Yes. It reminds me of a vintage party dress, so it's just so fitting, don't you think?"

"I do." I hate it, but I do think it's fitting. Now I know what we'll look like: insane. We will be one of those bridal parties that are pictured on line after going viral, in a *What Not to Do to Your Bridesmaids* article that lives on the internet for years to come.

Lily walks into the room holding a glass of wine and stops dead in her tracks just two feet inside the door.

"Holy shit! What is this? You opened a bridal store in your house?" There is the Lily I know and love.

"No!" Hannah yells at her and points towards the hallway. "No wine in here, it would just ruin everything if it spilled."

I watch Lily slowly back out of the room, eyes big and eyebrows raised. That was quick, her completely offending Hannah only an hour into our trip. I thought for sure it would take her until at least later tonight.

"I'm sure you could use another glass of wine, Ems," Lily says sarcastically as she rolls her eyes. "You should come have a glass." She nods towards the stairs, acting as if convincing me to come have a glass of wine is some difficult challenge. Obviously, Lily is starting to understand why a glass or two of wine might be necessary on this trip.

"Sure?" I look to Hannah who nods her head with a smile.

I follow the two of them down the grand staircase and into the open plan living room and kitchen. One full wall is black stone with a huge fireplace in the center. All the furniture is stark white, the walls are white, the curtains are white, the decorations are variations of white. The room merges into a wall of the kitchen with an island almost the full length of the room. Again, everything is white, except the stainless steel appliances.

"My God, how do you keep this clean?" I ask them, glad it's not mine.

"I have no idea. I have a lady who does it daily." Hannah pours herself a glass of pink champagne before hopping up onto one of the metal barstools that sit just below her white sparkly quartz island counter.

"What *is* your life?" I ask my brother who is sitting on the counter holding a beer. "My whole apartment could fit in this room alone."

"I don't know why? It's not like you don't have money."

He's right. When our parents died, they left us enough money that neither of us would've had to work for a good ten years even after paying off our student loans and college debt. I do have money, but after looking at this house I don't know if he will for much longer. He and Hannah appear to have a very rich taste. They bought the house right after the last time I saw them both. I've seen pictures and I knew it was fancy, but I never ever expected this fancy.

It's at moments like these, when I'm with my coupled up happy friends, that I find my mind wandering to what Jack and I might have been like if we'd made it all the way down the aisle. What would the wedding have actually been like? Would we be sitting here, blissfully happy, having found our soul mate in one another? Or would I ever have caught him doing his assistant?

Four

The Wedding Planning

One year, six months ago.

Tigard, Oregon

"How many people are on your guest list?"

Megan, our wedding planner, is sitting with a huge schedule book in front of her, covered in a rainbow of sticky notes. Every time I give her a number or an idea she writes it in three places: the pastel pink notepad at her right side, the notes section of the day planner, and then she quickly taps it into her opened laptop.

"Just over three hundred invitations need to be sent out. I doubt that many will come, but my fiancé is from... uh... money..."

"Socialites?"

"Yes. Rich socialites that know everyone in the city. That's a great definition."

Definitely a crowd I've never been welcomed into until now. And I'm still unsure if I'd like to be there or not. Besides knowing I'll stay for Jack, the rest of them make me a tad nervous.

"No problem. Did you have a theme or colors picked?"

"A theme?"

"Yeah, a lot of couples pick a theme for the wedding and that's where we get our colors, decoration ideas, and venue from. It really sets a tone for the wedding."

"Well, I don't know. I'm gonna be honest with you..." I pause – not to intentionally be dramatic, but because any time I tell someone this I get a gasp, moan or hanging jaw. "I was never the girl who was planning out her wedding or her Prince Charming. I never really cared about any of this. But because I'm marrying into this particular family, I'm expected to throw this seriously over the top wedding, and I have no idea what I need or want."

Just as suspected, Megan's jaw drops open and her eyebrows pinch together like she's confused, or maybe constipated. "You've never dressed up and played bride, or even brought bridal magazines?"

I shake my head with a frown, "Nope."

"That is a little weird! But don't worry, I did, and I know everything about weddings. I'll make sure yours is fabulous." She smiles as she jots down a note in each of her three devices.

"Can I tell you what I see for you guys after finally meeting you?"

"Absolutely," I nod.

"I noticed the ringer of your phone earlier was *Fly Me To The Moon* by *Frank Sinatra*. What would you think of something Old Hollywood style? Classy, elegant, and very vintage."

I feel the smile grow on my face. "I like that. I have no idea how you'd pull it off but I do love it."

"It's one of my favorite weddings to do," Megan grins.

"Now is probably a great time to mention that I'm marrying Amelia Cabot's son." I chew my fingernail as Megan slowly looks over her laptop at me. Of course she would know her by name, everyone seems to.

"Oh. Wow." She takes a deep breath.

"Yeah, she tends to like to do things her own way. When I'm done here she's going to drill me on what went on and insist that I give her your number so she can get her ideas to you. She can be a little overwhelming and demanding, so just remember you don't have to do anything she says unless I've approved it or you think it's a good idea. But like I said, I'm pretty clueless when it comes to weddings."

"Are you OK with her wanting to help plan the wedding? For some brides that is a definite no-no."

I shrug my shoulders, almost unsure of how to answer this question. If I say no, there will be instant strife between Amelia and me, but if I say yes, I might not even know what I've gotten myself into until I'm on my way down the aisle.

"If she comes up with something fitting then I don't mind at all. She's got flawless taste if I'm honest. Just be ready to put your sassy pants on and feel free to tell her no, blame me if you have to because she can be a bit exigent."

Megan lets out another small groan, "I know all about her. I've heard horror stories from other event planners. I'll stand my ground, though. You have nothing to worry about."

Her suddenly discouraged expression tells me she could be nervous about meeting the great Amelia Cabot. I don't blame her even one bit. I once witnessed Amelia fire a waitress at an event she threw because she dropped and broke an entire box filled with unopened expensive bottles of wine in the middle of the party, after tripping on a tiny teacup poodle that had escaped someone's bag. When that someone finally realized that her precious, yet annoying 'child' had nearly been severed in a gazillion pieces by breaking glass all around it, she demanded Amelia fire the waitress on the spot. And so she did.

"So, I will get started on a proposal tonight and we can meet up on..." Megan flips through her book quickly and scans her computer screen. "Can you meet me on Saturday? At my office? I'll have samples and outlines for you to go over with me, and we'll make a lot of the bigger decisions right then."

I nod, "Absolutely, it's a date." I grab my bag and coffee from the table, ready to be done with wedding planning for the day.

"Oh, and Emi..." Megan touches my hand as I start to leave the table. "Keep your afternoon open because we'll go look at venues that day too."

"OK. Should I bring Jack with me?"

"For sure. Actually, if he wants a say you'd better bring him to everything."

"Everything... OK. Thank you so much, Megan."

I don't know if Jack will go to every planner appointment with me, but if I should have to suffer all this just to get married, he should have to as well. It's not fair that men don't have to do anything for the wedding but show up, yet women are expected to be frazzled, irritated, and short on time for months on end for something that's over in a single day.

*

"I'm to come to everything?" Jack asks later that night as we fall into our nightly routine of dinner on the couch while watching *Drunk History on Hulu*.

"Well... maybe not *everything*, but some stuff, yeah. I can't do it all myself."

"You know if I could I'd be there for every meeting and every decision, Em, but with work, I'm just not sure I can squeeze it all in. What about Lily as a fill in for when I can't make it?"

"I'm sure Lily would be glad to go, but this is our wedding and you know how bad I am at this stuff. Surely, you care a little about every detail of the wedding?" I say with a half laugh knowing that it's only partially true. Men really don't care and if they say they do, they're probably lying.

"Sure, but napkins and china, aren't exactly my specialty. That's probably best left to you and Lily who seem to have an eye for those things."

"What about venues? Any ideas?"

"As long as we don't get married somewhere weird like a graveyard during a full moon," he laughs. "Then I'm up for anything as long as you're there."

"Sweet as that is, what I'm hearing is that I could come back here Saturday evening and say that I chose Thornbury Castle in England, and you wouldn't wonder about the cost?"

Not that this would ever happen. In fact, the only reason I know the name of this particular wedding venue is because I've been watching far too many wedding reality shows whilst trying to get into the groove of planning a wedding. The Cinderella wedding may be most girls' dream, but for some reason, it's just not mine.

"That's *not* the plan, is it?" He pauses, his fork midway to his mouth, suddenly realizing that I could really throw a million dollar wedding with a completely free rein.

"No," I laugh. "But I could if you aren't interested. I just need a bit of help. I'm not good at this stuff."

"I know. Look... I'll help as much as I can. I'd love for you to pick anywhere in the city as a venue. I think that would portray the two of us since neither of us are exactly country dwellers. And I'll come check it out with you this weekend. Otherwise, let's just try to keep it under a hundred thousand. Deal?"

A hundred thousand dollar wedding almost makes me hyperventilate to even just think about. Who spends that much money on a wedding? It's a one day party. I was thinking even twenty-five thousand seemed too much.

"Also, I have a surprise for you on Saturday afternoon..." Jack carries his plate from the couch into the kitchen.

"A surprise? You know I hate surprises."

"I know you'll love this one," he grins. "And before you tear the apartment to the ground, just know, it's not here," he smiles, snuggling himself next to me on the couch. "And you'll never guess it, I'll never tell, so just try to enjoy the moment."

I sigh a defeated sigh, as I squeeze his hand in mine. Now would be the perfect time to tell him that I've sort of invited his mom to have more than a little say in the wedding.

"I, uh, gave your mom's number to the wedding planner." I quickly fill my mouth with the rest of my wine, staring across the room at the TV so I won't witness the reaction of the news I've just tossed over at him.

"You what?" he laughs, sitting a little straighter on the couch.

"You know she'll just find a way to her eventually anyway. I was thinking about it on the way home and she's so much better at this stuff than me, so why not just let her do it?"

"You're just going to hand over the wedding planning to my mother?" His brows are raised and his voice is tight. If he never thought I was completely nuts before, he sure does right now.

"Well, no. I mean... maybe?" I shrug my shoulders. I didn't really think it through all the way, but I know I've been to Amelia's parties and they are the parties everyone who is anyone dies to get an invite to. "I just thought she'd have such better ideas and contacts than me."

"You are a brave girl, Ems." Jack pulls my hand to his lips for a quick reassuring kiss. "My mom is going to turn this into a reality TV show." He shakes his head as the disbelieving laugh he's been stifling emerges.

"But it'll be the kind on the E! channel, and that's not a terrible party if you ask me." I force a laugh, knowing how much he hates watching the Kardashians and their ridiculous parties with me, for the few moments before he asks to change the channel

He leans over and kisses my lips softly, "I hope you're ready."

How bad could it be? Amelia is one of the top socialites in the city, and if she throws a party, not one invite is turned down. She'll make this wedding beautiful, elegant, and probably way over the top. I won't have to do a thing. In fact, to tell you the truth, I doubt she'll let me have much say at all.

*

"Oh, great! You brought Jack *and* Amelia." Megan immediately looks more nervous now than she did the day of our interview. "It's so great to meet you both." She shakes their hands as if she's just met Portland royalty. Hardly. I don't think rich qualifies you as important. Or does it?

"Yes..." Amelia and I speak at the same time.

"We are excited to see what kind of ideas you have for us." Amelia sits in one of the two chairs facing Megan's office desk.

"I have so many ideas, so, let's get started."

I squeeze Jack's hand in mine, nervously. He kisses my forehead and directs me towards the single empty chair next to his mom, taking his place behind me.

"OK." Megan sounds enthusiastic before pointing towards the board with a gazillion fabrics, photos, and ideas. "Here is my idea based on what we spoke of the other day, the Old Hollywood feel for the wedding. Please do stop me with any questions as we go."

For almost twenty minutes Megan continues to talk about venues, fabrics, colors, food, flowers, souvenirs, photographers, decorations, cocktails, entertainment, the first dance, wait staff, and music. Who knew you needed so many things to have a wedding? I am kind of thinking eloping might be the way to go. All of these options may too easily find a way to become disastrous.

"What do you think? Is there anything you hate or love?"

"I'll start," Amelia stands from her chair, making her way to face the idea board head on. Jack and I exchange nervous smiles and prepare ourselves to watch what's about to unfold before us. This is it. This moment will define our wedding.

"I love the Old Hollywood theme, very classic and elegant, let's do the main colors as black and white with a touch of something like pastel blue or ruby red. The flowers should be crimson roses, none other, and the centerpieces should blow guests away with their grandeur and sparkle. We will, of course, need crystals, dozens of crystals, as well as crystal place settings and glasses. I like the idea of a champagne color thrown in for maybe the linens with gold and silver pops in the metals. I want full out décor from floor to ceiling, it should all match our theme. If we're going with the Old Hollywood theme the music should match, bring in a big band, Sinatra style. I have a caterer I'll give a call today, we can do a menu of choices for dinner and dessert, and cocktail hour will not take place in the same room as the reception. I'd like to set up a swanky sort of cigar bar for cocktail hour. No hard liquor, we don't need any drunks, so let's do a Champagne bar with a signature drink of each the bride and the groom's choices." Amelia glances over at Jack and me, never having taken a breath through her whole slew of ideas. "What do you think? Of course, if I'm bringing in a big band you would have to take a few dance lessons. I know it's been a while since Jack stepped foot in a ballroom..."

I look at Jack with a smile, 'I forgot you've had dance lessons."

"The skill seems to have faded a bit," he squeezes my hand. "I think everything sounds great, mom. But really, it's all about how Emi feels about it..." he looks to me, very willing to agree with anything I say. That's just Jack.

I nod. "I couldn't have come up with all this in a million years. I can't really picture it, but it sounds beautiful."

"Perfect," Amelia says with a smile, turning to Megan. The two of them start jotting things on the board, removing samples that weren't quite up to par, and poor Megan typing frantically into her phone as well. "Leave it to me, kids, and we'll have this planned in no time."

"Ready to sneak out?" Jack whispers into my ear, his breath on my neck sending chills down my spine. Even though we've been together just over four years, he still takes my breath away. "I have a surprise for you...

remember?" he adds, a coy grin on his face as he backs towards the door.

Really? I mouth over him, standing slowly from my chair. I watch as he turns the doorknob slowly, letting the door open without even as much as a click.

I know it's wrong to sneak out of our own wedding planning meeting, but I really can't help at this point and Amelia clearly has it under control. Megan and she haven't even looked at us or run by an idea in a couple of minutes, so I'm thinking my work here is truly done. I tiptoe over to the open door where Jack is now standing just outside against the wall.

"Emi?" Amelia suddenly calls my name, causing me to quickly spin her direction.

"Yes?"

"No need to look at venues today, I've already booked the Hilton Exec Tower for July the fifth," she grins with a nod.

"Oh, you chose the date too?" I didn't even consider her choosing the most important parts like our anniversary date or my wedding dress. I glance at Jack standing just out of sight of his mother. He shrugs his shoulders with a smile.

"Of course," Amelia waves a hand at me. "You kids get to your next appointment. I'll do what needs to be done here and I'll give you a call later this week for your input."

"Are you sure?" I ask, feeling more than guilty. "I don't want you to feel like you're doing everything."

Amelia walks over and wraps an arm around my shoulder, pulling me in for an awkward side hug. "You're like a daughter to me, Emi. It's not a bother! My only son is getting married, and to a woman that I actually like. I'm just so thankful to be a part of it."

I nod. I bet she wouldn't be quite so eager about it if I didn't offer to let her plan the entire thing.

"OK then," I say, glancing over at Megan. She's staring at Amelia, and to be honest looks both a little star-struck and a little deer in the headlights all at once. Obviously, this is not what she originally signed up for, but if she can succeed in planning a wedding for the great Amelia Cabot then she might earn herself the business of Portland's richest of rich.

*

Jack takes my hand as I get to him in the hallway, leading through the building and onto the sidewalk out front.

"I told you she'd take over..." he says with a hesitant laugh.

"What day is July the fifth anyway?" I pull my phone from my bag and scroll six months into the future. "Well, at least it's a Saturday."

"It's going to be a beautiful wedding, Em." Jack kisses my cheek.

"I really don't need to do anything, do I?"

"Maybe pick your own dress, I hope, and show up for appointments?"

"Did I do the wrong thing?" I bite my lip and stop walking, pulling Jack to a stop with me. "Is it going to end up being some stuffy middle aged richey rich party and not us?" The what could go wrongs are swirling through my head.

Jack pulls me against him, kissing the top of my head. "Not at all. She knows us and she thinks of you as a daughter, she'd never intentionally do anything you wouldn't like. You know that. Now come on... I've got a surprise for you..."

He leads me a few blocks down the road, my hand in his as we weave through people until we finally stop in front of a place called Uptown Dance Studio.

"What is this?" I ask, knowing full well what it is, just not having expected Jack to be the one to arrange it.

"I've heard that after weddings, couples sometimes do this first dance in front of their guests. I just thought... that maybe we could actually look like we knew what we were doing? What do you think?"

I laugh to myself before wrapping my arms around his neck and kissing his lips. "I think you're perfect."

He opens the front door, allowing me to enter ahead of him.

"Hello! You must be Jack and Emi?" a woman wearing a flattering and very fluid dress sashays across the floor in our direction. She greets Jack with a kiss on each cheek and then the same for me. "I'm Miranda, congratulations on your upcoming wedding. What a gorgeous couple you are! Any ideas on a first dance song? If not, I have a book full of ide—"

"I know what song," Jack interrupts her, pulling a CD from his jacket.

"You already picked the song?"

Miranda takes it from his hand and pops it into her CD player sitting at the front of the room. The second the sounds of the piano intro start my heart starts to melt.

"Just beautiful," Miranda says as I watch Jack lay his suit jacket on a chair near the wall.

"Hand around her waist, and her free hand in yours, and let's just try to follow the music..." Miranda gives instructions as I still try to make sense of the song he's chosen.

My mom used to sing this song, *Someone to Watch Over Me*, by *Ella Fitzgerald*, when I was a kid. She'd dance me around the living room and tell stories of her mother doing the same when she was young. It's amazing how a single song can induce so many memories even long after the last time you've heard it.

I rest my hand on Jack's arm with a sigh. Mostly a sigh to attempt to settle the gallop that my heart is on. We are actually getting married and so far, he's perfect.

"Too old fashioned?" he asks.

"No," I shake my head.

"Too emotional?"

I shake my head again, "It's like she's right here with us. It's perfect, thank you."

Just the fact that he remembers I told him this story is enough to make me fall for him all over again.

Jack knew I wanted to do something to honor my parents at my wedding but I didn't know what without it seeming too cheesy. I think adding in something that is as personal as a memory through a song, is absolutely the most romantic thing ever.

"It's like you two have been dancing together your whole life, I think *I* just fell in love..." Miranda laughs as she follows us around the room, making tiny suggestions here and there. "You'll wow the whole room."

Five

The Escape

Present Day

Northwest Portland, Oregon

You know when you visit somewhere you haven't been in a while and all the memories of when you were there last come racing back? That's been happening since I got here. All the memories of Jack and my life seem to be just around every corner I find. I've tried to avoid it but it seems to just not want to give up in surprising me. And I hate surprises.

I've been hiding out in the den watching *Friends* reruns because they can always make me feel better about anything.

"What's for lunch?" I make my way into the kitchen where I hear someone tinkering away on something.

"I invited some friends over for a barbecue this afternoon. Just a casual thing to relax before the wedding." Evan has at least ten different cuts of meats in different marinade bowls lined up across the counter in front of him. Platters, tongs, and bottles of sauce surround him.

"All of this is just for a casual thing?"

"No," he opens the fridge to platters of prepared food, beer, and what appear to be very fancy bacon wrapped appetizers. "All of this," he motions to the counter in front of him, then nods into the fridge, "is for a casual thing."

"How many friends did you invite?"

"Mostly just the wedding party."

"The entire wedding party?" I ask, knowing good and well that the one face that's been haunting me since I got here is in that exact bridal party and I'm just not ready to face him.

"Yes, bridesmaids, groomsmen, and their families." Evan stops brushing sauce on a plate of burgers and turns towards me, sauced brush still in hand. "I know you aren't particularly keen on seeing Jack again after what you guys went through, which I'm not sure I even fully know the details of what that was, but I think if you're here to prove you're over him, the weird, jittery, and nervous Emi thing you've got going on will have to get lost. Don't you think?"

I cock my head with a glare, "You don't have to make such sense to make your point."

"I know you, well. And I know you don't just get over things. You're still mad at me for that time I told Mom and Dad you stayed out all night with Max, your high school boyfriend, and that was thirteen years ago." Evan laughs as he goes back to swiping sauce on a tray of chicken.

"There was no reason they needed to know. There was also no reason you needed to give that kid a black eye when you found out *why* I was out all night..." Max took my virginity, *with* my consent, and Evan seemed to find out practically before I did and like big brothers do at times, he took matters into his own hands. Needless to say, Max and I broke up the next day. I didn't blame him one bit.

"Go do whatever it is you need to do to prove you're the girl who's moved on because they'll be here in thirty."

I grab a bacon wrapped appetizer from the tray in the fridge, just barely avoiding Evan trying to whack me with a spatula as I do, and race up the stairs to Lily and Josh's room.

"There's a wedding party, *party?*" I ask, wondering why she didn't let me in on the secret when I was vegging out downstairs.

"So?"

"Jack will be here?"

"Probably, I mean he is in the wedding party as your brother's best friend."

"What do I wear?!" I ask as I race back to my room, pulling every clothing option from my suitcases and piling them on my bed.

"Wait... why are you so worried about impressing the one guy here you are supposedly over?" Lily asks, following me into my room.

"I am over him, but that doesn't mean I can't make him wish I wasn't. I just want him to be miserable. There's a difference."

"You want him to see you and wish he wasn't such a fucking moron?"

"Exactly."

Lily rolls her eyes as she sits on the side of my bed going through the clothing I'm tossing at her.

"I just wish I didn't have to see him so soon. I'm not ready."

"You'll never be ready..."

"I can't say you're wrong about that. But now, I have to force myself to be ready to see him, and this woman he's seeing. That's some serious stress."

"Just be you!" she grabs a shirt in mid-air "And stop throwing things at me."

Just be me. Such great advice. If I did that, then Jack would know the exact fantasies I've had about him over the last two years. Not the sexual fantasies I'm sure he'd expect either. At least not most of the time. These ones involve revenge.

"I jus—" The doorbell interrupts me and I can feel my face doing things I'd rather it didn't. "Shit." I can't help it. I don't know exactly what I feel towards Jack anymore but, after being brought back to where it all ended, memories are coming at me left and right and making everything much more confusing than it needs to be.

"Can you just relax, you psycho. Get dressed..." she grabs a pair of jeans, sleeveless top, and flip-flops from the pile and throws them my way. "And come downstairs when you're ready."

I pull on the clothing Lily suggested, pull my hair from its nearly permanent bun and run my fingers through my curls, dab some lip gloss on my lips, and voila! I don't look like I've just spent the last few days a nervous, frazzled mess. Now if only the butterflies racing through my insides would die off.

"Emi! Come down and meet everyone," Hannah yells up the stairs.

I do one more mirror check and then force myself to casually make my way down the stairs to the empty foyer. I hear voices on the back patio and peer around the staircase in their direction.

I thought Evan said he invited just the wedding party and their families? There are a good forty people mingling out there. Hannah has tables set up with decorations and flowers and everything is very put together. How did I miss this as I vegged in front of the TV hidden away from the world?

"There you are!" Lily comes up behind me carrying the tray of bacon wrapped appetizers that could have called me in by scent from Mars. "Come on."

I follow her out, almost hiding behind her as she sets the tray on a table full of food. "Is he here?"

"Yes," she turns to me. "Now stop acting like a weirdo. Do you really want him to think we had to request leave from the lunatic asylum for you to join us this week?"

I shake my head, grabbing another bacon wrapped piece of heaven, shoving it in my mouth before I can give an appropriately witty answer.

Looking around the patio I can see there aren't a lot of singles here. In fact, I might be the only one. "Lil... Everyone here is in pairs." A kid maybe six years old skids past me on the heels of his tennis shoes. "Some of these people even have kids!"

Lily jerks me by the arm behind a curtain separating the patio from the hot tub area. This is where I should be hiding out, in the hot tub.

"Stop it!" she hisses at me, her face only two inches from my own. "You will stop acting like a pathetic, heartbroken teenager and you will get your ass out there and act like the amazing, confident, Emi we all know and love. Jack does not control you."

If ever there was a moment that felt like my mom was still here, this was it. I nod my head in shame and follow her back out on to the patio. Evan walks towards the outdoor kitchen, to which is attached a bar complete with a keg and all. I make my way to it and fill a glass. Now is not the time to not like beer. All I need is a distraction, and a few more of those bacon wrapped appetizers.

"Emi, come meet everyone." Hannah grabs my arm before I can make it back to the food table. "You know quite a few people but there are some that you might not. And don't be nervous about May, she and Jack haven't been together long and if I didn't know any better I'd bet she's as nervous to meet you as you are her."

"How much does she know?" I ask, wondering if I should fill her in on how much of a big turd Jack is.

"About what? About you and Jack? Oh, I'm sure she knows what we all know."

My heart sinks a bit because, besides Jack, I'm pretty sure I'm the only one who knows what truly happened that horrible day and thereafter. So, if what Hannah says is true, some unwanted truths may end up revealed this week. And I promise they won't come directly from me.

"I just don't know if I'm ready to meet—"

"Oh stop! She's just fabulous, I'm sure you'll love her like the rest of us do" Hannah glances over at me and frowns. "I'm sorry, you're right, this is an awkward situation and I'll do my best to not push you two together. You can't avoid Jack, though. I hope you know that?"

"I've done OK at it so far..." I say with a sly smile. Not that it's been easy. Jack still emails every couple of weeks and once I figured out how to block his number it was easier to avoid his phone calls so thankfully, technology has made things easier in that perspective.

"Guys!" Hannah pulls me into a group of people, some faces I know, some I don't. "This is Evan's twin sister, Emi!" Hannah puts her arm around me and hugs me from the side, which is a nice change to my face being shoved up against her girls. "I can't wait until we're officially sisters, finally!"

"Yeah, finally..." I nod, hoping no one will ask exactly what the addition of the word actually means. "Nice to meet you all." I glance around at all the faces who nod excitedly back at me. I only recognize a few but still don't see the one I'm the most anxious for. Hopefully, these people don't expect me to remember the names that Hannah is now rattling out because my head feels so stuffed with cotton wool that I can hardly even remember my own name right now.

"Where are Jack and May?" Hannah asks Evan, who points towards the edge of the house.

"They ran to their car." Evan walks past now wearing an apron with a woman's body in a bikini on the front. "They'll be right back."

I follow Evan, stopping momentarily at the appetizer table, grabbing a handful of meatballs and shoving one in my mouth as I walk.

"What are you doing?" Evan asks as I wash the meatball down with the now warm beer.

"Nothing... I uh" I shove the next meatball in and wash it down quickly.

"Please tell me you're leaving some appetizers for the actual guests?"

"Of course, I am. I'm not a total glutton. I'm just nervous."

"This might sound weird to say out loud but I'm honestly a little nervous *for* you. It's a weird situation you're in, for sure. I promise it won't be that bad though. Their whole relationship is pretty new."

"What does that even mean? New like, she's here to make me jealous, or new like, he's just not yet taken the next step?"

"Jack's different since you left. I don't know how to explain it."

"Is he worse?" Please let him be worse.

"He's not standing over here shoveling in the appetizers alone if that's what you mean."

"Ha, ha… that's not what I mean," I turn to the appetizer table again only I don't quite make it and run right into none other than Jack himself. "Shit, Jack!"

Jack lets out a small laugh, both his hands now resting on both my shoulders. "That was quite a hello…" he says, an awkward smile on his face, staring down at his now soaking wet pants that very much match my own.

"I'm sorry. I didn't mean to—" I momentarily look up at him and immediately wish I hadn't. He's not worse than he was. He hasn't gone bald or gained weight. He's still just as gorgeous as he ever was. His dark hair and eyes, his comforting smile, and his intoxicating cologne, they all sink straight into my feelings. Damn it.

Evan hands us each a towel from a cupboard near the grill. I pat myself dry, trying to avoid any more eye contact with him at all if possible. While he and Evan laugh at my lack of grace, I slip past him and through the doors of the house.

"Oh my God," I mumble to myself and make my way into the kitchen where I can only hope is where Lily disappeared to.

"What happened to you?" She looks at my sodden clothing and laughs.

"I spilled my beer."

"How?"

"By running right into Jack," I glare at her, whilst trying to squeeze beer out of my top into the sink.

"Oh no, did you get him too?"

"Yup," I nod. "Of course, I'd have preferred to have dumped it over his head, but he too, looks like he's wet his pants." I sigh, feeling more than defeated and lean against the counter behind me. "I can't do this right now. I wasn't ready to see him tonight and I'm definitely not ready to meet his girlfriend, *May*." Even just saying her name out loud makes me sick.

"You never will be ready. So, go change and *get* ready." Lily glares at me with her motherly charm. "Now."

I take my sweet time changing, trying on just about everything I brought with me besides the one thing that I know would absolutely drive Jack wild. My lucky dress.

I'm definitely not ready for that move yet. I don't even know what I feel right now, so it's way too soon.

The smell of the food wafting up to my room eventually coaxes me back down to the crowd of people now lined up at the bar waiting to fill their plates.

"Finally!" Evan smiles over at me. "I wasn't sure you were coming back at all. Come grab a plate."

I make my way to the back of the line, smiling politely at the faces turned in my direction. One particular face though stops me in my tracks.

"Greta?"

She nods up at me with a fake grin. "Emi, long time no see." Her perfectly made up face half glares at me.

"Why are *you* here?" I know she's not friends with Hannah or Evan so she can't possibly be a part of the bridal party. I look over at Hannah, who looks back and forth between Greta and me with a stunned look on her face.

"How do you two know each other?" Hannah asks us both.

"I... uh"

"Oh, we go way back, don't we, Emi?" she slides her free hand down Jacks arm, entwining her fingers with his, stopping my heart dead in its tracks.

My breathing gets heavy as I look at Jack who pulls his hand from Greta's quickly and takes a step towards me.

"You two are—" I swallow hard, trying not to choke on the feelings rushing through me. "You and Jack?"

This cannot be happening. "You're Jack's—"

"Girlfriend, yup. Just about two months now, right, babe?" she asks him with a grin that I'd like to slap right off her.

I look at Hannah, Evan, and Lily, confused. "I thought you said her name was May?"

"Oh, I go by May now, Greta is just so... old fashioned." She rolls her eyes.

"How could you?" I ask Jack as the tears well up in my eyes. "You knew how much I hated her. I can't believe you chose her..."

I set my plate back on the stack and turn to make my way into the house.

"Emi, wait..." Jack and Evan both follow me to the sliding doors.

"Ugh... she's always been *so* over dramatic." Greta rolls her eyes and goes back to filling up her plate while everyone else watches me try to escape the situation.

"Please talk to me, Emi," Jack asks as he reaches me before Evan can.

"You," I point right at him. "Are the last person I ever want to speak to again. I thought you loved me. I can't believe I was such an idiot." I turn to the front door.

"Where are you going?" Evan asks.

"I need to think or walk to clear my head, or something. I need to be alone..." I take one more quick look at Jack, who's entire face has dropped towards the floor in shame.

"Should I come with you?" Lily asks, standing just behind Evan.

"Nope," I shake my head. "I'll be fine. I'm an adult and I just need to figure out what's going on in my head. It was nice to meet you all." I glare over at Greta, "most of you, that is."

I pull open the door, slamming it behind me and stand on the porch nearly unable to move. How can your heart break over the same thing so many times? I just don't get it.

Maybe if I start walking I will be able to somehow work the clouds out in my head. I'm sure I've heard somewhere that walking can clear your head. I'm not exactly a frequent flyer at that gym I mentioned previously. I even intentionally bought the apartment above my coffee shop so I wouldn't have a commute to work. With hindsight, a short walk to work may have helped ward off this extra thirty pounds that found me.

Where am I walking to? Who knows, but if I keep at it maybe I'll get lucky and end up all the way back in Texas, avoiding everything that this shit show might be this week.

I glance up at the sign on the building *Old Tex*. It's no Texas but it'll have to do. I push open the giant, heavy front door with a porthole window just at head height.

The room is in semi darkness with small lights hanging over each table. TVs on the walls play CNN News, and the patrons are few and far between. Mostly older men, a few with a friend, a man behind the bar and another one sitting at the bar corner.

Drinking is probably the worst idea I've had yet but it's not like I've got better plans.

"Can I get a shot of vodka?" I ask, as I catch my breath from the quarter mile walk that only reminded me that I'm definitely not ready for any kind of marathon. Maybe food is a better option. "Do you maybe have a menu?"

"A menu?" the bartender asks me with a tilt of his head.

"Yeah, like for food?"

"Nope. There's a vending machine in the back."

It's not exactly the burgers and gourmet appetizers Evan made, but it'll have to do. Most of the time vending machines have all my favorite foods anyway. Salty and sweet. Perfect for my possible impending hangover whether it be of the emotional or physical kind.

"Can I also get a water?" Vodka isn't exactly thirst quenching, and considering I feel like I've just done a set of five hundred jumping jacks, I should probably help myself to not have a stroke in a strange place.

The bartender nods his head, unenthusiastically, sitting both drinks on the bar in front of me. "Eight bucks."

Oh no. I reach into all my pockets, hoping I accidentally shoved some cash into them the last time I wore them. No such luck.

"I...uh..." I stumble over my words. "I'm so sorry, I just had the worst afternoon of my life and I stormed out of my brother's house without my purse, or cash, or anything. Is it possible to bring it by later?"

Bartender stares at me, no emotion on his face. His head is bald, he has a tattoo showing out of the neck of his shirt, and he's more than a bit intimidating in this environment.

"You have no money?" he asks with a grunt.

"No," I shake my head, quietly hoping I sound as apologetic as I am. "I mean... I do, just not on me. Like I said, I'm here staying with my brother who's getting married this weekend and he decided to have a barbecue for the entire wedding party tonight without even so much as warning me and he invited my ex, who brought his new girlfriend, who is a girl I know... knew... and, well... I just needed to get away quickly to clear my head and think straight before I go—"

"I got it," the man sitting at the corner of the bar a few stools away from me says to the bartender, who nods before walking away from me without further questioning.

"You don't have to do that. I'm good for it, I swear."

"It's not a problem," he says with a quick glance in my direction.

"Are you sure? Because I promise I can bring it into you later, tomorrow even. I just can't really go back there and face them all tonight and if I was to call my best friend to bring me the money I guarantee they'd all just show up here."

He laughs as he turns in my direction.

As I catch the full view of him my jaw nearly drops open in surprise. I just assumed from the atmosphere of this place that all the men in here were old alcoholics who use this place as a second home away from nagging wives and irritating children. But this guy is not old. His sandy blond hair is a bit unruly, and the five o'clock shadow across his jaw looks almost intentional.

"Don't worry about it," he shakes his head with a small smile. "We all have bad days, and yours sounds..." He stops speaking and looks me over. "Sounds brutal." His southern accent could make any normal woman's heart swoon, but all it does for me is remind me of home and how I wish I was there right now.

"It *was* brutal, that's a good word for it. Thank you." I smile before turning back to the drinks now sitting in front of me, downing the vodka in hopes it will relax all the emotions flooding through me, and taking a sip of water while trying to keep my face from showing just how bad the shot really was, since cute barfly next to me seems to be watching. "You have an accent, where are you from?"

"Does clearing your head always consist of this much talking?" he asks.

"Oh, I'm sorry. I'll let you get back to your... uh..." I glance around him looking for whatever it is I'm interrupting, but all he has sitting on the bar in front of him is a bottle of water, during happy hour. "Water drinking."

"That's not what I meant," he laughs to himself with a shake of his head. When he stands up from the barstool, I can clearly see that he really should be an underwear model on the side of a giant billboard. Not a guy hiding out at the bar from whatever problems he's running from. My heart jumps into my throat as he takes a seat on the stool right next to me.

"I'm Liam Jaxson. I own the bar. And I didn't mean that to sound as rude as it did. I apologize."

I reach out and shake his now outstretched hand. His touch makes my skin feel like it's on fire and I pull it away quickly, not wanting my face to relay what this stranger is doing to me internally. I'm not normally the sort of girl who's attracted to men she's only just met.

"It's totally alright. I'm Emi."

"Nice to meet ya, Emi. Can I get you another drink?"

"Oh no... I'm not a drinker and this is my second so if I don't slow down, you'll be carrying me home." I hear it as it comes out of my mouth and realize how it could be taken. "I mean – not carry me home... but you know, take me—" I take a sudden horrified breath, "Oh my God... I didn't mean you'd take me as in *take me*..."

Sweet Jesus, Emi, shut up.

His laugh is intoxicating, luckily because otherwise I'd be more than mortified at how this clearing my head is going.

"No worries. I got it."

"Good." I sigh and take a sip of my water, glancing around the bar in front of me. I'm not sure if the situation I'm in now is any better than the situation back at Evan's. The silence between Liam and me is awkward as I slowly sip my water and inspect the room.

Mirrors line the wall in front of me, and all kind of liquor bottles and glasses sit on the floor to ceiling shelves. You can tell the place wasn't recently, or ever, remodeled. Southwestern objects are occasionally placed around the room, making me feel a tiny bit like I'm back in Texas.

"So, besides this ex and his new girlfriend, tell me something about Emi." Liam finally breaks the silence, an awkward smile hesitating just at the corner of his lips.

"I thought I was talking too much?" I ask ironically.

He shrugs, "I changed my mind."

"About me, huh?" I guess considering that he's paid for my drinks I at least owe him a conversation, even if it's forced.

"Sure."

"Hmm... I own my own coffee shop in Dallas." I'd much rather talk about work than about Jack. I own a successful, albeit, new, business. That makes me look a bit better than broken hearted, frazzled, forgot-all-my-money Emi.

"Dallas, Texas?"

"The one and only."

I'll be the first to admit that moving to a state I'd never even visited was nerve wracking. Had Josh and Lily not been with me I'm not sure I could have done it. I kind of stumbled upon a coffee shop that had recently shut down, and in order to quit thinking about everything I'd just lost with Jack, I put my heart and soul into opening it. It helped more than I could even explain. I wasn't sure I'd ever consider Dallas home, but I've come to love it.

"What a coincidence, I grew up in Fort Worth."

"That's the accent, then." I smile at him, relieved to find someone who isn't a part of this wedding or my past. "Oregon is a long way from Texas. What brought you here?"

"A woman," he winks at me with a shy smile. "Isn't it always a woman that drags a man across the country?"

"I wouldn't know. I don't have a lot of exper—" I stop before I can announce how few men I've dated. "I mean… wow. So, you're married to a girl from Portland?" I glance down at his hand but see no ring.

"Nope. Not anything actually." Liam shrugs his shoulders with a sad smile.

"Why not?"

"Why not what?"

"You said you moved here for a woman and now you're not anything, what happened?" I ask him, being far too nosey. If we're gonna talk, though, why not talk about anything but me?

"Hmm..." Liam is taking some time pondering his answer, which makes me worry that I've asked a question far too personal for someone I've just met. "She broke my heart, actually. It sounds like we have that in common."

"Oh, I'm sorry." I frown as I stare down at my drink. "Wait," I look over at him, "Why do you think *I'm* broken hearted?"

Liam raises a single eyebrow with a smile. "Seems kind of obvious, you see him again, meet his girlfriend and you run away. It kinda screams broken heart, don't you think?"

"I guess maybe..." I force a shoulder shrug as I reluctantly agree with him. I don't want him to be right but he is making complete sense.

"Ah. And this ex, he's moved on before you have?"

"I'm not still in love with Jack if that's what you're getting at. I *have* moved on; he just has a girlfriend before I found a boyfriend, that's all."

"Why run then? If you've moved on, shouldn't you be OK with seeing him?"

I sigh and drop my head in shame. "I'm starting to not like you," I laugh. It would figure I would meet someone who could read me better than I can read myself.

"Can I get another shot?" I ask the bartender before turning on my stool to face Liam. "Fine, I'm not exactly moved on, *per se*. I don't want him back or anything... He just... He's dating a girl who made my life miserable."

The bartender hands me my shot and I swallow it as quickly as humanly possible. "I'll tell you the story but only because I don't know you and because of that you won't tell my family and friends."

"Fair enough," Liam says, his dark eyes almost sparkle with intrigue as he sets down his water and gives me his full attention.

It's far easier to explain your devastating past to someone who knows nothing about you and can't judge you based on anything but the actual story. Maybe, since he seems to be able to read me as well as he has so far, he can give me some insight as to why I'm acting like a complete loon. After all, he too, is suffering a broken heart. He said so himself.

Six

The Mayfairs

One year, seven months ago.

Downtown Portland, Oregon

"Tonight is the Christmas party, so please tell me you've made sure you can be home by five to get ready?" I ask Jack who's standing near the kitchen counter waiting for his coffee to brew.

"Yes," he nods. "I'll be home by six at the latest and ready to go by seven. I promise, babe."

"Good, 'cause I hate work functions alone."

"You hate work functions at all," Jack laughs.

He's right. I'm not the biggest fan of work functions. I do all the PR and advertising for Mayfair Homes, so I should probably go and show my face and pretend that I love spending my evening with the people I already spend eight hours a day with.

"I know. How about we go out for drinks afterwards?" Jack suggests. "We haven't been out just the two of us in a while and I would love nothing more than to just have a romantic night, just you and me." He wraps his arms around me, softly kissing my neck. Which is pretty much a move guaranteeing that I won't say no to anything he requests.

"Perfect! Maybe we can just make a quick appearance and leave early"

"Maybe, but then how would you mingle with all the contacts you've brought the business? You're good at your job, Emi. You should put on a smile and be proud of that. I know I am."

"Why do you always have to be so good at making me feel better about myself? Perhaps I wanted to pretend I'm always irritated, instead of proud of what I've done." I can't help but laugh because even though I put on a serious face at work and around the clients, Jack knows I love what I do. I may not love the furniture business, but I love that I've helped grow this company into one of the top home stores in the area.

"You're good at everything you do, sweetheart, and it shows. I'm so proud." He pecks a kiss on my lips before he heads to the front door.

Never once has Jack made me feel like his job is superior to mine. In his mind we're equals and I could never thank him enough for putting me on that platform, level with him.

He loves his job and he says he went into it because his dad was in the business and he wanted to please his father. I know that's a part of it but I also know there is much more to it. He's such a hard worker, he cares about people, and well, he's really good at what he does. I'm the luckiest girl alive to be with a man who treats me the way Jack does.

"I'll see you tonight, babe."

*

As I get to my desk, my boss, Aron Mayfair, is waiting for me, perched on the edge of it.

"Emi, I have an idea that I wanted to run past you."

"Shoot..." I click on my computer, as I put my things away in the bottom drawer.

"Have you seen those commercials from businesses in town wishing their clients a Merry Christmas?"

"I have," I nod. Every year dozens of local channels churn out Christmas commercials wishing the city a magical Christmas.

"Can we turn this Christmas party into one of those? We've got just over three weeks until Christmas so you should have some time to get everything lined up. What do you think?"

"I think that's a great idea, Aron. I'll get started on everything right now and arrange for our film guy to be there tonight. Leave it to me and it'll be great."

"One thing, though..." Aron stands away from my desk, pacing. "I want Greta to be the host of the show. Maybe she could walk around and ask questions of our employees."

"I'm not sure what kind of *show* it will be?" I ask, thinking he was talking a less than one minute commercial here. "Really the ad can't be more than about sixty seconds at most."

"I know, I know, but Greta gets so much attention everywhere she goes and she wants to become the face of the company. I'm thinking what better way to start than with the Christmas and New Year ad?"

"OK, maybe we can have her ask clients and employees about their New Year's resolutions and just do a Happy Holidays ad, as opposed to a specific Christmas Ad? That would give us more time to run it."

"Perfect! I'll let her know. What time should she be there tonight to get started?"

Shoot. I didn't want to come to this party at all, and now I have to work it. So much for arriving with Jack. I guess we'll just meet up there.

"Maybe have her meet me at five, that will give us an hour to work through her questions and get ready."

In all reality, five minutes would be more than long enough to get ready for this tiny ad but I have a feeling this is going to be a much bigger process than I'm hoping for. I've never met Greta but for her to suddenly make her way into my life via an ad centered around her can't be a blessing.

"I knew I could count on you, Em. You're a star!" Aron says as he walks across the room.

*

I've been at the venue for the party for an hour making sure everything goes off without a hitch. Morgan arrived about fifteen minutes ago and is in the process of getting his gear ready to film. "You do know who Greta Mayfair is, right?" Morgan, my favorite camera guy, flips open a magazine he's pulled from his messenger bag. A tall, thin, half-naked blonde woman stares back at me.

"Whoa." I stare down at the picture even though I suddenly feel a little more than dirty. This girl has no shame and apparently not a lot of morals either from the looks of it. "Disgusting."

"That's just the pic I felt comfortable showing you. She's done full out nude."

"Then, why come work for her dad's furniture store, if she's basically a Playboy bunny? Why is she not canoodling up to dirty old Hugh Hefner himself in the Playboy mansion?"

"They fired her. Not the Playboy mansion, but everyone else she's ever worked with. I guess she's a real bitch. No one wants to work with her anymore. Even E! the same channel that airs the Kardashians pulled a contract from her recently, she's *that* vile. So, her daddy is saving her."

I stare over at Morgan, the same guy who I offended when we first met by asking if he was the assistant to the adult camera guy. I swallow away my nerves. She can't be that bad. Can she?

"How do you know so much about this?" I ask him as he sets up his camera and technical supplies.

"You saw that picture. Every man knows about her."

"Gross. Well, let's just make sure she's fully clothed tonight and everything should go fine."

"I hope so." Morgan nods towards the front doorway.

If this was a costume party she'd have just won an award. She's channeling Jessica Rabbit, with a slit up to her hip and her cleavage falling out of her barely there top, demanding the attention of every man in the room. If I didn't know any better I'd think I was seeing a hint of a gold colored flask tucked into the garter belt she's wearing on her one visible leg.

She looks exactly like her picture, just wearing a tiny bit more fabric. Clearly, no one told her there would be children at this party. She's got to be almost six feet tall, probably something like a size double zero, her long blonde hair is perfectly curled into beachy waves, with not a strand out of place and her skin could make a porcelain doll jealous.

"Are you Esmeralda?" she asks as she finally makes her way to me across the room. She walks incredibly slowly, as if she is expecting the flash of paparazzi cameras all around her. I'll be honest and say I've been stunned silent, staring at her making her way across the room in the heels I couldn't imagine wearing.

"No..." I reach out and shake her outstretched hand. "I mean yes, but I don't go by Esmeralda, you may call me Emi."

"Emi, great. So, what kind of show are we going for here? Daddy didn't really elaborate so I'm not sure what my character is?" She flips her hair behind her shoulder, dropping her hands to her hips to wait for my answer.

I'm standing stunned, eyebrows raised, jaw agape, unable to speak. Morgan pokes me and wakes me from my trance. She's a grown woman calling her father, Daddy. I might be sick by the end of the evening if it continues.

"Character?" I ask more than confused. "It's not really a show *per se*; but more of a one minute commercial slot. We're going to have you work the room and ask people about their New Year's resolutions before getting a group shot of everyone shouting Happy Holidays."

Greta rolls her eyes so hard it makes my own eyeballs hurt. "So... You're telling me that I'm doing a commercial?"

"Yes?" I ask it as a question, unsure of what her father told her. I glance back at Morgan for help but he's staring at her, stunned as well. His stare bores through her barely there dress, though, as if he's trying to use X-ray vision. Although what he just showed me in the magazine, I'm not sure there is a lot more to envision.

"Ridiculous. I told Daddy that I could do so much more than this. I should not have ruined that contact with E! for my own show. I'm so much more than a silly commercial." She stomps a single heeled foot to the ground, clearly ready to throw a fit for all who will watch. There has to be a way to defuse this.

Morgan and I exchange glances, wondering just what planet this girl thinks she's on. Not that I have any doubt, what-so-ever, that she'd be perfect for the E! channel. She could really give those Kardashian's a run for their money.

"This will be fun," I reassure her with a forced smile, hoping that the diva in her stays away long enough for us to shoot this commercial.

"Whatever," she rolls her eyes and waves me away. "Where is the dressing room? I need to touch up my makeup."

A laugh suddenly escapes my throat, causing Morgan to start coughing behind me to cover it up.

"We don't have an actual dressing room, but the bathroom is down the hall and to the right and it's really nice I'm told."

Greta's face stays stone still, her eyes never leaving my own.

"Can I show you the way?" I ask. "But in all honesty, you already look amazing." That brings a small smile to her face.

"I'll take your word for it." She flashes an obviously fake smile as she looks around the room. "Who decorated this?" she asks, only looking half impressed.

The decorators, caterers, and employees are still here, tirelessly working at getting the place ready for the party that starts in less than an hour. I'm far from a decorator so I contracted everything out to only the best of the best. It looks amazing.

I made sure it looked Christmassy since we are also shooting a commercial tonight. There are six eight foot tall Christmas trees around the room, fully decorated, loaded with fake presents. Garlands and twinkle lights hanging from the ceiling, and the tables have center pieces that I'm sure would make a Christmas bride jealous. It's truly gorgeous and cost far more than I would ever, ever pay myself.

"We hired a company," I say, grabbing the list of questions I made up for her from the table beside me.

"They did an OK job," she shrugs her shoulders. "Is that an open bar?" she asks noticing the bartender on the opposite side of the room. "I'm just going to grab a drink."

"Great," I rush to her side, hoping that getting trashed is not on her agenda. "I actually have a list of questions I need you to look over."

"I already know what I'm going to ask," she waves my paper away and bee-lines it to the bar.

Five minutes ago, she asked what character she needed to play and yet suddenly she's prepared with questions she didn't even know she had to ask? I find that more than hard to believe.

"This is gonna be a nightmare." Morgan stands at my side watching her sashay her tiny ass to the bar and immediately flirt with the bartender who seems mesmerized by the spell that is Greta Mayfair.

*

"Hi, babe." Jack leans in and kisses my cheek.

He's here right on time, but since I'm a tad preoccupied with not bringing out the evil from within Greta I don't even have a minute to spend with him like I'd planned.

"I'm so sorry I have to work during this. She's proving to be a bit of a nightmare."

"It's no problem," Jack says with a smile. "Did you get something to eat?" He asks, being the great boyfriend that he is, he's always concerned with my wellbeing and happiness.

"I haven't," I shake my head. "You should, though. I've heard the food is fantastic." I'm starving, so knowing that I might not have time to eat, from the menu that I worked so hard to get perfect, is irritating, to say the least.

"I'll bring you a plate. How about you?" he asks Morgan, who shrugs his shoulders before glancing at me for permission.

I nod with a roll of my eyes. Like I'd say no.

Morgan grins, "I can always eat."

"I'll be right back." Jack heads in the direction of the buffet while I turn back to Greta who is now giggling at anything said at the bar she's still parked at.

"Greta?" I approach her carefully, as to not startle her from her buzz. "We just need to get started. Maybe you could just work the room and start asking partygoers questions about their New Year's resolutions? Is that something you can do right now?"

Her eyes narrow, "What'sh your name again?" she slurs, almost knocking me over with the smell of liquor on her breath. I'd say she's drunk as much as possible, as quickly as possible in the last thirty minutes and is now the most flammable thing in the entire room.

"Oh my God, she's drunk," I say in a whisper to myself. I force a deep breath and a smile. "Emi is my name. Do you think you can still do the commercial?"

"Of course I can. I'm a *professional* actress and model. Why would you even ask me that? You obviously didn't see me in that L'Oréal commercial a few years back." She stands, staggering a bit on her stripper heels. "How about you worry about the camera and I'll do the rest?" she breathes it in my face, making me wish I could request that she brushes her teeth before doing the same to another partygoer.

"Perfect," I say, hoping she's too drunk to notice the condescending tone in my voice. I turn to Morgan who starts filming, a grin on his face. "Just start following her around I guess."

111

"This is gonna be epic."

I glare at him. "Stop it. It's going to be fine." I hope. If nothing else, at least we'll have a potentially viral video on our hands that she can submit to the next *Big Brother Auditions* or maybe *Celebrity Rehab*.

Morgan and I follow Greta halfway around the room and film her asking a few people some questions that she doesn't slur through. She's obviously had experience of keeping her cool on camera when wasted. I'm sure she'd make any reality TV station a fortune. The tabloids would eat her up.

"OH!" She suddenly yells and turns towards me. "I found a co-shtar." She points towards the table where Jack is setting up plates of food for him, Morgan, and me. "*He* ish... delishish."

There are a few too many shs in her words for me to deny the fact that she's completely lit. And now she's after my delicious (I can't deny it) boyfriend.

"What? No, he's actually my fiancé. He doesn't want to be in the commercial."

"That'sh *your* fianshe? No way?!" Her emphasis on your makes my skin crawl. Why would she be so surprised that Jack is with me?

"Come on," She loops her arm through mine, prancing us both across the room, hardly even wobbling on her platform heels. Her drunken strut is nowhere near as clumsy as mine would be.

Morgan follows us closely behind, which seems to be at the speed of a moderate jog. I motion for him to stop filming and he wastes no time setting the camera on the table and tucking into the plate of food Jack brought for him.

"Hey, Ems." Jack smiles as he pats the empty chair next to him.

"You. Are. Beautiful." Greta collapses into the chair obviously meant for me and breathes into his ear.

"I, uh..." Jack looks to me, eyes wide, and obviously stunned at the drunk woman now hanging off him.

"I'm so sorry, Jack, this is Aron's daughter, Greta. She's supposed to be my host for the commercial we're trying to shoot."

"Oh." He kindly reaches into his lap and removes her hand from his upper thigh, then scoots his chair further away from her. "Nice to meet you, Greta."

I bite my bottom lip hard to keep from completely losing it at his disgusted face. From the looks of it, you'd think Greta has some kind of infectious disease that Jack is trying to keep away from. I'm sure there's an STD or three floating around areas I'd rather not picture.

"Yhou are perfect," Greta slurs. "We should do thish together." Her drunkenness is really starting to show now. The extra sounds within her words are becoming more exaggerated.

Out of the corner of my eye, I notice Aron heading in our direction. Shit.

"Greta, your dad is coming." Why can't he mingle instead of choosing now to check on how his star of a daughter is coming along in her so called performance?

She immediately straightens up and loops her arm through Jack's, holding onto his elbow as if he was walking her down the aisle. Or maybe she's just using him as a stabilizer in case she loses her balance and starts to fall from her chair.

"Daddy, have you met my date?"

"I haven't," Aron shakes his head as he makes his way to Jack, hand extended. "It's great to meet you, son. What do you do for a living?" Leave it to Aron to immediately quiz a potential suitor of his daughter's on what he does for a living.

"Um... I'm a lawyer at *Morgan, Steller & Cabot*?" Jack says it like he's not even sure, and glances at me for assistance.

"A lawyer—"

I cut Aron off. "Actually, Aron, this is *my* fiancé, Jack Cabot." I get a confused look from both Greta and Aron. "You actually met him last summer at the company picnic?" I stare at his shaking head and scrunched face. He obviously doesn't remember.

"He *belongs* wifth me." Greta glares over at me. "Daddy, tell himm."

"Greta is a fine young woman. But if Jack belongs to Emi, I respect that." It's as if we're talking about an object, which I can tell by looking at Jack is not something he's very impressed with.

"WHAT?!" Greta yells, gaining the attention of the people near us. "No. Look at him? He'sh gorgeoush, he'sh well off and she is jusht... ugh!"

The disgusted noise coming from her makes me want to crawl into a hole and die. If only she would hiccup randomly through her sentences she'd be the archetypal obnoxious drunk.

"Shhe should be wifth hims," Greta points at Morgan, who has a steak halfway to his mouth without using a fork. "He'sh like, ew, and she'sh like, ew. Jusht trusht me... I'll take good care of him." She pulls Jack to standing, patting his ass with one hand and attempting to plant a kiss on his lips, but stumbles over her own feet, tightening her grip on Jack's arm that is now outstretched to keep her away.

"I don't think so," Jack somehow manages to sit her in an empty chair and escape her grip. She slumps forward as he makes his way quickly around the table to me, pulling me as close to him as possible before clearing his throat and loosening his tie with his free hand. "I'm with Emi and I'm perfectly happy with that. But I've no doubt, any man would be lucky to have you." He politely smiles at Aron but avoids direct eye contact with crazy Greta. Likely for fear that she'll take it as some kind of marriage proposal.

My Jack. Always the gentleman, in even the strangest of situations.

Greta suddenly starts wailing some kind of snorting cry or distress signal, and Aron kneels down by her chair. A few sniffs of the air around her and I've no doubt he's discovered she's had more than just one drink.

"What did you do to her?" Aron asks me, pointing at a now slurring, sobbing, slumped over Greta.

"*Nothing*. We were trying to prep her for the commercial—"

"SHHOW!" Greta yells the word at me.

"And she was only interested in the bar so we uh—"

"So, you just *let* her get wasted?" Aron stands so that we are again at eye level, Jack directly behind me should I need him.

"No." I shake my head. "No, sir. We didn't *let* her, she's an adult. I just… She's quite a handful and—"

"So, let me get this straight, I'm paying for a film crew," He glances at Morgan, who is hardly an entire crew. "And the host is slurring, crying, *and* being humiliated by *your* fiancé."

"I didn't humiliate anyone, actually," Jack takes a step forward fully ready to defend my honor.

Aron lets out a frustrated sigh. "Emi… I thought you were right for this job. But with Greta coming into the picture, I can see that jealousy has taken over, as it always does when women are around my Greta."

"WHAT?!" Jack, Morgan, and I say in unison. He has got to be kidding me. Jealous? Of Greta? I don't think so. Maybe I'm a little envious that I can't pull off the dress she's wearing, but that's it.

"I am *not* jealous of Greta." The disbelieving laugh I've been trying to stifle surrounds the words I'm using as my defense. Which makes me sound completely disrespectful. Although, in this particular situation, who would be married to respectful at this point? I mean, come on, I'm in trouble because a grown woman decided to get wasted when she knew she was working. How is this my fault? Babysitting a full grown woman most definitely isn't in my job description.

"It's funny now?" Aron throws his hands in the air.

"No. Not funny, just... crazy! You can't be serious about this? She's an adult. I can't make her not drink. I suggested it, but she wouldn't listen. In fact, she's been talking down to me all night long. What did you expect me to do?"

Jack squeezes my hand. Probably as a signal that I should shut up and not make the situation even worse, but I can't seem to go down without at least defending myself.

"I'll have you know that this entire situation has been utterly humiliating for me. If you're now upset because she's turned into this..." I point over at her. Her mascara is running down her face and her skin is now a pale shade of green.

The retching noise she makes as she leans over to throw up on her father's shoes turns all the heads that weren't already turned in our direction.

"Ohh... That's never good," Morgan says behind me.

Aron momentarily closes his eyes with a giant heaving sigh. "I'm sorry, Emi. I'll need you to pack up your things. Unfortunately, I'll have to let you go."

"You're firing me?!" I yell. "For what?!"

"For letting Greta become wasted at what was supposed to be our company Christmas Greeting recording and party. I expected you to be able to handle anything thrown at you in this job. This entire situation is hardly professional, and I think you and I both know it." He directs his statement at both Morgan and me.

"You're right," I shout. "The entire night has been completely unprofessional. Your precious daughter is the most conniving, manipulative person I have ever met, and I've only known her for an hour. She didn't need a commercial director, what she needed was an AA meeting. The fact that you are punishing the only person who tried to keep things professional is a testament to her manipulating even her own father. Good luck keeping your company afloat with her as the face of the business." The grip I have on Jack's hand is probably injuring him.

Holy Sweet Moses, I've snapped. A drunk, nude model has caused me to have a complete breakdown, and I'm standing in the middle of a party screaming at my boss.

"You can excuse yourselves now." With a wave of his hand, Aron expects us to be gone for doing absolutely nothing wrong. "You though," he points at Jack, "you will apologize to my Greta for making her feel badly about herself."

"I don't think so! If anything, she should be apologizing to everyone in the room for her out of line behavior towards a guest." Jack looks between Greta and Aron for a moment. He finally rolls his eyes skyward and nods towards the door with an irritated laugh. "Let's go."

Jack and Morgan work quickly, grabbing his equipment and bags. "This is insane," I bark at them as I grab my bag. "I'm taking these." I pile the three heaped plates of food on top of one another and quickly shove the full bottle of wine chilling in an ice bucket in the center of our table, into my bag. I did all the work, so I should at least taste the food.

My heels clack across the floor as I follow Jack and Morgan through the room. The eyes of my co-workers are following my every step. If I was really evil, I'd post whatever video Morgan got on the internet as soon as possible. But I can't. I may have just had an epic meltdown in front of hundreds of people, but I can't ruin anyone. Not even Greta.

*

"I don't even know what just happened?" I look up at Jack when I catch up with him.

"Me neither." Jack's face is netted with confusion. "That was... insane," he shakes his head.

We've all made it to the front of the building and now stand staring at each other in disbelief before all bursting out into laughter at the ridiculousness of the entire thing. This definitely was not the Christmas party experience I was expecting this evening.

"I stole our plates... and this." I pull the bottle of wine from my bag and watch both Jack and Morgan break out into more laughter.

"Wow... You're a fighter and a thief. I'm learning all kind of things about you tonight." Morgan takes a plate from the pile of three in my right hand. "Want me to upload this video? I got the whole thing."

"You were filming that?" I ask, surprised I didn't even notice.

I shove the unopened bottle of wine back into my bag before handing Jack a plate of food.

"Well... I thought it might be useful for the impending lawsuit," Morgan winks.

"It's tempting," I look over at Jack who shakes his head with a small smile. "But my lawyer says it's not a good idea."

"I know. If you ever change your mind, though, I'll save it."

"I'll keep that in mind," I say, suddenly feeling overwhelmingly bad about what just happened. "I'm so sorry about tonight."

"Don't worry about it," Morgan shrugs his shoulders. "They're assholes."

"I hope you find another playboy bunny. Maybe one that isn't quite as insane?" I try not to scrunch my face in disgust as I say it, but I can tell my face isn't co-operating.

Morgan laughs with a wink. "No worries there, I've got a whole stack of 'em."

"Ew," I say as he makes his way across the road to the Max Train Platform to wait for his train.

Jack's phone pings in his pocket.

"Oh no, is it work?" Could this night get any worse?

His face suddenly tenses as he looks at his phone before handing it over to me.

> Jack, I have connections. You'll be hearing from me. Greta.

"What the fuck?" I yell, nearly dropping my plate on the ground and startling an older woman walking past us with a bag of groceries. "She could barely speak a straight sentence five minutes ago. Now she's suddenly become Nancy Drew? How on earth did she get your number so fast?"

"She's going to be a real pain in the ass," Jack growls in irritation. I watch as he hits *Delete* and shoves his phone into his pocket. "Don't worry about it, though, I want nothing to do with that woman." He gives me a peck on the cheek and nods in the direction of the waterfront park trail not far from us. "Dinner on the street as we walk to our car, there's a date we've not had yet."

"True. A walk in the freezing moonlight could be romantic?" I suggest before he drapes his jacket around me. He takes my hand in his with a squeeze, "Everything will work itself out for the best, you'll see." As if reading my mind Jack sends his usual positive vibe into the atmosphere exactly when I need it most.

Seven

The Bridal Shower

Present Day

West Hills, Portland, Oregon

"What happened to you last night?" Lily asks. She, Hannah, Josh, and Evan are all sitting around the dining table with me the next morning, coffee in hand, all awaiting my answer.

I never intended to hang out at Old Tex until final call chatting, with a virtual stranger about the mess that is my life. But Liam was very easy to talk to and really not judgmental. Which was nice for a change. Talking to him also made me realize that I guess now is as good a time as any to spill all the secrets I've held back about the last day Jack and I were together. As I rattled it all off to Liam last night I felt kind of bad that I was telling it detail for detail to a complete stranger before I told even my own brother and soon to be sister-in-law.

"There are some things you guys don't know." I glance at everyone except Lily and Josh, who already know too much and have been sworn to secrecy. "Greta and I have a bit of a history."

"How?" Evan asks.

I know that supposedly Greta and Jack haven't been a couple for long but it makes me wonder just how much he's told them about her, or us even.

"Remember when I worked at Mayfair Homes?"

"Oh yeah... I forgot about that. You quit right after you and Jack got engaged, right?"

I shake my head. "Not exactly," I purse my lips together. I hate it when I lie and then get caught and need to explain it later. Right now, I honestly feel like I'm twelve years old. "I didn't quit, I got fired."

"How did you get fired?" Hannah's voice is high pitched and unbelieving. I can't blame her; I'm not the girl who normally gets fired, and even she knows it.

"Greta," I sigh. "She was supposed to be the face of a commercial we were shooting, but she got wasted, took a liking to Jack, and wouldn't take no for an answer. I was accused of being jealous, not keeping a close enough eye on her, not keeping her sober, and being irresponsible. So, her dad fired me."

"WHAT?" Evan and Hannah say in unison.

"Oh my God, Ems." Hannah stares at me, a frown on her face. "I'm so sorry. If I'd had any idea at all about this, I never would have even invited her to the wedding."

"She's invited?" I assumed she would probably be going as Jack's plus one but somewhere inside me, I hoped she wasn't.

"Everyone got a plus one so I couldn't possibly tell Jack, no. Although with his response when you left yesterday I can't say he'd be all hard up if I did."

"What response is that?" I ask. I knew I saw the Jack I once knew when I was trying to escape. He was more worried about what was happening with me, than even with Greta. Something just doesn't make sense.

"No, Hannah, just let it be," Evan says to her with a shake of his head.

Hannah purses her lips together, a sign that she'd rather explode than keep a secret.

"You know what you need?" Lily interrupts the awkward silence. "A date for the wedding. A plus one. It's only fair to make things even. Don't you think?"

"And how exactly is she going to find a plus one in just a few days..." Evan asks all smug.

"Actually," I think back to chatting with Liam last night. He might not be romantically interested in me, and that's totally fine, but he might be himself just heartbroken enough to help me make sure I get the final say in my own heartbreak. "I may just have the perfect person. I met him last night."

"My God," Evan shakes his head as if I'm a complete whore. I'm not sure why he still feels as if he's got to protect me when I'm in my thirties.

"It's not like *that*, you *perv*. It was innocent. We just talked. He owns a bar up the street. He agreed that my entire situation this week is more than rough, so maybe he'd help me out?"

"Do you have his number?" Lily asks.

"No," I shake my head. "But I know where he works."

"Well, you don't have time to go there and proposition him this morning. We have my bridal shower in an hour." Hannah smiles through clenched teeth. She knew I was hoping they would have had this bridal shower before I got here. Mingling with my ex-fiance's mother is not something I'm looking forward to.

"I'll go by there afterwards. I'm sorry if this whole thing is becoming weird," I say, even though I don't think it's entirely my fault.

"Don't apologize, I only wish I'd known all this earlier." Hannah frowns, obviously upset that she isn't in on all of my secrets. But it's not like I intentionally kept all this from her. Until yesterday, I didn't even know Greta was back in the picture.

"I'm sorry. I was... I *am* humiliated." I sigh deeply, knowing the only way for me to feel better about everything is to tell the rest of my secret to Hannah right now before she finds out on her own and hates me forever. "There might be something else between Greta and me..."

"There's more?"

I nod. "Yeah, it gets worse. I could have lived with the Christmas party thing. But..." I pause, trying to find a delicate way to say this next part. How do you tell someone their cheating brother was somehow in cahoots with Greta the bitch the entire time? "The day I caught Jack... you know. With Lily's advice, I went over later that day to talk to him but, it didn't go as planned."

"How did it go?" Evan asks, much more interested in the story than I expected him to be. He's never been one to be interested in every detail of my drama, but right now, he appears to be all ears.

"When the elevator doors opened, I heard Jack's voice so I peered around the corner before leaving the elevator, you know, so he wouldn't see me, and I saw..." I have to stop and take a breath to keep myself from becoming emotional. It happens every time I relive this part of the story. "I saw her, at our front door, telling him she heard he was newly single, and kissing his cheek. I'd know her blonde hair and voice anywhere. And then... he invited her in."

"*WHAT*?! *He did*? No way!" Hannah's voice is high and whiney, almost like she's having a hard time believing that this girlfriend of Jack's could do something so brazen. "What did you do?"

"Nothing. I never spoke to him again. I just couldn't unsee what I saw and I can't see how it could all happen the way it did, if he wasn't at least a little bit guilty. Now they're a couple, so what does that tell you?"

"I am *so* sorry, Ems." Evan reaches across the table and pats my hand. "I had no idea. I can kick his ass if you want?"

I smile. Part of me wants to take him up on that but that's not the adult part of me even a little bit.

"No, you can't, because no one is going to mention this. He chose her even before we broke up, so, no matter how much any of this appears to bother me, he gets to keep her. He's obviously not the Jack I once knew."

"Emi, I'm sorry," Hannah hugs me. "I promise to keep a fair distance between you and Greta at the bridal shower." A thin apologetic smile spreads across Hannah's face before she stands from the table. "I hate to cut this short but we have to get ready. Is there anything else we should know?"

I shake my head. "That's it." Thank God that's it. "I'll try and not let my emotions get the best of me the next couple of days."

It won't be easy, and I definitely can't make any promises, but for Hannah's sake I'll at least try and do my best and not over think the situation. No matter how much my head hurts over all this, Hannah and Evan deserve a stress free wedding.

*

"Emi!" Amelia greets me before even her own daughter when we walk through the door. "My dear girl, how

I've missed you!" She surprises me by pulling me in for a hug so tight I think I might never get away.

I kind of figured after I bailed on the huge wedding she was planning that she'd be more irritation, and less 'missed me'.

"You look..." She looks me over for a minute, probably trying to find another, less obvious, word for fat. "Fabulous."

I've noticed in life that when people tell you that you look 'fabulous' you really don't. You look just slightly less great than they had expected, and 'fabulous' rolls of the tongue so quickly and easily in a tense situation.

"Can you believe that we finally get to be family?" Amelia asks with a grin.

"Well... Not me, but Evan."

"Pfft! That includes you. Who'd have ever thought that instead of you and Jack, we'd end up with Hannah and Evan getting married?" She smiles sweetly before putting her arm around my shoulder and walking me into her lavish living room. "Still such a shame about you and Jack, though." She leans closer to me. "The man was heartbroken for ages. Even now, I sometimes wonder."

"What?" I force my face to not look stunned at what she's just said. She still sometimes wonders if Jack is broken hearted over me? But he's got a girlfriend?

"Hannah mentioned you ran away from us for some type of internship? How did that go, dear?"

"Internship?" I ask, with a shake of my head.

"Emi, I just remember something I need to talk to you about, urgently." Hannah grabs my arm and pulls me away from Amelia and Lily, dragging me across the room and into the pantry. A pantry that's bigger than my bedroom. "Shit," Hannah hisses. It's unlike her to use my favorite curse word.

"What is it?"

"There is something I forgot about. Please don't hate me."

"Spit it out." I should have known I wasn't the only one with secrets this week.

"When you and Jack broke up, he didn't want to tell Mom what actually happened. So, we – *He* told her that you had an amazing opportunity with an ad agency in New York for an internship."

"*WHAT*?" I squeak, in a weird high pitched, trying not to make a scene from the pantry, voice. "Why would he tell her that?" Having said that, I'm not entirely sure why I'm surprised by this. Jack has refused to admit any wrongdoing even when he was pretty much caught red-handed. Why would I think his family would know the truth?

"He thought he would win you back, Ems. It's not even been a year. He didn't want to break Mom's heart by telling her why you actually broke up."

"So instead of telling the truth he *lied* to her and made our break up *my* fault?"

"Well, no... He said it was a great opportunity for you and that you just didn't feel right getting married without at least giving it a go. He said you two just grew apart and amicably broke up. She's not mad at you. She's more frustrated with Jack. I don't know, actually. Things have been weird whenever you're mentioned." Hannah bites her freshly manicured nails nervously.

"Hannah…" Her name leaves my lips tinged with irritation. I can't be completely mad at her. It's not like *she* made it up. She just went along with it. Plus, she did kind of just forgive me earlier when I told her a secret she knew nothing about. If I don't just let this go, guess who will be the bigger bitch here? "Whatever, it's fine," I sigh through clenched teeth, annoyed at having to lie some more. "What do I need to say?"

"Just go with my story, at least until after the wedding, and then I'll tell her the truth. I promise."

"Fine." I scan the pantry and see a basket full of sample sized bottles of liquor and shove a few into my bag. Hannah's eyes grow wide as she pinches her lips into a disapproving, judgmental pucker. "What? I've earned these. Go mingle…"

She rolls her eyes with half a smile before giving me a hug, a quick one because she knows I hate hugs, despite her giving them to me every opportunity she has. "Thank you," she says with a relieved smile.

As she disappears through the door I grab my bag and straighten my dress. The last thing I need is someone spreading the rumor that I was getting busy with god knows who in the pantry.

"Emi?" Lily calls my name as I click open the pantry door. Lily spins around to face me. "*What* are you doing?"

"Hiding." I reluctantly leave the pantry and peek around the corner at the room full of plastic, made-up, glittering rich women. *Hannah*, they each squeal one by one as they greet the bride-to-be.

"Well stop it. You look more than crazy." Lily grabs two glasses of champagne off a tray sitting near her on the counter. "Drink this and let's go out there and try to blend in. And no more acting like a loon, pull it together, would ya?"

"Is Greta here?"

"Yes, and if you don't get out there she'll look much, much saner than you. Which is probably harder to do than we can imagine considering she's nearly certifiably mental."

"All right." I down the champagne, set the empty glass on the counter and grab another off the tray. No use letting them go to waste. "Let's go do some lying."

"Wait," Lily grabs my arm. "What? Why are we lying?"

I sigh. "Hannah and Jack didn't want to tell Amelia what really happened when we broke up, so they told her I took a business internship in New York and that we just... grew apart." I half laugh at the ridiculousness of it as I down my next champagne and exchange it for another.

"That's uh... wow. OK then, let's go lie."

"You're on board?" I ask her, surprised she's going to help me after she's been so up my ass about being half cracked.

"Well... not really. But this week can't get any weirder, so why the hell not?"

"Great!" I say, only the tiniest bit worried.

We join the buzzing room of ladies and I'm suddenly very afraid of what exactly might be said. I feel like I should have a notepad to keep track of my lies, just in case I need to follow up with them later in the week. Lying isn't exactly my forte so convincing someone that I'm telling the truth is a challenge on its own.

"Just smile and nod, and maybe they won't even approach,"

"Emi! I was wondering where you ran off to in the middle of our conversation? Now come say hello to everyone. They are all dying to catch up." Amelia guides Lily and me over to the group of women on the patio.

I glance around at the faces of Jack's aunts, family friends, and a few strangers. Obviously, the few family members Evan and I have are standing along the far wall, leaving little distance between themselves and the buffet. I wave over at my Aunt Maggie who waves back, a proud smile on her face. As I scan the room I see her, front and center as any good narcissist would be, Greta. Her fake, forced smile blends in with the rest of these plastics.

"Have you had the pleasure of meeting, Greta, Jack's new uh, friend?" An almost malicious smile hangs at the corners of Amelia's lips as she walks me over to introduce us. If I didn't know any better, I'd think she was up to something. Amelia has never played games with me, though. Somehow once she decided I was family, I was safe from any hurt that I imagine she could cause should she want to.

"Greta, this is Emi, Jack's former fiancé."

I grin, and almost want to do a little curtsey, but I hold back. "I've heard so much about you," I say sweetly.

Amelia nods with a grin. "Greta and Jack have been seeing each other for a short time now, isn't that right, Greta?"

"Well, two months is long enough to elope in my mind. And we have gotten pretty close recently."

Amelia gasps, causing me to force away a smile of my own. She pats my back and suddenly shouts hello at a woman who's just entered the room, leaving Greta and me together.

"This must be so hard for you, to have to watch the love of your life moving on?"

I shake my head with a nasally laugh. "First of all, I don't exactly see a ring on your finger... and second, Jack is hardly the love of my life." I down the champagne I'm still holding in one gulp. They are going down easier and easier, which considering I'm not a drinker, can't be good. "You can actually have him. In fact, I hope you two are very happy together. You're made for each other: both cheaters, both over the top, and both sad pathetic liars."

"Oh, little do you know just how serious our relationship is. Not that it's any of your business, but I'll have you know, Jack has never cheated on me. He doesn't need to, look at me." She waves her hands down her body. How arrogant can someone be? "But, I warned you I was more his type. I guess you should have listened and saved yourself some heartache." She smiles with a lift of her shoulders. "I really should get back."

"Yes, you should, maybe you could tell everyone how you're just dying to be given a second hand ring after cheating with your boyfriend while he was still engaged to be married to someone else? You'll fit right in with everyone here, just like the Stepford wife that I've no doubt you'll one day become."

A sound comes out of her mouth that is anything but pleasant. She quickly stomps her foot and turns away from me, sidling up to some rich old broad I've never seen before.

"Well, at least you haven't had to lie yet," Lily laughs beside me and motions to a free seating area. "Let's sit, away from the action. Maybe it will keep us out of trouble."

A clapping comes from the far side of the room. Amelia is gathering everyone's attention.

"Today we celebrate my lovely daughter, Hannah. She insisted I don't embarrass her, so I'll do my best. Let's play a quick introduction game. We'll go around the room and point to someone and say how we know them. Obviously, we will start with my Hannah. I know her because I'm her mother, Amelia, and I suffered many hours of labor bringing her into this world." Her laugh fills the room as she points to a now blushing Hannah.

The game goes on and on, and Lily introduces herself as my best friend which throws the introduction game to me.

"I'm Emi Harrison, I know Hannah through her brother, Jack." Hannah's eyes widen for a second, worried about what might come out of my mouth. "But, since he wasn't invited to the party I guess I'll just use his good friend, Greta. I once worked with Greta's father at Mayfair Homes and she and I once worked on a project together, well, kind of... didn't we?" I point over at Greta who looks momentarily horrified before she spits out an uncomfortable laugh.

"Actually, I'm Jack's *girlfriend*. And yes, we did once work together, if I remember correctly, you were fired that day? Right?"

I nod with a smile, Lily's elbow now wedged into my ribs. "Yes, yes I was and as a lovely little parting gift I was given a video of the entire evening. Maybe we'll have to sit down and have a watch, all of us?"

When I glance towards Amelia, her smile is vague, but there is enough to know that she knows more than she's saying.

"Anyway," Greta says, moving the game along.

I should have got hold of Morgan and asked for the video proof of what a nut job Greta really is, once I knew she was going to be here this week. That certainly would have thrown a wrench into her snide remarks aimed at me.

"Still haven't even had to lie…" I whisper to Lily as I take another sip of my champagne.

This last sip doesn't settle as well as the others and within seconds I know it's not staying put where it should be.

"Oh no!" I hiss to Lily, barely able to turn my head without the entire room spinning around me. Things are taking a sudden turn for the worse. I knew I shouldn't have kept drinking these things, on an empty stomach. "I'm gonna be sick." I lean into Lily, who grabs my arm.

"Where's the bathroom?" she whispers anxiously.

"Too far." I run to the patio, her at my heels. I try to make it at least past the decorative centerpiece fountain, but I don't. The heaving sound coming from within makes even me jump. I don't have to turn around to know the whole room is watching me defile this very expensive water feature.

"She'll be fine. I'm so sorry." Lily is standing in front of me, profusely trying to apologize on my behalf.

I finally look over at her, her face scrunched up in a horrifically embarrassed look. "This is not good, Ems," she mumbles under her breath.

All I can do is nod as I go for another round into the once crystal clear water of the fountain.

"Oh my!" Amelia bolts to action and runs to my side. "Let's get you lying down. Help me get her to the guest room," she says to Lily.

With Amelia on one side and Lily on the other, they drag me through the crowd of women and to a small guest bedroom on the first floor of their house.

"Grab her some Tylenol, Marion." Amelia barks an order at the woman dressed all in black in the doorway behind us. Before I can object I'm sipping water with Tylenol and have a cold rag being held against the back of my neck. "Was it something you ate?" Amelia asks, sitting by my side and attempting to nurse me back to health. Or in this case, an earlier, more sober version of me.

"No, no. Probably it was something I drank on an empty stomach. I shouldn't have done that." I will not tell her how much something I drank. That part isn't important.

"Of course, she's *drunk*." A voice echoes from the doorway. Greta is leaning against the edge, glaring at me. "What a way to ruin the party."

"Greta! Go gossip somewhere else," Lily snaps at her before closing the door in her face.

"Are you drunk?" Amelia asks, looking almost more concerned than angry.

"No, not really. I just had a lot of champagne on an empty stomach, and then Greta... it's like she's made it her job to make sure I'm as miserable as possible. I'm so sorry, Amelia. Really, I am. I feel a lot better, though."

That's mostly a lie. The room is still spinning, but I don't feel nauseous any longer so there is an improvement. That poor fountain, though.

"Emi." Amelia's motherly voice fills the room. The same voice she's used on me since my mother died. "I know that this is a trying week for you and for Jack. I knew it before it was even here. But I would hope that we could set all this aside and focus on Hannah and your brother Evan and make this as perfect as possible." She takes my hands in hers and looks me right in the eyes. "I love you like my own daughter, Emi, and while I don't know the exact truth over what happened between you and my son, I do know that he is still heartbroken over you to this day."

"But he's going out with Greta," I say, wondering what she meant by 'exact truth'.

"Please," Amelia waves her hand in the air. "Greta is there when Jack needs someone to talk to. She's pushed her way in wherever he is, invited herself to be at the same functions as he and yet even as in love with you as he is, he's convinced himself that Greta is all he deserves. His heart is still with you, should you still have it. So, please use some compassion when dealing with this tricky and emotional situation that we have ahead of us." She pats my hand, telling me her speech is done and that no questions will be allowed. As she heads for the door she stops just prior to opening it. "Stay in here if you like, but I do hope you'll rejoin the party soon." The door clicks closed and Lily and I are left alone.

"Whoa. She is a tad intimidating, isn't she?" Lily says with a nervous laugh.

"What do you think she meant by all that?"

"That Jack is still in love with you. Still pining, still waiting for his chance to sweep you off your feet. Which is exactly what we all thought anyway."

"It can't be right, Lil. He knew how much I hated Greta. How could he ever think that him being involved with her was a way back to me?"

"Life is complicated, Em. Sometimes in order to figure out exactly what you want, you have to figure out how far you'll travel to get there. How much of a challenge it's worth? Obviously, both you and Jack have some kind of unfinished feelings for one another. It doesn't take a rocket scientist to see it." Lily sits down where Amelia was a few moments ago. "I think it's time for you to make a decision about this. Either you're over Jack and you stop doing all of this..." she motions at my current drunken state, "or you figure out how to tell him how you really feel and you two have a sit down serious talk."

I stare at Lily, then close my eyes. "I don't know what I want and I really don't know how I feel." Maybe if the room would stop circling me, I'd be able to figure it out.

"Good. After the party then, we'll stop by and see your new friend. Nothing helps you make the right decision like a rebound guy. What's his name again?"

"Liam," I say, wondering if a rebound guy is really the right move to prove whether I am or am not over

Jack? It's definitely risky.

*

The party lasts a couple more hours. Thankfully, I'm able to avoid any more episodes and I'm somehow able to steer clear of Greta and any of Jack's family members who ask too many questions about my supposed internship and failed almost-wedding.

Hannah gets everything she could possibly need as an almost-married woman, and for the last hour I've watched Evan and Josh load it all up into two trucks as I've sat on the step of the front porch recovering from my recent embarrassment.

"Listen," I say to Lily who's helping Josh tie down the last of the boxes in the truck. "I think I should go make a fool of myself to this guy on my own."

"Why?"

"Because it's weird, and I've already looked like a ditz in front of him once. Not to mention that it's probably a totally bad idea that he'll laugh at. And let's face it, this week alone I've had enough humiliation to last me a lifetime."

She sighs heavily and glances at Josh as if she's making this decision against her better judgment. Which probably isn't far from the truth. "Fine, I'll drop you off there. But promise me you'll come home immediately after, and that you won't do anything completely stupid?"

"What stupid thing could I do?" I ask.

"Vomit in the elaborately landscaped waterfall in the middle of a party, maybe?" Josh laughs at me.

"Ask a random man to be your date for my wedding to prove you're over Jack?" Evan adds to Josh's suggestion.

"You guys aren't funny." I would add to my defense, but come on, I've got none.

"We should start a list of Emi's unintentional screw-ups this week," Evan says, avoiding direct eye contact. Clearly, he's not impressed with my ridiculous behavior. I can't say I blame him. I'm not normally this nutty.

"I prefer that we don't," I say, knowing full well that writing it down isn't necessary. They'll be telling this story from memory for years to come.

*

When I walk into the bar it's as dark as it was the other day, but this time I notice it's because there are no windows apart from the porthole in the door. It truly is a dive bar. I imagine having no windows makes it easier to hide from the problems you're trying to drown.

"She's back!" Bald Bartender yells, and I see Liam pop out of a doorway behind the bar.

"She certainly is. What brings you back? More troubles with the ex?" He winks at me as he walks around the counter to where I'm standing.

"Yes, and no. Actually..." I fidget with my bracelets and pick at my freshly painted nails. "I... um..." I force out a nervous breath. "I wanted to ask a favor of you."

"A favor? We're already at that point in our relationship?" He laughs and motions to the table near the back of the bar.

I'm nervous, like the-nausea-is-starting-to-return nervous. I take a couple of deep breaths, hopefully unnoticeable, and sit at the table.

Liam flips a chair around and straddles it, leaning against the back. "What kind of favor are we talking here? Do you need another loan? Or maybe a hit man?"

"No, no, neither of them. Yet."

His smile brings dimples to his stubbled face.

"It's actually kind of pathetic. I just... uh..." I take another breath and stare at the gold candle holder in front of me. The candle in it is dusty and melted down to the metal wick bottom.

Come on, Em, just say it out loud, it's not like it's going to get any less weird.

"I was wondering if you would come to the wedding with me as my date?" I rattle it out, laying my whole pathetic self right there on the table in front of the man I only met yesterday.

Liam leans back for a minute, his lips pursed and his eyes clouded with confusion. "You want *me* to be your date, to your brother's wedding? The one where your ex will be?"

"Yes," I drop my head towards the table. "I know, it's totally ridicul—"

He cuts me off. "I'll do it."

"You will?" I say completely shocked.

"Sure," he shrugs his shoulders with a smile. "You're beautiful, sweet, desperate, and you never know when I myself might need a favor in return."

"As long as your favor doesn't put me in jail, I'm in."

"I'll try to save that one until you know me a bit better then." He runs his hand through his hair before leaning against the chair back in front of him again. "Just one question: are we making him jealous so he'll dump the new girl and beg you to come back, or just going for heartbreak that he's lost you all together?"

"Why do I feel like you've done this before?" I ask him with a nervous laugh. "I think the later one, at least for now."

"Perfect..." He pulls a black leather wallet from his back jeans pocket and slides out a business card, handing it to me across the table. "This is me, my number, email, measurements," he winks. "Everything you need to get me the details of this wedding date."

"OK."

"Is it black tie?"

"No," I shake my head. For a guy, he pays attention to the details a lot of men would miss.

"I'll be there." He stands from his chair and puts his wallet back in his pocket. "And Emi?"

"Yeah?" I clutch my purse as I stand, still nervous even though he's just agreed to do this.

"When this wedding is over, he'll know just how crazy he was to do what he did. Sound good?"

I nod with a hesitant smile. This could go great, I could achieve whatever it is I think I'm looking to achieve, or it could become a disaster. "Sounds great, thank you."

"It's totally my pleasure." With a nod of his head, he stands up, walks around behind the bar, and disappears through the same side door he just came from.

Eight

The Proposal

One year, nine months ago.

Lincoln City, Oregon

"Pack a bag," Jack says with a grin as he walks through our apartment door.

"But I was just getting ready to make dinner."

He looks at the counter covered in sauce jars, spaghetti noodles, and seasonings. "I love your spaghetti." He wraps his arms around my waist. "But I'm thinking maybe tonight we go fancy and head to the coast for the weekend? It's all booked, paid for, and I promise high amounts of romance."

"What kind of romance? The kind that gets me into bed or the kind that makes me swoon and fall even more in love with you?"

Jack raises a single eyebrow with a smile "Hopefully both?" He laughs, before kissing my neck, sealing the deal that my answer will not be no. How could I ever resist the guy who is full of romantic surprises even though he knows I hate surprises.

"How fancy?" I ask, following him into our room. I pull out our two black suitcases from the closet and lay them on the bed.

"The blue dress fancy?" His smile grows and his brown eyes sparkle as he pictures me in the one dress he loves.

I only have one blue dress and he requests it anytime he can. I've actually started considering it my lucky blue dress because somehow, every time I wear it, something great happens. He actually picked it out one day while we were shopping and even though it's a few years old, I don't think he'll ever get tired of it.

It's the dress I wore for the first time to one of his office parties. It's really nothing special, just a midi dress with a slight flare to the hem with spaghetti straps in a blue color I fell in love with the second I saw it. It's figure flattering, even now, and fits like a glove (the regular kind).

"Whoa, we are going fancy. Does that mean—"

Like the soul-mate that he is, he reads my mind. "Yes, the pinstripe suit."

A girl can have her favorite clothing too, you know? One of the perks of Jack being a lawyer is that I can swoon over him looking all sexy and dressed up even if it isn't specifically for me. Today though, it will be.

"Yay!" I start tossing clothes into my suitcase, not forgetting the dress and my highest of high heels that make me stand at least above Jack's shoulders when wearing them.

*

It takes Jack and me all of an hour to pack our cases, and we speed through the mountains towards Lincoln City. Normally when we come, we stay in tiny motels or cool little bed and breakfasts, but when Jack pulls up to the entrance of the most expensive hotel in the town, my heart does a tiny pitter-patter as I imagine a fancy life I say I never want.

"We're staying here?"

"Yup."

"But we never stay here."

"I know, I thought it would be a nice change?" He grabs my hand and walks me into the hotel, chatting with the woman behind the counter as I walk around gawking at the fancy interiors. Everything is shiny and new with a modern sleek design. White flowers are on every counter and neon blue lights are under every eave.

When he's done checking us in I follow him into the elevator and watch him push the button for the eleventh floor.

"We're on the eleventh floor? Is there a balcony?" He knows my only requirement when staying at the beach is a balcony overlooking the ocean. I could spend hours sitting there, reading, or just watching the waves crash. It's mesmerizingly beautiful.

"Of course, there is. I have a reservation in the restaurant in an hour so let's dress up?" He flashes a sly smile as we walk out of the elevator and towards room 1124.

I admit I'm getting a little curious as to why he's going to all this trouble? It's not like Jack to be so secretive. That's part of what I love about him. I never have to wonder what he's up to, he normally tells me up front because he loves seeing my reaction as much as I love not waiting to have one. This time though… it's like he's hiding something from me. If I let myself go to what I think it might be, I'll be really nervous. I'm sure it's some kind of bad omen to expect what I think it is. If there is anything I've learned from watching far too many romantic comedies, it's not to expect a proposal. It never ends well.

"What did you plan, Mr Cabot? Should I be nervous?"

"Not at all. I just wanted to do something special for you since I've been working all the time lately. It's only fair," he presses his lips to mine, which I admit, is a pretty unfair way for him to immediately make everything OK.

The room door beeps and pops open when he inserts his key revealing a giant suite of a room.

"Whoa..." We walk into a sitting room bigger than our own living room at home, with a floor to ceiling window looking out at the sunset. There's a big TV on one wall and a plush couch on the other. A pair of French doors opens to a king-sized bed facing yet another wall of windows, which is the perfect way to wake up in the morning. I immediately spot the balcony stretching across both rooms.

"Jack," I squeeze his hand. "This is... expensive, and *so* beautiful." I know Jack comes from money but he doesn't normally live the fancy, rich life that he could if he wanted. He's more down to earth and laid back than that. This is extravagant and way out of the ordinary. Something is definitely up.

"Worth it." He leans down, kissing my lips with a hand on my neck, giving me all the feelings possible. When he finally pulls away he tosses his bag onto the bed, then unpacks everything and puts his things into the empty drawers in the dresser against the wall.

He's totally the opposite of me. He will unpack the moment we get somewhere whereas I will gladly live out of a suitcase for a month.

"Get dressed, gorgeous." He nods towards the bathroom near me.

I plug in my curling iron and do long loose waves in my hair. Pull on my dress and slip on my heels. A quick touch up of my already done makeup and I'm ready.

"OK…"

As I walk out of the bathroom door I am stunned. I thought I was quick getting ready but from the looks of this place it took me a lot longer than I thought.

On the balcony, there is a table set for two: candles, covered plates, and wine.

"How did you—"

"Madam, Sir." A man in a tuxedo interrupts me, directing me to my chair near where Jack is now standing.

"Who's this?" I ask, unsure of exactly what is really going on. I swear it was just twenty minutes ago I was standing here staring at the ocean, and now there is a full dinner and waiter in our room.

"This is Elliott, he's our chef and waiter for the evening." Jack pulls my chair out for me like the gentleman he is.

"You hired a private chef?"

"I did." He grabs the wine bottle and pours us each a glass of wine, pink in color. "I also instructed him to bring dessert first, because I know how you love eating cake for dinner." He laughs as he sets the wine back in the bucket. "But first…" he walks over and pulls open one of the dresser drawers he just laid all his clothes in and pulls out a small black box with a bright white bow.

Oh my God! It's a tiny gift box! The squealing going on inside me would embarrass even the coolest of people. A tiny box as in the size of a small piece of jewelry. Holy shit. I was right, he *is* up to something.

This is it, Ems. He's proposing.

How did he keep this a secret until right now? I can't believe this is happening! Is it totally wrong that I want to pause this moment and call Lily right this second?

"I wanted to give you this," he hands me the box and pulls his chair over near mine. "Open it."

"What did you do?" I ask him, pulling the bow off and lifting the lid off the box to reveal a white jewelry box the perfect size for a ring. "Is this—" Thank God he can't hear the squealing going on in my head right now.

Before I can finish, Jack takes the box, moves his chair, and kneels beside me opening the box to reveal the most beautiful engagement ring I've ever seen.

"I know you didn't want me to do this in a public place with a room full of strange eyes watching such a private moment, so here we are, in one of your favorite places, and I just have one question..." He smiles at me as he pulls the ring out of the box before taking my left hand in his. "Will you do me a favor, and spend forever making me this happy?"

"Oh my God!" I can't contain the squeal any longer and lunge out of my chair, knocking Jack over and causing the ring to go rolling across the floor towards the bed and thankfully, not the balcony. Jack spots it first, laughing as he collapses on the floor to reach it.

We're both laughing uncontrollably now, "Well, that was smooth," he holds the ring out to me, both of us now sitting on the floor in front of one another. "Marry me, Emi?"

I stare down at the ring, tears burning my eyes as they spill over uncontrollably. "It's all I ever wanted. Of course I'll marry you!" I hold my hand as steady as possible as he slides the gorgeous three carat ring onto my third finger like it was made to fit. I wrap my arms around his neck and stare at the ring over his shoulder for a moment. "I can't believe you did all this!"

He kisses my neck and lets out what sounds like a relieved sigh. "I love you more than anything." When his lips finally meet mine, they make me forget dessert, engagement rings, or even the fact that I'm wearing the most uncomfortable six inch heels. It's just us, and we are newly engaged.

*

"I can't believe you're engaged!!" Lily stares at my hand even weeks after she originally saw it. "This is quite the party, too. Who are all these people?"

"I have no idea. I actually don't know half of them. But isn't it just incredible?" I glance down at the ring again before taking a sip of my champagne. "It's like a dream." Truly.

"Have you set a date?"

"No. In fact, I didn't even arrange this party, this was all Amelia. I have no idea how to plan a wedding. You know me."

"I do know you," Lily laughs as she sips her champagne. "Want my advice?"

"Would saying no stop you?"

"Doubtful," she gives me a quick playful glare. "Hire a wedding planner. You can give her basic ideas and then let her do all the hard work. Really all you'll have to do is show up. In hindsight, I wish I'd hired one."

"Congratulations, you two. I knew she'd say yes." Jack's partner, Andy and he are shaking hands.

"You knew?" I ask, surprised to hear that Jack told anyone at all. He kept it so quiet I figured he was the only one that knew.

"I did, and I told him if he didn't do it soon, I would." He laughs, making me feel only a little dirty. "Let's see the rock." I hold out my hand, the overhead lights of the bar causing it to glitter to life. "Wow! No wonder she said yes."

"I know..." Jack laughs. "I probably should have asked before showing her the ring to know how she really felt." He winks, resting his hand on my lower back. Even now, almost four years into our relationship, his touch still sends sparks up my spine.

"You knew my answer long before you asked." I playfully smack him in the chest.

"We're gonna be sisters!" Hannah, Jack's younger sister, unintentionally presses her new boobs against my neck in a giant bear hug. If I was just a tad taller I wouldn't have to be in constant contact with her chest. "I'm so excited!" she squeals.

"Me too, Hannah. It's so exciting!"

"Oh my God..." She stops in her tracks, her gaze directed at the bar. "Who is *that*?"

I follow her gaze across the room to none other than my twin brother. "That's Emi's brother, Evan," Lily says for me.

"Wow! He is..." she glances at me, then back at him. "Gorgeous."

"OK..." I smile nervously up at Jack. Hannah is not exactly known for her great success with relationships, and neither is my brother, which is exactly the reason they've not met yet, but now I've no more excuses as to why they shouldn't meet. "I can introduce you. In any case, you will practically be family soon."

"Please do."

I wave Evan over as Hannah waits, almost patiently. "Ev, this is Jack's sister, Hannah. Hannah, this is my twin brother, Evan."

"You guys are twins?" She glances back and forth quickly like she doesn't believe a word I just said.

"Unfortunately," Evan laughs, holding his hand out for Hannah. "It's great to meet you. I'd love to hear all the dirt on your brother. There's got to be something to keep him from being as perfect as Emi claims." When their hands touch, you can almost see the spark between them.

I know it's not my place to come in-between possible true love but I also don't want to over think what could happen if Evan and Hannah get too close. My fear is that they will add each other to their never ending lists of one night stands. Then they'll somehow piss each other off, and we'll never be able to have a family gathering without some strange tension in the room. Not exactly the family gathering I'd like to initiate during the engagement party.

"Buy me a drink and I'll show you the photos that go with the stories." Hannah flirts, making me a little sick to my stomach.

"Ew... Go do it over there, maybe?" I glance towards an open table and watch Hannah loop her arm through Evan's, leading him across the room. "And by *do it* I don't really mean *do it*," I call after them but Hannah only waves a hand over her shoulder in my direction.

"That's bad news, isn't it?" I ask Jack, who's still talking to Andy.

"Could be, but they're grown-ups."

"Emi, Jack," Amelia and her husband Robert approach us, dressed to the nines, and looking like this party was meant for them. "Isn't this just lovely?" Amelia air kisses each of my cheeks. A gesture I despise. Whenever I see people do the whole air kiss greeting it looks like they were told to make sure others think they're getting along, when really, they hate each other.

It is lovely, and she would know since she planned the entire thing. I didn't want to have a party at all. I'm not a huge fan of socializing with a room full of strangers, but she insisted it was the thing to do. Of course, she would pick a swanky downtown bar and hire it out for a private event like some local elitist. Not surprisingly the room is full of at least a hundred people, only maybe a dozen of whom I've ever actually met.

"This ring..." Amelia takes my hand and inspects it like she's doing an appraisal to make sure it's all still there. "was Jack's grandmother's ring. Of course, he added a touch of his own to it before giving it to you, but still, it's just beautiful and so sentimental. One day you can pass it down to your son."

"Son?" I choke on my champagne. I've only been engaged for three weeks and now his family has me popping out sons already. "I don't know if a son is in the plans for quite some time."

"Well, of course not immediately, let's get through the wedding first, but I'm sure you will be blessed with the most beautiful of children, don't you think, dear?"

Robert nods his head, he's always been a man of few words. He's chatting with Jack about whatever grown men talk about at engagement parties, which I doubt is producing sons. I'm not exactly listening because the idea of me being responsible for a child is still swirling through my head like a tornado.

"Come, dear," Amelia says. "Introduce me to your family."

"There's only a few of them, I'm afraid." With my parents being deceased, only a couple of aunts and uncles and my brother could make it. I don't know if that makes me look as pathetic as an orphan or not, but it doesn't raise me up to the Cabot status in life. "Evan..." I say his name before reaching the table he and Hannah are still sharing, hoping that they aren't already doing the dirty things they are both so known for. "Evan, this is Jack's mother, Amelia."

"Evan, look how handsome you are. And you've already met my Hannah." She pats Hannah's shoulder with a questioning stare before turning her attention back to Evan. "What are your feelings on the upcoming nuptials?"

Evan quickly stands up, following the instructions our father once gave him of standing when a woman approaches your table. He doesn't hide giving Hannah a somewhat guilty sideways look.

"I think Jack and Emi are absolutely perfect for one another, don't you?"

"I do, actually, they make a rather lovely couple."

Evan nods with a curt smile, "I've no doubt they'll be very happy together." He nods in my direction for approval. I might have told him to keep things classier than he normally would and so far, so good. Amelia looks sufficiently impressed.

"Who else is here that I should meet?" Amelia scans the room, probably looking for faces she's never seen on her side of town.

She knows my family history but it does make me feel good that she's making a big deal about meeting the family members that could actually make it.

"Our Aunt Maggie is here, and her brother Melvin is with her." Evan points in their direction. Both of them are standing in front of the buffet, probably looking for something not too fancy to eat.

"Let's go have a meet." Amelia pulls me along with her like a schoolgirl in trouble. "This is just so exciting, soon we'll all be family and you won't ever have to worry about ending up alone." She speaks excitedly, which surprises me. Amelia has always treated me like a daughter, but I've often felt a tad like she thought Jack could do so much better than normal, hardly any family, me, a commoner.

"Aunt Maggie, I'm so glad you came."

Maggie sets her plate on the table and wraps her arms around me for a hug. Maggie has always been that eccentric aunt who means the best but sometimes can throw a can of crazy into a completely normal situation. Sometimes I wonder if she had a hand in naming us. She used to tell us stories about a young Romanian woman coming to live in America after escaping a family who didn't believe in her connection with the afterlife. Maggie would point to a crystal ball that permanently sat on a high shelf in her home and tell us stories of their friendship as young girls, and how easily they still chat even though her friend passed on years ago.

"My sweet little Esmeralda. Your mother is so pleased with all this. I'm so sad she's not here to tell you herself."

I glance at Amelia, who, from what I have told her, knows this part of Maggie, but her wide eyes insist that she's since forgotten my warning.

"Me too. I'm so glad *you're* here, though. I do wish I could tell Mom about the proposal. He did it in true Jack style." I laugh, knowing my mom would know exactly what I was talking about. It was something we used to joke about with Jack's elaborate ideas and surprises and it was the way he'd first won my parents over. Me too, for that matter.

"I'd like to introduce you to Amelia, Jack's mother. She's really taken me in like I'm her own."

"Nonsense, I've just done what any mother would do. I'm so sorry about Molly's passing." Amelia takes Maggie's hands in hers, truly looking sorry about my mom's death.

"Thank you, so are we. I just can't believe she's missing all this in person. You're getting a great girl in Esmeralda, she's a real sweetheart, a beauty too. She's got great things ahead in her life, let me tell you."

"That she is." Amelia pats my hand.

"Oh, my! Look at this stone!" Uncle Melvin inspects the sparkling rock on my finger, his eyes growing wider by the second. "I wonder what something like that costs?" he asks Maggie.

"Priceless, it's a family heirloom." Amelia corrects him, her face shocked at his question.

"Jack is just a lovely boy, you've done a fine job on that one. I've no doubt these kids will get past the rough patch." Maggie compliments Amelia and quickly notices the look of dismay on my face. "I mean... they will get through whatever life throws their way. They're both such strong headed kids, they'll make the right choices in life."

Amelia nods. "I'm sure they'll go far in life. Tell me, though, about the rough patch you mentioned?"

"Oh..." Maggie forces a smile in my direction. "It's just an old saying, every marriage has rough patches, they're inevitable. I just know these kids will make it through with the right choices."

Amelia nods in agreement before they start discussing the food. A welcome topic in my book.

Leave it to Maggie to throw in an accidental psychic reading into the conversation, even though before the party I begged her not to. The last thing I need is her proving to Amelia that I'm far from the normal girl she thinks she knows.

"Have you seen the pile of gifts?" Lily saves me from having to chat about babies with Amelia and Maggie. "It's insane. I didn't even know people got these kinds of things at engagement parties."

"I've already had at least five people, whose names I couldn't even tell you, hand me envelopes with checks in them. It's crazy!"

The ping of metal against glass grabs both our attention and when we turn I see Jack standing at the front of the room waving me up to him.

"Gotta go," I whisper to Lily as I make my way through the crowd to him.

"If you haven't met her yet, this is Emi, my beautiful bride-to-be." He smiles sweetly at me before turning back to the crowd. "I want to thank you all for celebrating our engagement with us. It means so much that you're all here. I hope you'll join me in toasting Emi and me in our journey towards the altar." Jack turns to me taking my hand in his. "I want to thank you, for two things. The first is for saying yes," the crowd around us laughs, like saying no was even a possibility in my own head or heart. "And the second, the most important, is for allowing me to experience what the saying *All You Need Is Love* really means. You've truly changed my world for the better and I can't wait to become your husband and truly love you as you so deserve."

A unanimous "Ah" fills the room, myself included as I wipe away the tears desperately trying to escape. Thankfully Jack knows just how bad at on the spot speeches I am, and he gives me no opportunity to say anything more than *I love you*, through the kiss he's planted on me in a room full of strangers clapping.

__Nine__

The Rehearsal

Present Day

Downtown Portland, Oregon

"Well…" Lily corners me in the kitchen the next morning, her hands on her hips as she taps the floor with the toe of her shoe. "Is he coming tonight?"

I nod, an over excited, but totally nervous, smile on my face. "Yes, Liam is coming to everything wedding related, as if he came here with me for that exact purpose. Is it weird?"

It's weird. I already know it is. Not only because I barely know him but because I really don't know *why* I'm doing this. I mean, I know I don't want to seem like the only lonely girl in the room but besides that, why?

"I don't think so," Lily shakes her head. "As far as I know everyone else is a couple, so it would probably be weird for you if you didn't have a date."

"True. Here's the thing, though..." I glance around the doorway to make sure no one is within hearing distance. We've all just barely rolled out of bed so the chances that someone is up and already eavesdropping are slim. "He didn't really even hesitate to say yes, is that weird?"

"Maybe a little," Lily shrugs her shoulders. "But that is exactly what you wanted, so I don't know why you're over thinking it now?"

"Right. I know. I'm just nervous, I think."

"Maybe you're nervous because since Jack you've only dated a handful of men and it's never gone further than the first date." Lily rolls her eyes.

In my defense, Jack and I only broke up about a year ago. In my experience that's not exactly enough time to stumble upon Prince Charming for the second time. I've been asked out on dates, don't get me wrong. I've just never really felt like going. Why waste my time on the guy on Tinder whose profile claims he's twenty-nine but the crow's feet scream forty-five?

"What?!" Hannah appears from virtually nowhere and is staring at me with a shocked face. "You've not dated since Jack?" Her voice is high pitched and nearly shrill. Why does the only person that ever catches me in untruthful moments seem always to be Hannah?

"No, that's not what I—" Lily tries to save me from her accidental announcement but it's too late.

"I heard what you said. It's been almost a year since you moved away, how can you only have had a few first dates?" Her jaw drops open momentarily before she puts her hand to her face with a gasp. "You still love him!"

I shake my head frantically so that Lily does the same. "No, Hannah, I don't."

"Yes, you do. That's the only thing that would explain all this. You ran away from the barbecue the other night, you drank yourself sick at my bridal shower and you and Greta have been literally acting like jealous high school girls ever since you found out she's interested in Jack. You're still in love with him." She sighs, holding her hand over her heart romantically, pacing between Lily and me. "Ems, this could change everything. Like, *everything*. You have to tell him." She stops in front of me, grabbing hold of both my hands. "Seriously, you need to tell him how you feel. I get the feeling he's not really into Greta."

"Ugh..." Lily groans. "Who would be?"

I glare over at Lily. "I am *not* in love with your brother, Hannah." I drop her hands from mine. "Did he leave me an everlasting scar? Yes. Did he break my heart into pieces more than once? Unfortunately, another yes. Do I still love him?" I hesitate with my answer, not intentionally. I just don't have one yet. I've tried to work out my feelings and it's not as easy as one might assume. I want to be over Jack, trust me, I do. I just... there is something in him that I can't shake. The way he looks at me and the way he doesn't look at Greta, his supposed girlfriend. "No. No, I don't. I just didn't expect to get here and find him involved with my arch-enemy."

They both stare at me with amusement.

"What? I can have an arch-enemy, can't I? She's an absolute bitch. And you can't tell me that you've never thought it as well." I point straight at Hannah, who frowns but doesn't disagree. "I am not *in* love with Jack. In fact, I have a date tonight *and* to the wedding."

This is the perfect distraction from the conversation that seems to be going in circles.

"He said yes?" Hannah asks like it surprises her. Really though, it only surprises me. I forgot she knew about all this. Otherwise, I might not have called it a date. It's more of an arrangement. Which is totally pathetic.

"Of course, he said yes." Lily defends me as she wraps her arm around my shoulder. "Look at her, she's gorgeous."

"Enough kissing ass for the spot of best friend. I have to get ready to wow him." I give Lily a playful, almost not serious, glare.

"Which him, Em? The stand-in, or Jack?" Hannah purses her lips together, her face scrunched into a silent *you can't deny it* look.

She thinks she knows me so well. Damn it! I wish I was a faster thinker when I need to be. But, of course, I'm tongue-tied. Hannah's question is the exact question even I've refused to answer to myself for the last twenty-four hours. "I don't know yet."

"Told you," she snaps at me.

"UGH!" I moan to Hannah with an eye roll as I pass her on my way to the stairs. "I'll be down when I'm ready," I say, in my most irritated voice.

*

"Wow! You are going to turn some heads." Lily greets me in the hallway as I walk out of the wedding room carrying my dress that was sharing a bag with a few other options. Without options, I'd be even more frazzled because nothing would seem right for the occasion. "Wait, isn't that *the* dress?"

I drop my head, the tiniest bit ashamed that I'm going to this extent to woo a guy I don't even know if I still want. It is the dress, and she knows it well enough not to have to ask. The blue dress that Jack picked out. The dress we got engaged in at his request. The dress he's unzipped and watched drop to the floor many times.

"Maybe..." I respond, really not wanting to get into the whole reason of why I'm wearing it. "I just... Well, if he's moved on and is some kind of happy relationship, then I really don't have any way of making him miserable. Unless I wear a dress that I know makes him swoon."

"Your grand plan now is to make him suffer by realizing he's still attracted to you?"

"Maybe."

I'm just glad I packed the darn thing. So far, the only glances I'm getting from him feel like pity. And until I can see a look I recognise, I won't know how I really feel.

"OK, and not to be the bearer of bad news but how on earth is that thing ever gonna fit?"

"Is that a subtle way to call me fat?" I glare at her.

"That's not what I'm saying and you know it," she snaps back.

"I may or may not have had it altered before we left. I mean really it was a complete remake but never mind that, it now fits and if I don't at least try to see what happens when I wear it tonight, I might never forgive myself."

"OK..." Lily says slowly, "Now even I'm curious to know the answer to Hannah's question."

"That makes three of us..." I say to Lily, wondering if my head and heart can ever just get along and agree?

I really wasn't planning on trying to get Jack's attention by wearing my lucky dress tonight. I wasn't planning on wearing it at all. It was one of those last minute ideas I had and the exact reason I missed the original bridesmaid's dress alteration in the first place. I went to have this dress altered instead of the other. Thank God, I did it early because it truly did take a few days for the woman to practically remake the entire dress to fit my new, somewhat larger than I'd like, figure without adding any super cinching underwear underneath. Sometimes a girl just needs a secret weapon, you know, just in case. This dress is mine. I hope.

I glance in the mirror after I've got it on and yes, it was well worth it. Even though I'm a bit larger than I was the last time I wore it, it still looks incredible. Jack won't know what hit him. At this point, it's not just a dress, it's an insight into our prior life. Our happy life.

"Hey, Em?" Lily calls to me from the bottom of the stairs.

"I'm almost ready!" I call back, trying to do a few quick hair adjustments.

The tap on my door moments later reminds me that I can't spend forever putting myself together. "Come on in, Lil, I'm just about ready."

The door swings open and my brother walks in. "You've been up here an hour…"

"I know, sorry."

"Wow…" he takes a step back with a smile. "I know my job is to make sure you are properly tormented as my sister, but you look great."

I smile back. We maybe have had the torment thing down pat when we were kids but we've grown up at least a little bit since then.

"Thank you, Ev. You look very handsome. Are you nervous?" He's wearing a suit, his hair is slicked back and he looks the complete opposite of my normal, casual, chuck wearing brother. I can almost see what Hannah sees in him.

"Nah," he shakes his head. "Listen, I understand your friend agreed to..." His eyebrows narrow in confusion. "I guess I don't quite get why you need him, but he's here."

"I need him because I'm the only one without a date, and the only one who's been dumped in the worst of ways recently, so that also makes me the only one who needs to at least look like I have my life together. I can't keep showing up alone, it makes me seem like I'm not over Jack." I grab my bag off the bed and pull on my shoes.

Evan reaches out and gently touches my upper arm, "Are you over Jack, Em?"

"I – uh"

"Cause I for one would understand if you weren't." He smiles the exact smile that tells me he already knows how I'm feeling without me having to say it out loud.

I drop onto the side of the bed with a sigh, Evan sits next to me.

"You guys were together for a long time, that's not nothing. You can't just move on from a nearly five year relationship in a few months."

"He did..." I look over at Evan who nods with a frown.

"I know it does seem that way but, I know Jack, and I don't think Greta is the woman Jack wants. I think Greta is the woman Jack thinks he deserves."

As my emotions bubble inside I quickly stand. "That doesn't even make any sense."

"And you wearing your lucky dress does?" Evan touches the sleeve of my dress.

I pinch my lips together. "How do you even know about that?"

"Hannah talks, *a lot*." He laughs. Evan walks towards the bedroom door. "Can I just say one more thing?"

"Like you won't if I say no…"

"True. I really do want you to be happy, Em. We all do. Jack included. I think it would be to your benefit for you two to finally talk about all this. Don't you?"

I shake my head as I shove my phone into my bag. "I don't know yet." I look into the mirror, happy with the me that's looking back.

"You do look beautiful. No matter who it's for, Jack, or the new guy, they're both incredibly lucky to have any chance with my twin sister."

"Thanks," I say with a sincere smile. I know that was him apologizing for pushing the conversation a little further than I was comfortable with.

"Let's head down and hope for a rehearsal dinner that's as smooth as silk."

I cross my fingers behind my back. Seriously, please, *please* let there be no more incidents. I don't know who's in charge of that department. God? Or maybe Karma? But whoever it is, please give me some kind of break.

As I get to the top of the stairs I hear Liam talking to Lily and Josh. I try to peek at him before he sees me, but

I'm too short to see over the balcony. One more deep breath to try and calm my nerves and I'll be ready to go.

"Come on, EM!" Hannah squeals as she exits her room at the end of the hall, her arm now linked through Evan's. The two of them looking completely ready to walk down the aisle right now even though the actual wedding is still a day away.

"You look gorgeous!" she says excitedly, a quick smile at Evan.

"So do you, so beautiful..." I return her compliment.

"I know," she giggles, doing a small twirl before once again taking my brother's arm. "Now, let's go check out Emi's date!"

I follow her to the top of the stairs, much more nervous than I had expected to be. Why am I so nervous? This is basically a business deal. Favor for possible favor. Liam smiles up at me from the bottom of the stairs.

"Whoa," he says, wide eyed.

He's wearing a pair of black slacks, a nice green shirt, and a black and white striped tie. His normally ruffled hair is now slicked over to the side and I'm only just now noticing the tattoos showing below his rolled up sleeves. Which, I'll admit, is a little bit of an unexpected turn on.

"Whoa to you, too," I say back to him, feeling more than awkward knowing that everyone in the room is watching us. I haven't felt this weird about a date since I went to prom in my senior year. If someone pulls out a camera, I'll just die.

He approaches me and kisses my cheek sweetly. "I don't know if I can compete with you, though. You are gorgeous." I hear Lily *aw* sarcastically behind me and shoot her a look of death.

"Sounds good," Evan claps his hands. "Looks like everyone, invited or not, is ready to go." He ushers us all out of the front door and towards a black limo parked at the curb.

Liam is so close behind me that I can feel my heart nervously drop a little further into my stomach with each step.

"So, how are we playing this?" he breathes into my ear, making my brain momentarily stall with any rational or pure thoughts. "Am I boyfriend status, or just random friend date status?"

I step off the curb behind the limo and pull Liam with me. "Um... I'm not sure exactly what I'm expecting as an outcome yet. I haven't seen him tonight so, I was hoping just random friend date status to start?"

Liam nods, a sweet smile on his face. "Maybe we'll see what happens? Let's feel out the situation and see how it goes before we make any solid decisions."

"OK." I nod and turn towards the car door.

"And, Emi... you're the boss here. I don't want you to be uncomfortable."

"Thanks," I smile. Believe it or not, that tiny little statement made me relax that much more.

"What are you two doing?" Evan asks me as we crawl into the limo.

"Whispering sweet nothings to each other?" Josh adds his two cents, knowing it might rev up Evan and earning a glare from me.

"Nothing, I just... uh—"

"I just wanted to tell her again how gorgeous she looked. My bad habit, sometimes I just can't hide my inner romantic. So, introduce me to everyone."

"Right. So, this is Evan and Hannah, the bride and groom."

Liam reaches out and shakes hands with both of them. "Congratulations to you both, and thank you for letting me escort the second most beautiful woman in the limo." He nods to Hannah, who immediately projects her inner Southern Belle by blushing and fanning herself.

"And this is my best friend Lily and her husband, Josh."

"Nice to meet you, Josh. You and Evan are both very lucky men." He shakes both their hands with a smile before turning back to me, his eyes smiling with far too much enthusiasm.

"What do you do, Liam?" Evan, of course, is the first one to pile on the questions.

"I own Old Tex, the run down bar up the street. Just bought it about a month ago. It's really a dive bar right now, but my plan is to turn it into something a lot cooler."

"Ah... And why are you helping my sister?"

"Evan!" I hiss at him, mortified that he'd act like a douche about this after he was so sweet upstairs.

"Your sister..." Liam glances at me with a smile. "She's a sweet woman, a damsel in distress, you could say. How could I say no?"

"So, I guess I don't understand the plan?" Evan continues with the third degree.

"You all know our arrangement?" Liam looks to me for insight.

"No," I blurt out, before noticing Evan's eyebrows rise in confusion. "I mean yes, they know why you're coming."

Please, Liam, don't talk about how it's in exchange for a possible favor. Evan's mind will go right to the big protective brother gutter.

I plead with him silently and hope he really is as good at reading people as he was the other night.

"Emi just didn't really tell us why you agreed to go, you know, with you hardly knowing her and all?" Hannah follows up.

"Guys! This isn't a Dateline interview. I'm a grown woman, Liam is a grown man, can you give us a break? He's here so maybe Jack, Greta and I can be a little more comfortable in the same room, without a third wheel. That's all." I glare at both Hannah and Evan who both shrug their shoulders in defeat.

"Tell me about you two." Liam smoothly changes the subject. "How did all this come to be?"

It takes the entire ride to the wedding venue for Evan and Hannah to tell Liam their love story. Which gives me a chance to try and stop sweating from all the wrong areas.

"He is actually cute!" Lily grabs my arm the moment I leave the limo and walks me into the building, with Josh, Evan, and Liam all chatting like old friends behind us. "I think he might really like you."

"Stop it. This is just a favor, nothing more."

"We'll see..."

"Fabulous!" A woman with so much Botox in her face she can't smile, claps her hands the moment we walk out of the elevator. "We have wedding party members arriving, and right on time!"

"Hi, Muffy!" Hannah greets Botox Lady with the dreaded air kisses, while Lily and I act like we're twelve and mouth the name *Muffy* to one another as we stifle back a giggle. There are just some things you never grow out of.

"We are just waiting for a few more members of the wedding party," she tells Hannah before they walk away from us, inspecting the ongoing decorating.

"Here is the rest of our party now." Muffy follows them in with her eyes. "If you are part of the bridal party please make your way to me, otherwise, if you're a plus one, have a seat in the seating area.

Amelia smiles in my direction, Jack at her side and Greta hanging off him like a cancerous tumor. Jack's eyes meet mine almost immediately, a small smile starts to appear on his face until Greta takes his hand and the smile never reaches his eyes. This is not the Jack I knew. He looks defeated. I've not really let myself spend a lot of time admiring him since I got here, and I wish I hadn't right now either.

Here I was, secretly expecting him to swoon at the fact that I'm wearing his favorite dress, and his expression is more like he's just looked into the open coffin of a friend who's passed on. I force a smile at him but he only looks away, causing my heart to sink into my chest.

"Before we get started, I think the bride and groom have some gifts they want to hand out." A man walks towards us with a rolling cart full of gift bags.

"We do," Hannah says with a giggle. Evan starts handing gift bags to all the bridal party, one by one. "Evan had these specially made for his groomsmen, but please don't devour them right now. Maybe later, or even take them home."

"And I... had these made up this morning. I think you all should put them on right now for rehearsal. It'll be fun!" Her giddy smile tells me these gifts are either expensive or embarrassing or quite possibly both.

I watch as other girls start pulling black t-shirts out of their gift bags.

"Oh my God! This is so funny... I love it!" One of the other bridesmaids pulls their shirt on, and I'm immediately afraid to look at my own.

"The Bridesmaids..." Hannah points to the front before having the girl turn around. "I'm the sweet one..." She giggles, "Aren't they cute!?"

"Which one are you?" Liam leans over, quietly asking in my ear.

"I'm afraid to look." I hold the gift bag tightly against my chest, scared to pull my shirt out and see what title I've been given. All the other girls are pulling their t-shirts on. So far, I see *THE SWEET ONE, THE FUNNY ONE, THE LATE ONE*, and mine is the last not revealed. Greta is off in the corner, pouting that she didn't get one since she's not officially a bridesmaid. I have a feeling that if she had, revealing mine wouldn't be quite as nerve wracking.

"Come on Emi, it's fun. Put yours on."

I reluctantly pull the shirt out of the bag and turn it to read the back before anyone else can. Shit. It would be just my luck that she's chosen my weak spot as my title. I'm just happy she didn't choose *THE CONFUSED ONE* or *SHE STILL LOVES JACK ONE*.

"Read it out loud, Ems," Hannah encourages me with a smile.

"Um – *THE DRUNK ONE...*" I say aloud, forcing a giggle and immediately hearing Evan burst out laughing. If there was ever a cringeworthy moment that made you wish you could hide anywhere, this is it. I can feel my face flush as the room giggles around me. I know it's a joke, but it's a joke that's all too real right now.

"It's just a joke," Hannah jabs Evan in the ribs with her elbow. "Put it on!"

I glance at Lily and Josh behind me before looking back at Liam again who has a strange, almost smile on his face.

"Fine." I pull the t-shirt on over my dress and do an exaggerated spin so everyone can get a good look.

"She got that one spot on, didn't she?" Greta announces to the room with a laugh before being elbowed by Jack. "What?"

"Quiet!" Muffy claps us into silence. "Enough nonsense, let's get started!"

"Wait!" Hannah interrupts her quickly, scurrying to her side in the center of the room. "We have just one more thing to do." Evan walks up behind her with two white sashes hanging over his arm. "We haven't really announced who our Maid of Honor and Best Man are, we wanted it to be a surprise, so…" We all watch her take the sashes from Evan.

"As Evan's Best Man he chose the guy who he's been the closest to for so many years, a man who actually helped bring us together so long ago. A man who even took Evan in like a brother when his world fell apart after his parents died." She walks up to Jack and puts the sash over his head, like he's just won some sort of beauty pageant, straightening it so the sparkly words Best Man lie directly across his chest.

"We're brothers really, even before today, thanks for always being there for me," Evan says, then nods towards me "For us, really."

I finally see Jack smile, a real smile that reaches all the way to his eyes as he walks over to hug my brother. Despite all the nonsense Jack has been there for both Evan and me in so many ways.

"And... my Maid of Honor... This was really hard for me, but the last few days have really made it clear who it should be. Because of you, this day is even happening and I couldn't ever be more thankful for that. We may have had a rocky start, but I know you're forever supposed to be in my life, one way or another..."

When she's standing directly in front of me I feel myself shaking my head. "Hannah, I can't walk down the aisle with—" I whisper, but she purses her lips and glares with an intensity I can almost feel. It's time for me to shut up and listen.

"Emi, I chose you as my Maid of Honor because, after today, we'll finally be sisters forever. Just as we should have been last year." The sash is slung around my neck and straightened to show the glittery pink Maid of Honor squarely across my chest.

"Thank you," I hug her, thankful that she feels this way but unable to pull my eyes from a watching Jack.

Muffy claps again. "Now that the awards ceremony is over let's get to the rehearsal."

"Wow..." Liam laughs under his breath. "This is quite the wedding already."

"This is bad." I glance around the room looking for Lily but since she and Josh are only guests and not official wedding party, they've moved to the seating area and are both scrolling through their phones.

"Why is it bad?" Liam asks me.

"Because the Maid of Honor walks down the aisle with the Best Man."

"I take it the Best Man is the guy who broke your heart?"

I nod, "Yes, Jack."

Liam rubs the back of his neck for a moment, his face somber and staring into space. When his hand touches mine a spark of electricity moves quickly all the way to my brain.

"Then, before I take my seat in the plus one section, I think my status is now boyfriend." And in a moment too quick for me to even process the words he's just said, his arm is around my back, he's pulled me against him and his lips meet mine. I melt... like literally; my knees go weak and I don't pull away. I can't, the last time someone kissed me, it was Jack. My head and my heart are in a war and right now my brain seems to be on strike, fizzing like a shaken bottle of champagne.

"OK, *OK*... Enough with the love scene. Plus ones, find your seat in the audience." Muffy's stern voice causes us both to pull away. Liam's hand slowly runs along my back as he walks towards Lily and Josh.

When I finally glance around the room, all eyes are on us. Hannah's mouth is hanging open with a huge awkward smile and Jack's face is much the opposite of hers.

"Hannah and Robert move to the back of the room, Best Man and Maid of Honor in front of them..." Muffy is barking orders and maneuvering people exactly where she wants them.

Hannah skips to my side and slides her arm through mine, pulling me from the daydream and towards the back of the room with her.

"Oh my God. So, what is this then?" She tries to be quiet, but I'm sure half the room just heard her.

"Shh... Hannah. I don't know. He just... kissed me."

"And?"

"And what?"

"Was it good?" She raises an eyebrow.

"What? This isn't a sleepover where we talk boys. I don't know what it was. It was, uh..." We stop at the back of the room. The only person there so far is Robert, who isn't listening anyway. "It was surprising."

"I bet! He is cute, but, are you sure you want this?"

"*This* is nothing. It's just an act, remember?"

"Right..." Her gaze moves to my side, and when I glance around Jack is quietly standing there waiting for us to drop into walking orders. "Right," Hannah says again, walking away from me towards her father.

"Emi," Jack's voice is unemotional, and he doesn't look directly at me.

"Jack," I match his tone as if we're in a poker game.

"You look beautiful, as always." He finally looks down at me with a hesitant, shy smile. "Who's the guy?" He nods towards the seating area where Liam is now sitting behind Lily and Josh with Greta getting a little too comfortable right next to him.

"Just a friend," I answer.

I watch Greta chat with Liam, laughing at his every word and honestly making me a little bit sick that she's got some kind of power to continue to weasel her way to men I'm close to.

"A friend you make out with?" He looks at me with a disapproving look on his face.

"Why do you care? You appear to be hot and heavy with my arch-enemy."

He shakes his head with a frown. "It's far from hot and heavy."

"I'm a grown woman, I can see anyone I want to see. Just as you can date the one woman I *hate* if you want to. No one is holding you back. These are the things that happen when people break up."

He sighs heavily. "I'm not worried about the guy, Ems. I'm worried about you."

"Why are you worried about me?"

"I just am. Believe it or not..." he stares down at the floor for a moment before finally looking up at me. "I miss you."

"When the music starts," Muffy yells, interrupting the moment where my heart stopped. "You are to count to three and then take your groomsman's arm and start slowly walking up the aisle."

I force myself to stare at the front of the room. Watching Liam and Greta chat, Lily and Josh laugh at something on their phone.

"Please talk to me, Emi," Jack whispers, holding out his elbow for me.

I sigh, "Why?"

"Because if you actually expect me to move on I need to say some things. I'll walk away forever if that's what you want but not until we talk, can you give me at least that?"

I look to Greta, who's now got her attention turned on the two of us.

"No." I finally take his elbow with a glare.

"Fine." We both take a step forward. "I'll say it right now then."

"What?" I say, a little louder than intended, seeing Josh and Lily both turn towards us as well. "Jack, no, now is not the time."

"It's never the time for you. But you *have* to know, I never cheated on you."

I roll my eyes and take another step forward.

"That day, I know it looked bad, but it wasn't the way it looked."

"Just stop." I look up at his sad face. "Please, I've heard all this before, but I know what I saw."

"You don't, and you need to know this." His eyes plead with me in a way that makes my chest hurt. For the first time since I've been here, I see actual remorse in Jack's face.

"Can we STOP the conversation back there and pay attention?!" Muffy yells back at us, her finger waving from across the room and silencing us both, which honestly is a relief on my part.

Another step forward but Jack leans closer to me, allowing his cologne to wash over me and affect every unclouded area I still have.

"We will talk this week, whether you like it or not, I need it." He whispers into my ear, his breath making the hair on my neck stand straight up. And all I can do is nod.

Ten

The Wedding of Lily & Josh

Two years, nine months ago.

Cancun, Mexico

"Why did you choose a combined bachelor/bachelorette party? How will Josh have strippers if we're there?" I ask Lily, who still has the curling iron in her hair even though we were supposed to meet the guys at the bar twenty minutes ago.

"Because it's fun, there will be *no* strippers, and we're all friends. So why not?"

"Got it. I just hope this burrito Evan convinced me to eat earlier doesn't make a comeback."

"You're sick?"

"Not sick, yet, just... iffy. It's not like I drank the water or anything." I wasn't going to tell her this at all and just hope it passed. Literally.

"Well, hold it together."

Finally, Lily is the picture of perfect and ready to walk the few blocks from our hotel down to the bar where this magical event is to take place. I probably shouldn't have worn heels this high for this much walking, but I hate looking an entire foot shorter than Jack.

"Wow! This place is busy!" People are spilling out of the front doors, laughing, drinking, and just overall partying, as one does in Cancun on vacation. "Come on."

We push our way through the crowd and look around the busy bar for the rest of our party. Someone waving from the private balcony above us grabs my attention. Evan.

"They're up there!" I point towards his grinning face.

"Perfect! We wanted to get the balcony but weren't sure we could at such short notice." We squeeze through a crowd full of scantily clad half naked bodies towards the stairs, and the man guarding the VIP rope nods towards us without a word while allowing us through.

"It's *so* hot in here," I yell to Lily over the music, as I follow her to the top.

"It's Mexico, Ems. It's *always* hot, *everywhere*."

It's so hot that I think my hair is sweating, but I continue up the stairs and hope there is air conditioning in the VIP room.

"Finally! What took you so long?" Jack kisses my lips.

"Lily..." I roll my eyes with a laugh. "She just had to look perfect." I look across the room at her and Josh already making out in a corner by themselves. "I'm not sure why we are having a party to watch them have sex in public. It's kinda gross."

"They're not gonna have sex. That would be disgusting." Evan takes a swig of his beer. "We leave disgusting to me, remember?" He winks at the only other bridesmaid that made the trek from Oregon to Mexico.

"No," I shake my finger at him. "Lily will be pissed if you screw her cousin," I say, using the only demanding tone I know.

"Lily will never know," he and Jack both laugh. "Right?"

"I know you have like zero morals about this stuff, just don't do it here, please?" I beg Evan to try and keep it in his pants, but I know he'll never listen. He never does.

"I got you a drink," Jack points at the Cosmo on the table in front of him.

I take a giant slurp, hoping it doesn't go to war and piss off the burrito from earlier. "Please promise me that if we ever were to get married that we won't have bachelor/bachelorette parties?"

"Promised. Really, aren't they just an excuse to do something dirty right before the wedding?" I glance back at Josh and Lily, still making out in the corner. "I thought so, but apparently, in this case, it's just to make the rest of us feel dirty."

"They're just in love," Jack smiles over at them. "Dirty love." His scrunched-up disgusted face matches my own, as we laugh at his joke.

You can only drink in a hundred degree room for so long before you feel like you're going to have a stroke. An hour was about all it took for us to decide to take our party outside to the beach.

*

"Where's Josh?" Lily asks after she finally realizes he's not lying on the sand with us.

"Maybe he went to get another drink?" Jack says, never moving from his star gazing position.

"Evan's gone too, so I'm sure that's where they are." I glance around at the indentations that held all six of us just thirty minutes ago. "Wait..." I sit up and look around again. I may be seeing slight doubles of things, after a couple of Cosmo's in a hundred degree room, but I know I'm missing a complete person here. "Corinne is gone too."

"Yes, as close as she and Evan were getting in the bar I'd say—" Jack groans suddenly, probably because of my elbow in his ribs. "I mean..."

"What?!" Lily shrieks. "Evan is with Corinne?"

"No..." I quickly denounce the idea of Lily's engaged cousin Corinne doing anything she shouldn't with my brother. "Maybe she went back to the hotel? I'm sure Evan is wherever Josh is."

"Let's go," Lily jumps up but stumbles backwards, catching herself on a nearby lounger. "Your brother will not defile another of my friends or family members."

"Come on, Lil…" Jack is starting to slur his words, which is a rare occasion and I'm sure is only happening because absolutely no one from his family or work is even in the same country as us right now. "Evan has always had a way with the ladies, you know that." The perverted tone coming from my boyfriend is somewhat disturbing. He's supposed to be the gentleman of the guys. "It's not like he forces them to have sex with him. They just do." He bursts into a giggle as he lies back on the sand.

"Nice." Lily stares over at Jack with a glare. "It's good to know you lost your class at *my* wedding."

"I didn't lose anything. I'm just sworn to the truth right now because I've had way too much to drink today."

"Don't fight!" I yell. "Let's just go find Josh and Evan," I try to hold everything together but wrangling emotional drunks to get along is about as effective as herding a flock of seagulls.

"And Corinne," Lily adds, like I had forgotten her.

"Yes, Corinne too."

"There are at least five bars between here and our hotel, we're gonna search them all?"

"That's right. And no more to drink for you," Lily points directly at Jack who only grins.

"He's been demoted to bottled water, so no worries there," I say, hoping that the acid bubbling in my throat is just heartburn and not the attempted reappearance of the previously mentioned burrito.

The first bar we walk into appears to be a dirty dive bar. Like the kind you actually walk out of wishing you could take a shower. It's so dark you can hardly see but a few people ahead of you. There is a band playing with strobe lights flashing so the thirty minutes we search is pointless. If one more person grinds against me in here I'm gonna be sick for sure.

"I think this is an after hours bar." Jack glances around the next one, his eyes as big as saucers. On the bar are three mostly naked women (I'm not sure if sequined barely there underwear even counts as clothing) dancing in heels so high it hurts me just to look at them.

"Do you see them?" Lily yells over the swanky music playing overhead. I shake my head, trying to avoid eye contact with just about every person in there for fear of catching some kind of airborne STD. "I'm just going to ask the bartender," Lily shouts.

"Jack and I will wait outside." I turn to grab Jack but he's no longer at my side. "Shit." Maybe he's already gone outside? It is packed in here, and he's not exactly thinking straight this evening. Of all the places to lose him, why did it have to be a topless bar?

I shove my way through the crowd and reach the sidewalk only to see Jack sitting on a bench out front.

Sitting is an overstatement, he's kind of curled into the fetal position with his head hanging off the edge of the bench, holding onto a pole that acts as a bus stop sign. A nearly naked, definitely topless woman is sitting next to him, giggling at whatever it is he's just said to her.

"Jack!"

"Ems, I was just asking this lady if she'd seen them." He jumps up, still holding the pole for balance, and grabs my hand. "I found hher," he slurs to the woman, who is now looking at the two of us and is a lot less giggly than she was a moment earlier.

"They haven't seen them." Lily comes up behind us looking more than frazzled. "This is the worst party ever!" Her voice quivers as she says it, cuing me as to what is coming next.

"Please don't cry," I say, as tears start to roll down her cheeks. "Maybe they got confused and went back to the hotel?"

"Less go check," Jack slurs into my face, causing me to fan the beer smell away.

"How about we agree to not breathe directly onto one another?" I say with a roll of my eyes.

"Deal." He reaches down and takes my hand in his, pulling it to his lips to kiss it, missing on the first try but succeeding on the second. "See... Shtill a gentleman." He says to Lily with a hair lipped smile.

"Come on." I lead him down the street by his hand, my shoes in my other one. "I'm sure they're at the hotel," I say to Lily, but of course she's no longer standing next to me. "Lil?" I call out. "For Christ's sake, can we stop losing people?" I turn to Jack who is pointing past me.

"She went that way."

I follow his finger but she's not there either.

"Great. How did I end up the soberest out of all of us?" I look over at Jack's goofy smile and laugh.

"I know, normally that'sh me."

"I think I like it better that way." I frown at my grown man-child, stumbling along the sidewalk next to me, staring at the sky instead of where he's walking.

"I need to sssit," he says suddenly, lurching towards a giant palm bush and landing head first in the middle of it, his arms and legs flailing loosely until they hit the ground in a sort of star-fish position.

I drop my head back and sigh. "Let's lie down for a few minutes."

I help him to the beach just a few feet away, steering him towards a lounger and making sure he's not going to fall off before settling myself into the one next to him.

The air is warm, even with the slight breeze. The moon reflects off the ocean in a way that almost makes it so bright that you feel like it's not night time at all. I've never seen a sky prettier than the one above me. It's like you have to fall in love with the tropical atmosphere.

I look over to Jack who is peacefully sleeping off the few drinks he's had. He's a lightweight so I knew if he let loose this would happen. He never allows himself to lose control so I can't possibly complain about one time. Even though he's snoring obnoxiously, and all my friends are missing, there is something romantic about this exact moment.

"Jack?" I ask a few moments later, sort of checking to make sure he's still alive.

He mumbles something under his breath.

"If we ever got married, I'd want to do it here, with just the people closest to us, without all the alcohol and stress, but just us. Ya know? It seems so much easier than all the fuss of a real wedding. It would be so romantic."

He only groans over at me. I'm kind of glad he doesn't totally hear what I'm saying because we haven't talked about marriage at all. We've been together for three years and not once has he hinted that we should get married. He's always so focused on the next step in his career that I don't think it's honestly even on his mind.

Our relationship is great, so why change it? But with my friends getting married I'm starting to feel a little left out. I mean... I'm twenty-six years old; I feel like this is the marrying age if there was one. I'm done with college, I'm working in a career I don't hate and I've no doubt that Jack is *the one*, so maybe *I* should mention it... preferably when he's not passed out on a lounger next to me.

"Ems..." Jack groans at me, causing me to jerk awake and try to figure out where I am. I look over at him, no longer on the lounger but lying in the sand between the chairs we were originally in. "Why are we on the beach?"

I glance around. It's not as dark as it was when we sat down here so I pull my phone from my pocket and check the time. 4:33 a.m. We've been lying out here since just after 1 a.m. and we must've fallen asleep.

"We stopped because you were dizzy, remember? We can head back to our room now. Do you feel OK?"

"No..." he half laughs as he rubs his head. "But I can make it back." He sits up and looks over at me, his dark hair falling across his forehead, his skin pale, and yet he's still absolutely gorgeous. "I think this is the first time I've been this drunk."

"In front of me for sure."

"Well, that's a change," he laughs, as I try and pull him off the ground.

"That it is."

"I had a dream that we got married." His smile is faint, but his eyes are locked on mine. He must've heard me earlier. "We got married right here, with the moon in the background."

"Oh yeah?" I ask, pretending I have no idea why he'd dream that.

"Yeah, it was..." he stops walking, obviously searching for a word to use. "Beautiful," he reaches up, touching my face and gently kissing my lips. "Just like you."

My heart melts. How could I not be happy to hear that?

"Thanks, Jack. Let's get you back."

*

I slide the hotel card key into the suite we are all staying in and watch the flash of the green light before the door pops open and Jack pushes his way through like a bull in a china shop.

"Hello, bed," he says as he walks down the hall to our room.

"Let me just make sure everyone got back," I say, watching him fall face first into our bed.

I knock quietly on Corinne's door. She doesn't answer so I crack the door open to make sure she's at least in bed. She is... But so is Evan. Obviously, they have been up to no good, considering I'm standing on their clothes near the doorway.

"EVAN!" I half whisper, poking him in the back. "EVAN!"

"What?" He groans, opening one eye.

"Get back in your room or Lily will kill you when she gets up. What is wrong with you? Corinne is engaged!"

"So... It's not like we're the ones getting married tomorrow."

"Just go!" I toss his clothes at him and watch him kick off the blankets, holding his wad of clothes over his nether regions and tiptoe back to his room across the hall. "Not a word of this to anyone!"

"Whatever, Mom." His door clicks shut behind him.

I glance in at Jack, who isn't moving but has somehow managed to strip himself and is now lying completely naked on top of the covers, his bare ass exposed to anyone looking in through the wall of windows.

"Lil?" I crack her door enough so that the light shines directly onto the bed, giving me the perfect vision of her and Josh doing things I never even wanted to imagine they did. "OH MY GOD!" I squeal.

"EMI!" Lily yells and tosses a pillow towards the door.

"Sorry!" I yell through the crack, quickly shutting the door. "Shit." I race into my own room, shut the door, and close the curtains so Jack doesn't gain a crowd when it's light outside.

Right then it hits me: not the alcohol because I barely drank tonight, but the burrito. I barely make it to the bathroom before the burrito makes a second appearance.

I don't remember sleeping for the next few hours on the bathroom floor but I'm awoken by Jack, using the toilet in the same way I remember using it last.

"I'm never drinking again," he moans, lying down next to me and wrapping his arms around me. "Why are you in here?"

"Bad burrito last night."

We both lie on the floor, me using his chest as a pillow, for the next hour until he finally feels well enough to take a shower and get dressed.

"Wedding is in eight hours," he stands in the doorway looking as handsome as ever in his cargo shorts and white button up t-shirt. It's almost as if he didn't just have the first hangover of his life.

"I'm so sick," I cry from the floor, wishing I'd never had gone to that burrito stand with Evan yesterday. "Is Evan sick?" He'd better be; it's only fair.

"I dunno, sweetie. I'll go get you some aspirin and find out."

I hear the door open a few minutes later, but it's not Jack's flip-flops in front of me, it's Evan's chucks.

"What the hell? Jack said you're sick from the burrito stand yesterday?"

"You're not?"

"Nope..." he pats his non-existent gut. "I feel great."

"You are a disgusting human being." I push his calf in an attempt to force him out of my bathroom.

"Why's that?" He kneels down to where I'm still sprawled across the floor.

"Because you screw everything."

"Oh, come on now... not *everything*. I have *some* standards." His sly smile makes me feel even sicker.

"I brought you Evan's hangover cure," Jack walks in behind Evan. "Come on..." He helps me walk to the bed and sits a tray of burnt toast, juice, and aspirin in front of me.

"But I don't have a hangover, I have a burrito-over."

Jack laughs. "Eat, babe, and I'm sure you'll start to feel better."

He sits with me as I try to force down the toast, rubbing my back and being supportive even though I feel like I should be doing this for him.

The toast doesn't help. I race to the bathroom to throw up, collapsing on the bathroom floor until Lily comes in and maintains that she can't wait any longer. I have to get ready.

I sit in a chair on the balcony, the sun beating down on me, as she fixes my hair and makeup. Jack practically carries me to the beach and all the way down the aisle, insisting the entire way that despite my being sick, I'm still the most beautiful woman there.

Somehow, with Jack's help, holding me upright throughout the ceremony, I make it all the way through without even needing to use the prettiest trash can Lily could find for me to hold just in case, my bouquet taped to the front of it. Then nearly as miraculously as it came on, it was gone.

I lie on the bed in Jack and my room the next morning feeling terrible for how things went. "That was a miserable time, wasn't it?"

"It wasn't too bad."

"Did I ruin her day? I couldn't live with myself if I did."

Jack sits next to me, pulling me against him and allowing me to rest my head on his shoulder.

"She's as happy as she's ever been. So, it's safe to say you haven't ruined anything." He kisses my forehead. "I heard what you said the other night, about wanting to get married on the beach."

For a second my heart stops and my ears turn scalding hot, the same way they used to when I knew I was in trouble as a kid.

"You did?" Why on earth did I say it out loud? Every girl knows not to mention marriage first. It only scares men away.

"I did," He grins. "And I agree... It would be perfect."

"Yeah?" My heart starts pounding in my chest, wondering if he's going to ask me to marry him right this second.

"Well," he laughs. "Without the food poisoning and the hangover, yes."

"Yeah." I nod.

"I don't know if I'm quite there yet, but it's definitely an idea for the future."

My heart sinks a bit, and I have to force my face to not show the disappointment I'm feeling knowing that this is *not* him proposing. Not that I was ever really expecting it, but a girl can dream.

He strokes my cheek with his thumb and kisses my lips. "It's not off the table for the future."

I nod, my eyes still closed as he pulls his lips away from mine. I'll take it.

Eleven

The Wedding Day

Present Day

Downtown Portland, Oregon

"Everybody up!" Hannah is storming my room, pulling open the curtains and inviting in the rare Portland sunshine to invade my space.

"What time is it?" I ask, objecting to a sunrise wakeup call.

"7 a.m." She stands next to the bed waiting for me to pull the blankets off my face. "I'm getting married today! We have a ton to do so get up!"

"What do we have to do that can't get done in the next twelve hours?" She yanks the blankets off me as I say it.

"Just come downstairs and don't ruin my day."

She disappears through the door as I sit up on the side of the bed trying to force myself to wake up.

"*What?* I'm not even *in* the wedding party!" Lily objects from her room next door.

I throw on a bra, because when you have C-sized boobs no bra is a definite no-go, before heading downstairs to the smells of heaven wafting my direction.

A man in a black jacket and black chef's hat greets me with a wave. "Good morning, Miss. Is there anything I can prepare for you this morning?"

"Prepare for me?"

"Yes, Miss Cabot has hired me to feed you throughout the day. Whatever you'd like, I can accommodate."

I feel my eyes grow wide with excitement. "You can make me whatever I want for breakfast?" I ask, just to double check that I'm not still sleeping and having the best dream ever.

"Yes, ma'am." He nods his head enthusiastically.

"What do you suggest?"

"I have an omelet that most clients love."

"Let's do it... And for your information... I *love* cheese. I'm not one of these dieting women you probably normally cook for."

He smiles, showing all his teeth. "My favorite kind of woman. I'll bring it out to you as soon as it's done." He nods towards the counter filled with everything needed for gourmet coffee or hot chocolate. "Help yourself to some coffee if you'd like."

"I would like, thank you."

"Oh good, there you are." Hannah looks panicked already and we're still many, *many* hours away from the wedding. "Listen, as soon as you've eaten I need you to shower because the spray tan lady will be here at nine."

"Spray tan lady?"

"Yeah, you've never had one?" She watches me shake my head. "Oh, it's so cool. She actually brings all the equipment right to the house and does it here. It's quick and subtle, and when it's over you'll glow like you just got back from somewhere tropical."

I've never had a spray tan before, and I'm a little nervous for my natural skin tone is not much darker than the color of snow. What if something goes wrong? No, it can't, people do this all the time with no issues.

"OK," I say with a shrug of my shoulders, while I pour a few too many coffee flavors into my cup.

By the time I get to the table, Mr Chef is following me over with a plate heaped full of cheesy goodness. "Your omelet, Miss."

"You're not actually going to eat that?" Greta and her judgmental sneer come sauntering into the room, taking the chair across from mine. "Do you have any idea how many calories are in something like that?"

"I do, actually." I nod, pretending I don't hate her.

"Those are calories you definitely don't need."

"Why are you here again?" I ask as I shove a giant forkful of eggs and cheese into my mouth as she watches in disgust. "Last I checked you aren't a part of the bridal party. You probably could have slept in and saved us all some irritation."

Greta rolls her eyes, an exasperated smile on her face. "This whole morning of beauty is my wedding gift to Hannah."

"Ah, sweet. Now we can all look like plastic dolls just like you."

Greta shakes her head with a glare, "No wonder you lost Jack."

"I didn't *lose* him. For your information, I *dumped* him. If anything, you should be thanking me."

"Why would *I* thank *you*?"

"Because without me, you'd not be secretly wishing that one day you'll be wearing the exact same diamond that once sat on my hand."

Her jaw drops open. "Whatever, where's Hannah?"

I intentionally fork another pile of eggs into my mouth and shrug my shoulders.

"Oh good! Greta, you're here. I'm so excited you can get ready with all of us. The girl you recommended will be here any minute too."

"Great! I'm so excited to help so just tell me where I'm needed."

"They're probably looking for her back at the mental institution…" I say to myself watching only the Chef grin at my joke.

*

When I'm finally done with my second omelet, yes, second, I head upstairs to attempt the start of getting ready for this wedding. I look through the basket of expensive toiletries Hannah left in my room and grab the shampoo and conditioner before jumping in the shower. I take extra time shaving every part of me that may or may not be exposed today before lathering my hair in a shampoo that smells more than delightful. I can already feel my mood lifting. Maybe all I needed was a good shower? Or maybe it was the omelets?

"Hey Em, Hannah wanted me to—" Lily stops midsentence as I walk out of the bathroom, a towel wrapped around my chest.

"To what?"

"What did you do to your hair?"

"Uh, washed it, don't act so surprised."

"What did you wash it *with*?" Her face is anything but amused by my sharp wit.

"What do you mean? *Shampoo*... Actually, I used the stuff Hannah left in here." I point over at the basket of goodies.

"I don't think it was shampoo..."

"Why?" I walk past her back into the bathroom and glance in the mirror. "OH, MY GOD! Oh my God, what in the holy fuck?!" My once dark ash hair is now a muddy purple color.

"What's wrong?" Hannah walks in, her mouth dropping open in shock. "What did you do?"

"I didn't do anything, Hannah, except use the shampoo you gave me." I point to the basket.

"Why would it do this?" she asks me, getting closer to inspect it.

"I don't know?"

She grabs the shampoo off the shower shelf and squeezes some into her hand. "It's purple?"

"Why is it purple?"

"You didn't notice this while you were showering?"

I watch her squeeze the conditioner into her hand, also purple.

"No... I had my eyes closed."

"You shower with your eyes closed?" Lily asks.

"Sometimes, when I'm trying to relax. How do you shower?" I snap at her, wondering why my showering techniques are suddenly to blame for my hair turning purple.

"Beside the point." Hannah waves a frantic hand at her. "It's not so terrible, it's kind of a lavender gray color. If need be we could say it matches the dress." She lets out a nervous laugh. "When the hairdresser gets here we'll just have her fix it." She forces a deep breath, obviously a little more stressed out than she's letting on.

"Right." I take another glance in the mirror. "Of course, she can fix it."

"How about right now you go do your tan and then as soon as the hair lady gets here we'll get your hair fixed?" Hannah is doing her best to stay calm, but her voice keeps cracking when she speaks. I am going to single handedly ruin yet another wedding day.

I make my way toward the den, where the tanning lady is supposed to be set up. And, of course, right before I walk in, Greta walks out.

"Whoa... New hair for the wedding? It's an odd day to go purple, isn't it?"

"Funny... Shampoo mishap, that's all."

She nods her head and rolls her eyes.

When I walk into the room there is a tall tent with hoses coming from it and running into some contraption next to it. It looks more like a science experiment than a tanning booth.

"Hi, there! And you are?" A perky girl in super-short shorts and a skin tight sleeveless top turns toward me, a smile on her face.

"Emi."

"Emi! Perfect. I just need you to strip and stand in the tent then do exactly as I say. Have you ever done this before?"

"No," I shake my head nervously.

"It's easy peasy, so no worries there."

"You want me to strip naked?" I ask, hoping she says no, but fully expecting to hear a yes. There is one goal I have in life when it comes to naked and that is for me to be the only one to see it unless there are special romantic circumstances.

"Don't worry, I've seen it all before." She waves a hand at me as if there is absolutely nothing to worry about. There is, though. She just did Greta's tan – and *her* naked is a tad smaller and probably smoother, than *my* naked.

"OK." I shut the den door, lock it, and strip down to nothing. "Just in the tent then?"

"Yup. This is super-quick, maybe ten minutes." She positions me in the center of the tent. "Great. I'll start at your feet and spray upwards so when you feel it on your chest close your eyes tightly and hold your breath for a moment until I'm done with your face. Then I'll take a second and do another spray before we do your back."

"Easy enough." I stand where she told me to and she starts to spray a cool mist over my skin.

"Is that it?" I ask her ten minutes later.

"Yup."

"But it didn't do anything?" I'm still looking at my ghostly white skin.

"It takes a few hours for it to set in. Don't worry, you'll be glowing."

"I'll take your word for it." I pat myself dry with the towel she's handed me, just as instructed, and pull on the robe I carried down with me.

I walk back towards the buffet, which is the last thing I need, but secretly I'm hoping it's time to eat again. Hannah stops me just short enough to smell everything but not see it. "Delilah is here."

"Delilah?" I ask, secretly hoping it's another chef.

"The hair girl. Actually, Heidi is the hair girl but when I told her our problem she called in a backup to take care of just you."

"Great, I look so terrible I need my own team of beauticians."

"That's not what I meant, she's getting set up in your room. That way no one will wonder why you're getting special treatment."

"Is it really special treatment, though, Hannah? Or is it just solving a problem that might ruin your wedding?"

"Just go!" she barks at me, clearly getting more stressed with every passing minute.

"Delilah?" I walk into my room to see a large woman with a lot of hair setting out all kinds of potions and powders on a rolling cart I've never seen before.

"Oh my. Yup, that's purple." She points at the stool set in the middle of my bathroom. "Let's get started."

She doesn't waste any time washing it multiple times, conditioning it, spraying, drying, painting goo on and sealing me up in tin foil.

"So... What exactly is this?"

"You're going blonde... I assume you've bleached your hair before?"

I stare at Delilah, "Nope. That's kind of why the purple was such a shock."

"What kind of shampoo was it?"

"I dunno... Something Hannah gave me, but it was purple."

"Well, I think you'll look great as a blonde."

"It's really going to be completely blonde?" I stare at my tin foiled head in the mirror in front of me. I feel like this is a decision I should have had a say in. Marilyn Monroe platinum just isn't a color that ever appealed to my hair. Oddly enough the tin foil reminds me of the dress I'll be putting on in a couple hours' time.

"Hopefully. It looked like the washing got out most of the color, really it was just left in the bottom half of your hair, so this should strip it out."

Bleaching is not a fast process. I've flipped through every magazine I brought with me at least three times while I've been wearing this tin foil hat. My scalp is starting to burn and I don't know if this smell will ever wash away.

"Let's check it." Delilah hops off the bed and slowly starts unwrapping a section of my hair while I watch nervously in the mirror. When she gets about six inches down, the foil, complete with the bottom half of my hair, comes away in her hand. "Oh... No."

"No... No *oh-no's*, Delilah! What just happened? Did my hair just fall off?"

"You're sure you've not recently dyed your hair or anything?"

"You mean besides *this morning*? NO! Why?" I'm getting more frantic with each question she asks.

"'Cause this sometimes happens when people over color their hair. It will essentially melt off during another color application, and bleach isn't the easiest thing on hair anyway, so—"

"So, what?! Get it out then!" I yell at her and watch her quickly pull all the tin foil from my hair. About every third one pulls the bottom half of my hair right off all over my head, leaving me with big jagged shoulder length patches throughout my normally nearly waist length hair.

"Oh my God," I breathe out as slowly as possible, leaning over the sink, trying not to have a full on panic attack and wondering how this day could possibly get any worse. "Now what?"

"I'm gonna have to cut it."

"Cut it?! Do you have any idea how long it took me to grow it this long?"

"I know," Delilah nods her head apologetically. "But unless you want to look like this..." She points at one of the worst areas. "I suggest we cut it. It'll be really cute on you."

"NO!" I jump off the stool and down the hallway. "LILY! HANNAH!" I am screaming through the landing, looking into each room I walk past before I finally see everyone gathered at the bottom of the stairs. "She melted off my hair! But only *some* parts, so it looks awful, and now..." I try to take a breath between seethes. "*NOW* she wants to cut it. But *nooo*... I want the other girl to do it." Delilah stands next to me, now looking slightly irritated.

"I can totally cut it."

"Like you could totally get the purple out? No. You're on bridesmaid duty now. Send up Heidi!" I yell down the stairs, sending Hannah scrambling along the hall to summon Heidi.

By the time I'm back in my room and sitting on the stool, trying not to sob, a tiny woman who I assume is Heidi walks in looking scared. "Hi, Emi. I'm so sorry about this. Let's see what we can do."

I close my eyes as she works, worried about how my wavy hair will look shoulder length. I've been growing my hair since high school when I made the mistake of cutting what my mother insisted would be an adorable pixie cut. It wasn't. Not even a little bit.

"OK," she says, waking me from my almost nap, causing me to slowly squint open my eyes, afraid of what I'm about to see. The blonde surprises me but it's kind of cute. It's in layers with the longest layer being just below my shoulders and she's tamed my unruly curls into loose waves. "Do you hate it?"

I reach up and touch it, almost afraid if I do the rest will fall out. "No," I slowly shake my head. "I actually think I like it."

"Unfortunately, not all the purple came out, so there are still tiny streaks of lavender, but it looks intentional, and it kind of matches your dress."

"You are a lifesaver!" I jump off the stool and even to my own surprise I pull Heidi in for a hug. "Thank you!" I run down the stairs and into a room filled with dresses and makeup ladies. "She did it!"

"Oh my God... Look how cute that is on you! You look like a whole new Emi!" Lily touches my hair with a huge smile on her face. "I seriously love it."

"Me too!" Hannah nods her head in approval. "Now you can relax for a few minutes until we have a spot for you to have your makeup done."

"Nope, I'll be doing my own makeup, thank you. After that nonsense, I'm just not comfortable having someone else fix my face." I laugh but am all too serious.

"Are you sure?" Lily asks.

"Yes. Very, very." I head upstairs and load up YouTube to get some quick tips so I don't look washed out with my new blonde hair. Thank God for technology. I don't know how I ever got through my teenage years without it.

About halfway through my third video is when I realize it's not the makeup making me look streaky but the spray tan that is now starting to darken. When I say 'darken,' I mean, I look like I've just spent a week lying in the sun. It's not exactly turning me orange, but I'm definitely no longer a milky white.

"Hey, Lil..." I nonchalantly yell down the stairs, hoping not to send Hannah into a full on panic.

"What?" she yells back, obviously not quite reading my mind like I'd hoped.

"Can you come up here?"

"Is something wrong?" she yells back, leading me to the balcony overlooking the living room.

"Just get your ass up here!" I hiss down to her and watch her jump off the couch and run towards the stairs.

"What is it?" She walks in and stops in her tracks, looking me up and down. "Oh no… the tan?"

"As if anything else could go wrong. Yeah. The tan. What the fuck? How bad does it look?"

Lily bites her lip and looks me up and down. "It's not terrible yet, but it keeps getting darker for up to eight hours. So… with the wedding just a few hours away…"

"Oh, my God… oh my God, oh my God, oh my God. What do I do?" I sit down on the bed and drop my head down between my knees, hoping to avoid the rapidly setting in panic.

"I dunno… Give me a second." She's frantically typing into her phone, probably Googling how to remove spray tan. It can't be a problem never googled just hours before a wedding.

"This says, to slather on a layer of baby oil, let it sit for fifteen minutes and then scrub with lemon juice and baking soda."

"What about my hair?" I glance in the mirror at my new adorable hair.

"We'll just have to refix it. I have some oil." She disappears from my room, returning within the same minute with a tiny bottle of baby oil. "Get to slathering, I'll go down and make the scrub, I'm sure Hannah has everything."

Baby oil is not a fun product. Once I had my top half covered in it the bottle was hard to manage to cover my legs. But somehow, I managed and now I can't even sit because it's so thick I'd likely just slide off anything I sat on.

"Here." Lily comes back in with a stiff loofah sponge and a container full of yellowish goop. "It's probably been about ten minutes, so get in there, steaming hot and scrub till your skin bleeds."

"That seems a little drastic, doesn't it?" I take the concoction from her and walk into the shower. Right when I was happy with how my hair turned out, I have to mess it all up and hope that the outcome is the same.

"Either have pink skin from over scrubbing or look like you tried to change race?"

"Fine, I'll scrub till it hurts." I did, I scrubbed every area until I couldn't take it and then I moved onto the next and then, in the end, I had to rewash with a regular loofah just to get the oil completely off my skin.

"Better?" I walk out still in a towel to see Lily sitting on my bed watching TV.

"Oh... Yes. I'd say you're half as dark now. Still a little darker than I'd choose, but it looks almost normal."

"Really?" I glance in the mirror right as Hannah walks in.

"Time to get—" She stops and stares at me. "What happened to your hair?"

"The spray tan went wrong and we had to scrub it off."

"What?"

"I looked like I sat in the sun for hours."

"And this is the after-scrub?" She's got her jaw clenched through her forced smile.

"Yeah... Still terrible?"

"A little dark, but definitely not terrible. But... now you need to refix your hair, do your makeup, and get dressed." She sighs with a frown.

"Got it, Lily will help me, right Lil?"

"Absolutely. Nothing to worry about."

Lily and I both grin at Hannah, who eventually forces out a smile, even though it's not one that screams she's got faith we'll make it happen on time. We will though.

After today I'm not sure I want a girls' day ever again. The makeup, hair, and girly stuff has gone so wrong and taken so long, and now, an hour before the wedding, when I look into the mirror I barely see me, but a tanned blonde that I hardly recognize.

"You look amazing!" Lily stands back and admires all the hard work we've done in the last hour. "Seriously, I think all this makes even the hideous dress look better!"

"Really?"

"Yes, you are just, wow."

"Aw, thank you!" I squeeze her by the neck, causing her to giggle while struggling to get free. "After a rough few hours you totally just made my day. I was so afraid I was going to be the laughing stock of the wedding."

"There's no way for that to be possible now. In fact, I think you'll end up with all eyes on you." She grabs her bag and hands me my shoes. "I think you might even have a couple of men to choose from after tonight."

"No, remember, the Liam thing is just a favor. A business deal really." No way am I going to mention that this deal is favor for possible favor. I'm not sure what kind of favor I might be getting myself into at some point in the future, and I'm sure Lily's thoughts will go right to the worst possible idea.

"A favor, Right." She stares at me, eyebrows raised in disbelief.

"Will you stop?"

"Fine, but don't come crying to me when they've both fallen in love with you and you can't decide between the two of them."

"I promise that won't happen. Now let's go before Hannah has a stroke worrying about us." We are running late and we promised Hannah we would be there in plenty of time for the wedding. Liam agreed to pick us up the moment I texted him and that was five minutes ago.

"Hello?" I hear him in the foyer yelling up the stairs for us. I told him to let himself in if we weren't already out front when he got here.

"Be right down!" I yell through the doorway before slipping on my stripper heels. "Let's go."

When I reach the top of the stairs Liam's face lights up with a look that is half confused, half intrigued. "Wow! You are just..." He smiles and runs a hand through his hair. "You are gorgeous. I love the hair."

"You do?"

"Yeah. Seriously, I haven't been speechless for a while." He holds the door open as Lily and I walk out to his SUV. "I'm sure Jack will fall head over heels for you." His face drops a bit when he says it, and my heart hurts momentarily when I hear the disappointment in his statement.

"Doubtful, but thank you."

"I'm just glad to be the date of the prettiest girl in the room for the night." He helps push all the feathers safely into his truck before running around to his seat.

I can't believe it but we might actually make this wedding on time, and I'm looking even better than I did last night.

Twelve

The Funeral

Three years ago.

Northwest Portland, Oregon

"She's gone," I say with a cry. A cry that no matter how hard I try to hold it back, it surfaces.

"I am so sorry, babe." Jack walks around to where I'm standing, pulling me into him, allowing me to cry into his chest for the thousandth time.

"I'm sure she's happy to be with Dad again," Evan attempts to lighten the mood and make me feel the tiniest bit better.

"I've already taken care of everything," I hear Jack say over my head to Evan.

"I couldn't let you do that…"

"I wanted to," Jack reaches away from me, and pats Evan's shoulder.

"You can stay as long as you want to, we can send the chaplain in if you'd like?" A nurse tries to smile through a frown.

I know even the nurses were not looking forward to this day. My mom had become the mom of the ward for the last few months she's been here.

I'm not sure you can die of a broken heart, but it sure appears to be that way. One day she was fine, and a few months after Dad died she got weaker and weaker. When we finally convinced her to go to the doctor they discovered that her heart was failing. She refused most options they gave her, and only lasted a few more months living on her own before we had to have her admitted to the hospital.

Her only request was an en-suite kitchen so she could cook for the staff. Not exactly something they do for the terminally ill but the idea of it was nice. I dug up all the old videos our father made of Evan and me as kids and Jack hunted for a projector that could play them. When she wasn't playing games on the iPad Evan bought her, she was snuggled up in bed watching old home movies.

She was never alone in her time in the hospital. Either Evan or I slept here with her and if for some reason we couldn't, Jack and even Amelia had no problem taking a turn.

The last time I left her side was a week ago. I knew her passing was getting close so I couldn't force myself to leave or even take a shower.

Stop being sad for me Emi, I've had a good life. You just make the most of yours as I did mine.

She said it practically every hour, which would only send me into more fits of crying. I don't have a lot in the way of emotions unless death is involved. I just don't do well with death. Especially since I have such little family as it is.

*

"Ready?" Jack asks as I step out of the town car and onto the grass of the cemetery.

"No." I shake my head, pulling my sunglasses over my swollen eyes. I watch the ground below me as I follow Jack, my hand in his, Evan at my side as we make the trek through the graveyard to the burial site. It's spring, so the blooms on the trees and the birds singing their songs makes the day almost one to remember.

I half listen to the preacher as he speaks about earthly memories. One hand in Evan's and another in Jack's, and Jack's amazing family standing behind us to honor a woman they hardly even knew. A woman who will never see her children get married, or have babies, and never get to celebrate the big moments in life with us.

When the crowd starts to thin out Jack walks me across the grass to look down at her headstone.

"I wanted to give you something," He reaches into his pocket and pulls out a rectangular box, opening it to display a beautiful sea green Sterling Silver wrapped dichroic glass pendant.

"It's beautiful," I sigh.

"Your mom's ashes are spun within the stone. She'll be with you always." He pulls the necklace from the box and clasps it around my neck. "I also had one made as a keychain for your brother."

I stare down at the stone around my neck, a tear sliding down my cheek.

"You made this day perfect, not only for me but for Evan too. I know he's the manly, shows no emotions kind of guy but he needed you as well."

"It was nothing," Jack says with a smile. His lips touch my forehead and I know that he's now my normal. Even without my parents, I couldn't go on without him.

"Ready to go back to the house?"

"Sure." I nod, sliding my hand into his and taking one final look at my mother's final resting place. It's beautiful, just like her.

*

"Emi dear!" My Aunt Maggie engulfs me in a giant hug. "She was such a marvelous woman. She's happier now, though."

I nod my head and fight back the tears. Every time someone hugs me more tears seem to appear as if they are never ending. "You know anytime you need me I'm just a few miles away, right?" She holds me at arm's length with a serious look on her face. "You haven't lost everyone. You still have me, Evan, Uncle Melvin, Jack and his wonderful family too. We'll all be right here for years to come."

"But... what... about... when... I... get... married... or... or... or..." I try not to sob it out but it just happens.

"Or what dear?"

"Or get pregnant? Who will be there then?"

"Well, I will! Your mother was a good twelve years older than me so I'll gladly take her place in all those events. Anytime you need anything a girl would go to her mother for, you come to me." She says it sternly, as if I can't hear it over the sobbing.

"Emi..." Evan walks up to us. "Can I get you something?"

I shake my head.

"Has she eaten at all since we got here?" Jack asks, already piling food on a plate.

"Not that I've seen."

I'm sitting at my mom's dining table, a plate piled high full of food that will exceed any calorie counting I've been doing has just been set in front of me. Mac and cheese, scalloped potatoes, ham, everything but anything green. Jack knows me too well.

"Here ya go, sugar. I got you a coffee, just the way you like it."

I start to cry as he hands it to me. And he doesn't run. He smiles, sits next to me and rests his hand on my thigh. He's been here since she died and he's comforted not only me but Evan too. Even though I know he's tried to hide it, he's not doing well either.

"Emi! You poor sweet girl." Amelia's heels click across the tiled floor quickly towards me. "Evan, come over here." She pulls us both to her in a hug. "Anything you two need, you let me, or Jack know. You've been a part of our family for so long and this is no exception. Do you understand that?" I nod as she pulls away, trying desperately to keep the tears back and not make direct eye contact with Evan as for some reason that always seems to make things worse.

"My lord, girl, you look terrible. You can come to stay with me for a while." She glances at Evan, "do you need a place to stay too?"

"No," he shakes his head with a small grateful smile. "I'm thankful you all will help take care of Emi, though."

"But I can't—"

"Nope, there will be no buts. You will move into Jack's old room and I will make sure you get through this."

I shrug my shoulders, not having more of an answer than that. I guess staying with Amelia and Robert for a few days wouldn't kill me. Walking around this house I once shared with my mom is doing nothing but making this whole thing even harder. Every time a memory pops up I lose it, and I've been eating peanut butter and jelly for far too many months now.

"Alright," I force a smile and nod.

I pick at the plate Jack brought me, watching all the people I know and love share stories about my mother. They laugh, hug, and I'm just not there yet. I can't seem to talk about her as if she's in the past. To me, she's been my whole life.

*

"I'm nervous. Are you nervous?" I fidget with the necklace Jack gave me at the funeral as Evan and I sit in Jack's partner Andy's office.

"Not really."

"But what if there is more than we expected? Or less?"

"Either way, it's more than the five hundred dollars in my account right now." Evan grins. He's bounced back from this much quicker than I have. Which I guess considering he's a guy is understandable. The only thing different is how close him and Jack have become. Like true brothers.

"How are you always broke?" I ask him, wondering how Mom and Dad always considered him the more responsible of the two of us. "You're single, you live in a crap apartment, and you work all the time."

"I know how to have fun. You should try it sometime."

"What? I'm fun! Ask Jack!"

"No, thanks," he scrunches his face into a disgusted look.

"OK, kids." Andy walks in behind us holding a file full of papers. "First thing I need to say is how sorry I am about your mother. The few times I spoke with her she seemed like a great lady." He drops the file onto his desk and sits down in his chair. "As you know, your parents were quite well off."

We both watch as he slides on a pair of glasses while opening the file in front of him. "And while there are no stipulations on the inheritance, your parents have made some... requests."

"Requests?" Evan asks, looking suddenly nervous.

"Suggestions, really. Are we ready?"

"Oh, God," I mumble under my breath. I know what my parents were like. This could be very bad.

"Let's start with Emi... You will, of course, receive half of everything, and your parents have suggested that you start living the life you want. Don't rush it. Enjoy things and make the little things count. Forgiveness is the opposite of stubbornness." Andy says the last sentence with a single eyebrow raised as it makes completely no sense but sounds exactly like something my mom would've said.

Evan nods his head with a smile. "Even in death, they know you're stubborn."

"Not so fast, Mr Harrison. You too will receive half of everything, and their request for you is that you take care of your sister and stop trying to populate the earth with every woman you meet. They ask that you find a nice girl and settle down and remember that self-respect is more important than a one night stand where some woman walks away hurt."

I want to laugh out loud but I know those words cut deep for Evan.

"While they both agreed that you are relatively level headed, you don't always make the best decisions. That should change."

"So, we both suck?" Evan asks with a laugh.

"Essentially," Andy laughs. "Their final request is that we sell their house. You keep what you want from the interior and focus on the life that YOU want. Invest and save before pissing away the entire estate." He slides off his glasses and jots a note on two separate slips of paper before turning them over and sliding them across the desk to each of us. "This is the amount you'll each receive, and of course, this is minus any taxes or debts that needed to be paid."

Evan and I both take a deep breath before turning over our numbers.

"Holy shit," I announce, holding the note to my chest and glancing over at Evan.

"Yeah, that's a bit more than the five hundred I mentioned, earlier isn't it?"

"That it is, Mr Harrison, so be wise. You two are young, you have a lot of life ahead of you and you've now got a head start. Don't blow it, like I see so often with the young ones."

"I won't," we say in unison, both a little stunned at the turn of events.

"Emi, I know that you live in the house right now. The house was listed yesterday and we've already got interest, so I would advise you to be looking for a new place to reside, in the very near future."

"OK," I say, kind of sad that this part of my life is moving on without my parents. I've lived in that house my whole life so to leave it quickly, well... it's gonna hurt.

*

"That's a lot of money, Ems." Jack stands at the oven cooking dinner as I go over everything that happened earlier today.

I've got folders and papers spread across the island trying to get my things in order.

"I know, AND I have to move, like pronto. Where should I even look?" I scroll through the apartments for rent site I've got up on my laptop but nothing seems like somewhere I'd want to live.

"Actually... I had an idea." Jack disappears into his room for a moment before coming out holding a small wrapped package in his hands.

"You bought me a present?"

"I did. And if it's not something you're ready for, let me know, there is no pressure here." He nods at the gift now in my hands. "Open it."

I'm nervous. He already gave me the best gift he ever could, the necklace with my mom's ashes. I haven't taken it off since and now, there is more?

I can feel myself unintentionally holding my breath as I pull the ribbon off and unwrap the black paper revealing a tiny white box. It's too flat to be a ring box, unfortunately. I glance up at Jack who is standing at the edge of the bar, arms crossed, a smile on his face. I pull the lid off the box and stare down at a key.

"What's this?" I ask looking over at him confused. "Wait... are you...?"

"I am. I mean... unless you don't want to? You spend almost every day over here anyway, so why not make it official and move in?"

"Are you sure?" I ask, worried that he's doing this only because he knows I need somewhere to live. I guess we've been moving towards this, but I hate that he's asking during a moment where I'm just about homeless.

"I wouldn't have made the key if I wasn't sure."

"Do your parents know?"

"Emi, I'm almost twenty-eight years old. I don't need to run everything I do by my parents. Besides, you heard my mother the other day, she loves you. I'm surprised she didn't ask you to move in permanently first." His eyebrows rise in anticipation of my answer. "So... yes or no?"

It's not the ring I'm always hoping to get, but it's pretty darn close. I've never lived with a man before so I'm more than nervous. I do know I for sure do not want to say no. This is a big step towards true adulthood, and an even bigger step towards a possible husband.

"Yes." I bit my lip with a giggle. "Yes, I will move in with you."

Jack pulls me off the stool and lifts me off the ground before kissing my forehead. "Awesome."

"So, which room is mine?" I joke, looking at the extra bedroom Jack's turned into an office.

"That part is not negotiable… We share a room. Now go, call Lily because I know you're absolutely dying to tell her."

"You are seriously the best boyfriend ever!" I kiss his lips and grab my phone off the counter to call Lily on speaker phone so Jack can witness just how excited girls get over these kinds of things.

"GUESS WHAT?" I scream into the phone.

"What? God… Why are you so loud?" She laughs, but I can tell she's a bit annoyed with the screaming.

"Jack asked me to move in with him!"

"He did?!"

"Yup!"

"You know what's next, right? A proposal, I bet he'll go all out." Jack coughs in the background, probably in shock that girls think that moving in together automatically predicts a proposal. "Oh, oops, am I on speaker?"

"Yeah…"

"Well… At least I'm not calling to verify the reservation of a wedding venue, like on *Friends*."

"True," I respond, wondering how Jack would react if something like that actually happened.

"When's the big moving day?"

"As soon as Emi wants," Jack says before I can speak. "This weekend if you like?"

"Really?"

"Of course, Andy told me the house was already up for sale, and Evan and I are moving everything into storage this weekend, so we might as well do it all in one go."

"We can help if you want?" Lily volunteers herself and Josh to help me pack up my whole life and move.

"OK!" I enthusiastically announce. "Let's do it this weekend!"

Thirteen

The Reception

Present Day

Downtown Portland, Oregon

"Attention, wedding party!!" Botoxed Muffy claps as quietly as possible as she attempts to line us all up to get the wedding started.

"Let's all get with our partners! Make sure you haven't forgotten bouquets, tissues, rings..." She glances around at all of our faces. "Are we ready?"

I kind of feel like we should all yell, ma'am, yes ma'am here and watch her finally smile. She's been bossing us around, yelling, and just being generally obnoxious for the last thirty minutes. With it being so close to the wedding and the fact that the guests are just beyond the doors she's standing in front of, this is the quietest I've seen her yet.

"Once I open these doors we will walk down the aisle just like we practiced last night."

"Today is the day, Ems," Jack says, as he takes his place next to me in line.

"The day our siblings get married? Yes, I know, Jack. I'm here."

"No... The day we finally talk."

"I don't think this is the time or the place."

"No time or place has been right for you for months. Please," he looks over at me, pain filling his eyes. "Please let me do this, Em. If not for you, then for me."

Even though I wanted him to gain twenty pounds and lose his hair, I'm glad he didn't. He's still just as gorgeous as he was the last time I saw him and even though I don't want him to, he still stirs up something inside me.

I nod. "OK." I want to say more but there is something about the processional music starting and the entire atmosphere that prevents me from being the stubborn Emi I would usually be.

"Thank you." He nods with a smile, reaching down and pulling my hand into the crook of his arm and holding it there like he's taking me hostage until we've had this conversation.

"What are you doing?"

"Getting ready to walk down the aisle." He grins down at me, knowing full well that wasn't what I was asking and not seeming to care at all. "Do you like him?"

"What?" We take a step forward, me glancing at Liam in the crowd, now looking comfortable with Greta by his side, like a trophy wife. Which, now that I think of it, I'm sure is her destiny in life. She'll become some bitchy trophy wife and make anyone's life miserable who doesn't bow to her greatness. I can just picture her as the villain on *The Real Housewives of Portland* one day. I refuse to be one of her victims.

"The bartender, do you like him?" Jack stares towards the front of the room as he speaks. "Romantically?"

"How do you know he's a bartender?"

"I know things," he says, as we take another step forward.

I shake my head, "You don't know anything."

"I know you just met him."

"Wha—"

"SHHH!" Muffy glares at us, motioning for the couple ahead of us to start down the aisle.

"Why do you think that?" I whisper, as quietly as possible, but Jack just shrugs his shoulders and holds my hand even tighter. "You're wrong, anyway," I say with a clenched tooth smile. "I met him in Dallas."

Think Emi, *think*. I need a good lie and I need it fast. I can't believe I didn't think of a plausible back story before now. I should have known Jack would research him; he's a freaking lawyer.

"No, you didn't," he says under his breath, smiling at the crowd as if nothing is going on between us.

"*Yes, I did.*" I hiss through clenched teeth, moving my lips as little as possible so no one notices our conversation. I suddenly spot Lily's face, her eyes wide, a questioning smile. We obviously aren't being as subtle as I thought we were. Thankfully the end of the aisle comes quickly and we part before the music changes.

Hannah and her father step into the doorway, both beaming with excitement. Hannah truly does look lovely in her giant princess gown. When I glance over at my brother he's fighting back tears but looks as in love as anyone I've ever seen. They're absolutely perfect for each other. I smile at him when he looks my way but then notice that Jack and Liam are both watching me, with very different smiles on their faces.

Liam's smile is that smile every girl wants to see. The one they make internet memes out of that say something like *Find a man that looks at you like Joe Biden looks at Obama*. Honestly, that smile freaks me out far more than it should. I didn't really come here to find love or anything like it. This is supposed to be something just short of a business arrangement. But this smile, the kiss last night, and his flattery have somehow convinced everyone, but Jack, that we are almost a couple.

Jack, though? His smile is almost a silent plea that is piercing right through my soul. It's the same smile he would use when we were together and I was mad at him. Which was rare. How is he doing this to me? He's got me wondering things that have nothing to do with getting back at him.

I force a small smile back in their direction, but for some reason, my eyes are on Jack. Damn him. I can't get the memories to stop replaying in my head. It was so much easier to be in control when I was two thousand miles away.

If I'm honest, that's partly why I left. I wanted to be in control and I couldn't do that seeing him every day. I deserve the man who would do anything to make sure I knew how much he loved me and Jack lost that the day we broke up. He sat back and waited. Waited for me to decide to forgive him, to take second place to Madison or Greta, or whoever. I don't want to be in second place.

*

"Wasn't it beautiful," I say to Lily, as we walk into the reception room.

Amelia really spared no expense with this wedding. Sheer panels hang from the ceiling, backlit with soft lighting. Giant crystal chandeliers hang over every table with centerpieces of all white flowers taller than me. "Did you see Evan as Hannah walked down the aisle?" I ask, mesmerized by the atmosphere of the room.

"I did," she says, glancing at me as we stand near the bar. "I also saw you and Jack as you walked down the aisle. You both looked… happy? What was that about?"

"What?" I grab a glass of wine from the bartender and guiltily glance back at Lily.

"What happened?"

"I agreed to talk..." I spot Liam heading in my direction.

"I told you," Liam says, planting a kiss on my cheek.

"You told her what?" Josh asks.

"That she'd be the most beautiful girl in the room." Both Lily and Josh's eyebrows rise in confusion.

"That's too sweet," I force a pinched smile in their direction to gloat about me being the prettiest. "It's not true, but it's sweet." It might not be completely true but that doesn't mean I have to ignore it.

"I think it's true," Liam says, but his attention is on Lily and Josh.

"Thank you. How was Greta? I saw she made herself comfortable next to you. Sorry about that."

"She's an odd one, that's for sure. She kept asking what I thought of your hair. And your spray tan."

"Why would she care about those?"

"I don't know," he shakes his head. "But she made sure to tell me what a morning you'd had, and how everything had gone wrong for you. She said you're always this unlucky and that I should run as far as possible from you." He laughs when he says it. I, however, can almost feel the steam rising from my head. How dare she try and control the situation through my date!

Wait... Did she? The hair, the spray tan, the purple shampoo...

"You don't think—" I start to ask Lily, who is already nodding her head.

"It makes sense, considering nothing went wrong with any of the other girls, and she was there the entire time." She inhales through her nose, her nostrils flaring. "I can't believe we didn't see this before!"

"She sabotaged me? For what?" I say it far too loud, causing people near us to turn in our direction to see what the commotion is about.

Right then she and Jack walk into the room. Without a further thought, I start marching towards them until I feel a hand pull me to a stop.

"Emi, I don't think this is a great idea, not here." Liam tries to stop me but I pull away from him and stomp my way to them.

"YOU BITCH!" I spit at her in a hiss much louder than intended. "You did this!" I point to my hair. Greta starts to back away from me slowly, putting Jack between us as a human shield.

"What's going on?" Jack asks, glancing between the two of us, obviously more than clueless.

"She hates me... For what, though? You know she tried to make me look like a complete fool today?" I snap at Jack who tries to process what I'm saying.

"Come on..." he glances at a trembling Greta. "She would never..." His face drops in disbelief when she doesn't offer any explanation or denial.

"Ask her... Ask her about my hair, or my spray tan..."

"PLEASE WELCOME, OUR STAR COUPLE... MR AND MRS... EVAN AND HANNAH HARRISON."

The DJ interrupts us and we all stop speaking and look towards the doors that Evan and Hannah are running through, hand in hand.

"Emi, let's not do this here." Lily and Liam are now either side of me, trying to convince me to walk away from Jack and Greta. But I can't.

"Not until she admits it."

"*Girls*... What *is* going on?" Amelia approaches us, glancing between the two of us. "I'm not sure what's happening, but let's move it outside the reception." She corrals all of us out into the hallway, and closes the doors to the reception room. Greta keeps Jack between us as a buffer. "Now what is the problem?"

"Go ahead and tell them, Greta." I cross my arms over my chest waiting to hear the lie she's about to tell.

"There is *no* problem, Mrs Cabot." Greta shrugs her shoulders with a nervous laugh, probably trying to convince herself that she hasn't been caught.

"How did you even get in my room to change the shampoo?" I wait for her to answer, but she just rolls her eyes. "Or the spray tan, how did you set that up? The hairdresser who fried off my hair, was that planned or was that just a lucky coincidence?"

"Puh-lease. You can't prove I did any of that. You're just bad luck... always have been. By the way, I've heard about your so called lucky dress, and trust me, there isn't enough luck in the world to help *you* out, not even in an ugly, so two seasons ago, dress." Greta rolls her eyes with an irritated groan, as if I'm the most pathetic person on the planet to believe in something like luck. That dress *is* lucky. She might be right about it being from two seasons ago but who cares? Some of the best moments of my life have happened while I was wearing it. There is no other explanation for it *but* luck.

Amelia's glare towards Greta makes even me shiver in fear. "Maybe we should contact the spray tan employee and ask her? Surely that would prove your innocence, right, Greta?"

We all watch her open her mouth to speak, but then suddenly decide against it.

Liam steps up beside me. "Greta, I do find it unusual that everything Emi just mentioned are the very same things you asked me about just before she and Jack walked down the aisle. There is just one more thing I hadn't mentioned to Emi yet..."

"What?" I turn to Liam, worried about what other damage she's done.

Liam glances to Greta's left hand, everyone's gaze following.

My heart stops in my chest. Like freezes. "My ring," I look over at Jack who's now got a hand on the back of his neck as he turns away, walking a few steps and then turning back to look back at her hand with narrowed eyes. "You asked her to *marry* you?" I ask, when he glances back at me.

"No," he shakes his head before grabbing her hand and staring down at the engagement ring that once sat on my hand. "*Where* did you get this?" he says with his voice raised.

"I uh – stumbled across it in your desk drawer. Obviously, you were just planning it out, so I saved you some time. I thought maybe we could announce it tonight?" she bats her eyes as if trying to convince him telepathically.

Jack backs away from her, his head shaking the entire time. "No, no, no. *NO*, I wasn't planning anything out and there will be *no* announcements. I've had that ring in my desk since Emi and I—" he looks to the floor, obviously mortified that he's living this in front of his whole family.

"Did you do those things to Emi?" Amelia interrupts as Jack walks down the hall partially losing it with Greta's revelation.

Greta shakes her head in denial, but the glistening of sweat on her forehead isn't the physical reaction of someone who is innocent. I know from watching too many who-done-it TV shows.

"Fine, OK? I may have had something to do with them, but you totally deserved it. Look what you do to Jack when he's around you. He hasn't been the same since you got here. He's miserable."

I'm staring down the hall, my eyes never leaving Jack. When he turns towards us our eyes meet.

"I'm not miserable," he says to me in a near whisper. "I'm also not dating Greta. Not really…"

I look at Greta whose mouth drops open as if this is the first time she's hearing this from him. Considering she just shocked him by showing up to his sister's wedding wearing my old engagement ring, I'm thinking she makes her own rules and has a lot of conversations that no one else knows about.

"Greta, there is something I've wondered about quite often these last few weeks." Amelia's arms are crossed in front of her and her pacing between us is more than nerve-wracking. "There was a story a friend of mine brought to my attention at a party you and Jack both attended. I'd like to get a straight answer from you about it."

"Mom, don't get involved," Jack growls.

"This involves you too, Jack. I would think it would be of importance to you."

Jack looks back to me, all the same emotions on his face that I can feel in mine. Shock, regret, humiliation, and pain.

"Elsie Graham, the mother of a girl called Madison Graham, told me a story I couldn't quite believe at the time," Amelia continues. Greta sucks in her breath and suddenly looks completely terrified, unsure where to run. "You are friends with Madison Graham, am I right?"

"Not really," Greta shakes her head continuously.

Amelia frowns. "Maybe you're not close any longer, but you were close a year ago, correct?"

Greta is still shaking her head. "I wouldn't say close, I knew *of* her."

"You knew of her enough to send her in Jack's direction when he was looking for a new assistant?" This time, Greta doesn't answer, only shrugs her shoulders.

"Wait a minute..." Jack finally speaks as he walks towards Greta in the center of the room. "Madison Graham, my former assistant? That Madison?"

"Yes." Amelia nods her head, glancing back at me. "This would be the same Madison." She sighs heavily and walks over to speak to Greta, face to face. "I'm going to give you one chance to tell the truth. If you don't, I will make sure you never fit into my crowd again."

"You can't do that," Greta says, with a haughty look on her face. "I was already in that crowd without you."

"Go on then, let's hear the truth – or I'll tell the story Elsie filled me in on."

Everyone's head turns to Greta, but I look at Jack. Both of us know exactly what Greta is about to say and because of that, it's hard to breathe.

"It's nothing, really. I just... uh... That first time I met you," Greta turns to Jack and smiles sweetly. "At the Christmas Party, remember?"

He stares through her with no emotion.

"I... uh... I couldn't quit thinking about you, and you wouldn't answer my calls, so I... I heard that you needed an assistant and my fr... a girl I knew from college, was looking for a job. I thought she'd be a great fit so I sent her your way." She shrugs her shoulders as if that's the end of the story, but Amelia clears her throat and Greta sighs again. "I asked her to bring me up to you and get your reaction, but it didn't faze you even a little bit, because of *her*." Greta glares at me.

"Yes," Jack says with a nod, our eyes meeting again momentarily.

"Go on," Amelia says.

"So, I came up with a plan." Greta is speaking in almost a whisper at this point.

"What plan?" I finally ask her, deserving the truth.

"A plan to steal Jack from you."

"My God," Liam says next to me under his breath. "She is crazy." He looks at me, his eyebrows narrowed but eyes wide.

"I'm *not* crazy." Greta glares at Liam, presumably having overheard his comment. "I was just in love. I asked Madison to make sure that Jack dumped Emi. What happened is not what I expected, or planned, but it worked." The nonchalant shrug of her shoulders makes me want to run across the room and strangle her.

"You're telling me that you sent Madison into my office that day?" Jack takes a few steps backward as if just hit by a cannon.

"Not exactly." Greta follows him down the hall. "She did that on her own; I just told her when to do it. Madison knew Emi was coming to meet you for lunch that day, so she made sure Emi would catch you... uh... you know."

"No... I don't know. Catch me what?" Jack suddenly turns towards her, his face flushed and showing a glare I've never witnessed from him before.

"You know... you, *with* her." Greta's shoulders shrug again.

I look back at Jack, a tear rolling down my cheek. *She* did this. *She* ruined my life. She ruined *our* lives. She did it on purpose, and she doesn't even care.

Suddenly I find myself feeling dizzy, my hand over my mouth, unable to say anything. I slide down the wall behind me to the floor, dropping my head onto my knees.

"Emi," I feel Jack suddenly kneeling in front of me. "I *wasn't* with her," he says. "This is what I've wanted to talk to you about. I love *you*, Ems. I'd never hurt you like this. *Never.*"

I glance up at Jack, whose face is as pained as my own. "She was all over me but I didn't want any part of it. I was as caught off guard as you were. I'm so sorry it looked the way it did." He reaches up, touching my neck and leaning his head against my own. "I'm *so* sorry, I love you."

For a moment I breathe him in. I force a breath and quickly wipe away a tear. "It wasn't just Madison," I say in a whisper, for some reason not wanting to hurt him any more than he obviously already is.

"What?"

"Don't pretend you don't know. It's because of her." I look over at Greta, who has a proud evil grin on her face. "I went home that day, I saw her, at our door, when I went to talk to you. You let her in. You let Greta into OUR apartment, Jack. She kissed you."

"You saw that? Why didn't you tell me?" Jack stands up, a hand in his hair and his jaw hanging open. "She kissed me without an invitation. She showed up, *without* an invitation. She'd been harassing me for weeks and I'd finally had enough. I only invited her in to threaten a restraining order if it didn't stop."

"Come on..." I clamber to my feet. "I walked in on you doing I don't know what with Madison, and then later the same day I find you getting a little too close to the one girl you knew I hated. Then I get here, a nervous wreck to even see you again and I find out you two are dating. What was I supposed to think?"

Jack is silent as he stares at me from across the hall. "We aren't dating. Not really. She's just somehow everywhere I am. She's the only person I had to talk to about this because I've been humiliated for being such an idiot as to let all this happen. She seemed to be the only one who understood. I didn't know why until now." He glares over at her. "I have no romantic feelings for Greta."

He shakes his head, tears glistening in his eyes, before finally giving up and walking away from me. And in an instant, my heart breaks again. But this time it hurts so bad I'm not sure if I'll ever recover.

"Give the ring back to my mother, Greta." He says on his way past her.

"WHAT?" she squeals. "You're going to let her do this to us?"

The moment the words come out of her mouth, the sorrow in his eyes turns to rage and he turns his attention directly to her.

"*YOU* did this to us," he growls at her. "And I use the word us loosely. We were nothing. You lied from the very start, you manipulated your way in." He stops and stares at the floor. "I can't believe I didn't see it. I've been so hung up on—" he looks back towards me before turning back to Greta. "I don't ever want to see you again." He looks to his mother as if they are having a silent conversation. "You need to leave, Greta." Jack backs away before turning away from her altogether, not even waiting for her reaction.

I look at Greta, whose face is now a mix of horror, disbelief, and heartbreak. I've never seen anything more fitting for a girl who is pure evil. A piece of my heart starts to heal instantly, and I don't feel even a little bit bad about it.

I thought I wanted to see Jack miserable, and now that I have, I know it's the worst feeling I've ever had. That was before I knew what I know now. Seeing Greta finally get what she deserves is far better.

"Before you leave," Amelia says, "you may hand over my mother's ring that you've stolen." She holds her hand out to Greta who pulls her hand to her heart quickly.

"Wait, Jack..." She calls to him as he disappears through the doors into the reception. Only looking back at me.

"I've notified security, and if you don't go in the next five minutes, you will be escorted out of the building by them. It's your choice." Amelia once again holds her hand out for the ring. Greta jerks it violently off her finger, hurling it to the floor. The stomping sound of her exiting before security arrives echoes in my head in sync with my heartbeat pounding in my ears. I watch the elevator doors close behind her, almost as if it were a final dramatic exit of the woman who did everything possible to ruin my life for no reason at all.

"Let's all get back to the reception so we don't ruin Hannah's day." Amelia nods a small smile my direction before walking towards the doors into the reception room.

"We'll just leave you two alone." Lily and Josh sneak away, leaving Liam and me standing in the foyer.

"I... uh..." Liam runs a hand through his hair nervously. "I'm so sorry. I know I've only known you a few days, but that made even me sick. Is there anything I can do?"

I shake my head, fighting back the tears, again. I feel like walking in on Jack and Madison has only just happened, and I'm losing everything for the second time.

"Do you need to go and talk to him?"

"No," I answer quickly, turning to Liam, and forcing a smile. "Not yet. Let's get back."

"Emi..." Liam takes my hand, stopping in front of me. "You have every right to be upset. Mad even. I know this is a lot to deal with and I also know I'm very much an outsider but, I really think you and Jack need to talk." He sighs the sort of sigh you make when you give people bad news. "Can I give you some advice?"

He continues without waiting for my answer. "You are an amazing woman. For months, my heart and my head have been a mess because of my own break up, and then you wander into my bar and make me see things in a way I haven't in a while. But you have a lot going on here that needs to be sorted, and I think after all this," he motions to the now empty foyer, "you owe it to yourself to see what you still feel for Jack."

"You think I should get back with him?"

"I think only you know the answer to that. But I do think you should work out what all the information revealed tonight means to you."

I nod.

"I think it's best if I go. You know where to find me." He forces a sad smile as I watch him make his way to the elevator. He nods his head in my direction as the doors close behind him, leaving me alone with only my confusion to keep me company.

Another tear falls down my cheek before I can wipe it away. I can't just fall apart, this is my brother's wedding. I walk to the doorway, the doors now open and watch the excitement in the room. Our families are happy, chatting, and celebrating Evan and Hannah. People are dancing, eating, laughing, and here I stand with only half a heart left.

Lily waves over at me from the table she's been assigned to. The last thing I want is to ruin my brother's wedding day. Whether I want to or not, I have to pull myself together.

"Where's Liam?" she asks.

"He left."

"Oh. Ems..." She smiles a pitiful smile and pats the chair next to her. "I'm so sorry, but I think he did the right thing. You need to deal with this right now."

"I know." I sigh and look across the room at Jack. He's sitting at a table alone, staring at a beer bottle in front of him, looking as miserable as I've ever seen him. Even though I've no idea what should be said, I promised him we would talk today. That's not a promise I can break right now.

I slowly make my way across the room to his table, sitting in the chair next to him. He glances over and forces a hesitant smile.

"Are you OK?" I ask.

"THE BRIDE AND GROOM HAVE REQUESTED THAT THE MAID OF HONOR AND BEST MAN JOIN THEM ON THE DANCE FLOOR!"

Jack laughs to himself, then looks to me. "Did you know they were gonna do this?"

"No." I shake my head.

"There's no way out of it now." Jack stands, holding his hand out for mine. I follow him to the dance floor, Evan and Hannah are nowhere to be seen.

As he pulls me against him the song starts. *Safe Inside*, by James Arthur. I've heard it before because I fell in love with it a while back, as heart wrenching as it is, it's absolutely perfect for this exact moment.

It's awkward at first when I take his free hand, he pulls it against his chest with a sigh.

"I'm so sorry, Em."

I stop and look up at him, shaking my head. "I don't want to talk, not right now." I know I promised him I would, but I can't talk right now, my emotions would only get the best of me.

He nods, a hesitant and sad smile on his face as I lean my head into his chest, breathing him in. *We* didn't do this. *We* didn't cause this mess. For once we are a casualty of someone else's crazy.

A lot has happened in the last thirty minutes, really in the last year, and all I want to do right now is feel him hold me again like he used to. I just want to be still and know that I didn't do anything wrong to lose him. I know there is still a lot to talk through but this feels like a start. The silence of us, just existing in the same room.

Fourteen

The Fight

Three years, eight months ago.

Downtown Portland, Oregon

There are times I wonder why anyone would ever want to be a lawyer? It seems like all Jack ever does is work. If he's not working on an active case he's working his ass off because he's trying to become a partner at the firm. He's good at his job, he really is, but is it worth risking your personal life for?

"When is the last time you guys even had dinner together?" Lily asks.

I'm sitting at a table in the middle of a bustling restaurant with Lily and Josh. Without my boyfriend, I feel like I'm the third wheel. Again.

"Over a month ago," I sigh, pushing the food around my plate. "I try, really I do. I've even scheduled dinner dates, and he'll call at the last second and have to cancel. I just don't get it. Should I be worried?"

Lily's frown says it all. "I don't know? Maybe?"

"No." Josh rolls his eyes. "You girls think too much. Maybe he's just busy with work. It's not like he has any kind of malicious bone in his body. Jack's the best guy we all know."

I feel myself nodding but also wondering if it's actually true. "Maybe we missed some kind of signal?"

"Signal?" He grabs his beer and leans back in his chair, both Lily and I waiting for his response. "Maybe it's a signal that he worked his ass off in college and he's almost accomplished one of his goals. Do you guys have these conversations about me?"

"No," says Lily, wildly trying to silently signal me to agree with her.

"Yes," I say at the same moment, not quite picking up her signal quick enough and earning a confused look from Josh.

"Great."

"You haven't done anything completely stupid like this yet, so we haven't really had to." Lily plants a reassuring kiss upon his cheek.

"Jack's not doing anything stupid," Josh repeats to me.

"Maybe he isn't, but you don't think him pushing her aside for weeks at a time is a little risky?" Lily asks him. It seems I'm now just a bystander in their argument over my love life.

"How's that?" he asks.

"What if he's pushing her into the arms of some other attention giving man?" Lily replies, clearly disgusted by Josh's nonchalant attitude over this entire conversation.

"Is he?" He looks directly at me.

"Well... no," I sigh. "But he could be."

"But he's not, and it's not like you're going to get tired of him and dump him, so I say, learn to live with it. He's a hard working guy and he wants to make the most of a career he loves. Either accept it or move on."

"Have I ever told you I don't love your latest choice in men?" I say to Lily, who nods in agreement before giggling.

"He'll learn the ways of us soon enough."

A roll of Josh's eyes says maybe he won't.

He could have a point though. Up until now Jack and I have never had an issue, in fact, we've never really even had a serious fight. Maybe he really is just completely innocent and this entire problem is quite possibly just in my head.

But then again... maybe he's not. Men do these things; they get wrapped up in their work and decide they don't have time for a relationship and instead of telling us they get busy and disappear. What if that's what this is?

"I'm just going to have to talk to him about it."

"You should. Do it tonight... Surprise him at his office."

"Yeah, great idea. Men love that... when women surprise us anywhere. Don't do that if your relationship means anything to you. It seems desperate." Josh glances at Lily.

"I'll do it." I look over at Josh who's giving me the 'I warned you' pinched lips look. He doesn't know everything; He just knows one man's perspective. I respect that, but I know Jack. And something is wrong.

*

I order our favorite meals from *Pastini: tortellini gorgonzola* for me and *fettuccini alfredo* with chicken for Jack. *Pastini* is the restaurant I choose to eat at whenever it's my turn to decide. I stop by the *Piece of Cake Bakery* and grab an entire Fantasy Cake. Which is the best cake in the entire world... cheesecake on top of chocolate cake with cream cheese icing. It's like a chocolate cheesecake heaven. I even get a bottle of wine that cost more than fifteen dollars. Jack should be more than impressed.

I probably should have considered how I'd get this all into the building before ordering every food item I adore, but sometimes the stomach speaks louder than the brain.

"Do you need help?" a voice behind me asks. When I glance back I see Rachel, Jack's assistant, coming out of the stairwell. "Oh! Emi, it's so good to see you."

"Hey, Rachel. I'd love some help. I'm just bringing up dinner to Jack, I feel like I never see him anymore."

"Oh... Jack actually isn't in the office; didn't he tell you?"

"Tell me?" I ask out loud wondering how the look on my face doesn't say everything she needs to know?

"He and Andy were meeting with a client in Seattle. They left first thing this morning."

I drop the *Pastini* bag on the ground. "In Seattle?"

"I'm sorry," she nods. "Can I help you at least get everything back out to your car?"

For a moment, I stare at Rachel, confused. Why wouldn't he tell me he was leaving the state?

"Yes, yes... That would be great," I say to Rachel, hoping she doesn't notice the panicked look on my face.

She and I load the stuff into my car, and Rachel, the sweet girl she is, waves as she walks towards her car in the garage nearby. Now, as if never calling or showing up for our dates isn't enough, he's running off out of state, without even telling me.

I violently jab his number into my phone only for it to go straight to voicemail. Either his phone isn't on, or he's intentionally ignoring me. The asshole. I dial Lily and thankfully she picks up on the first ring.

"He left town, without even telling me."

"What?" she asks, obviously confused by me starting my conversation yet again in the middle of a sentence. You'd think she'd be used to me by now, but I'm still able to surprise her with my over thinking.

"Yeah... I went through all the work of picking up all of our favorite foods to surprise him with dinner at work, and when I get here Rachel tells me that he went out of town with Andy – *this morning.*"

"And you're sure he didn't tell you?"

"Yeah, of course I'm sure! We've hardly talked in a few days and I don't remember him mentioning this at all. I'd remember that!"

"OK, OK, that is weird."

"Do you think he's cheating on me?"

"No..." Her hesitation doesn't match her words.

"Great. Now what?"

"Let's go to his apartment and see what else he hasn't told you?"

"I don't exactly have a key, Lil."

"So? That's a minor, workable detail." She laughs. "Well just tell the super that you left your medication in there and you have to get it back before Jack gets home from his business trip."

"That could work."

This is not the right thing to do. I just need it on record that I know this.

"I'll meet you there in ten." I hit the *End call* button.

It might not be the *right* thing to do but I'm doing it. What can it hurt? If he doesn't want to talk to me, I'll figure out why on my own.

*

The super was more than easy and let me into Jack's apartment with no questions asked. Apparently, I'm on the list of accepted people in his life so he didn't even stay to make sure I got what I lied that I needed in the first place.

"Now what?" I glance at Lily who is already going through drawers in the kitchen.

"Start looking for things." Clearly, she's done this before.

"What am I looking for?"

"Proof that he's not always at work. Women's underwear, condom wrappers, toothbrushes that aren't yours, photos..."

"Ew..." It's at moments like these I question my friendship with Lily but also thank the Lord that I have her.

"Well... it's what some men do, Ems."

"I hope it's not what Jack does..." I walk into his bedroom. Everything is perfectly clean, the bed made, no dirty clothes and the curtains are closed. I glance through a couple of drawers but he's so anal about everything that there isn't a reason to dig: the shirt drawer has shirts, the sock drawer has socks, yadda, yadda, yadda. Nothing exciting anywhere.

"Find anything?" Lily asks me as she enters Jack's room.

"No... you?"

"This." She holds up a bright purple bra.

"That's mine!" I snatch it from her just as the front door clicks open. "Oh my God!" I hiss at her, hoping to God it's just the super checking on us.

"Hello?" Jack's voice comes booming through the apartment.

"I left my purse out there," Lily whispers, running to my side.

"Emi?" He walks down the hallway, our eyes momentarily meeting before his gaze moves to the bra still hanging from my fingertips. "What-" He looks around the room, spotting Lily cowering behind me. "*What* are you doing here? How did you even get in?"

"Jack... I... Uh... wanted to surprise you, with dinner, so I went to your office but Rachel said you were here."

"So why is Lily hiding behind you then?" He asks with no emotion on his face.

"We couldn't find you so we thought we'd check in here. We just got here too." I pretend my day has been exhausting as well so I just really don't even have time to fight about what's really going on.

"And how did you get in?" He's being really hard to read right now with all the questions.

"The super let me in." I watch Jack's brow furrow and his lips pinch together.

"I'm just going to wait for you in the car." Lily runs past us and is out of the front door before I can even object.

"If you thought I was here, why did you get the super to let you in?" He grabs a picture frame still in my hand and sets it back on the dresser where it belongs. "I'm confused. And where is this dinner?" He glances around the room.

There is no way I can continue to lie my way through this. "I must've been so excited to see you that I left dinner in the car. I got our favorite, though. *Pastini*." Obviously, I'm going to try the lying. At this point, what else do I have to lose?

"Ems, Rachel called me a few minutes ago to tell me you were upset I didn't tell you I was going out of town."

"Oh?"

"I was going to call you after I got back but... here you are, sneaking around my apartment. Why are you really here?"

Of course, he sees right through my lies. As he should, it's not like we've been dating for just a couple of weeks. It's been a couple of years.

"I don't know, Jack... You act like I'm at the bottom of your list lately, so I wanted to find out what you're really up to. Why you don't treat me like you used to?"

"So, you snuck into my apartment to – what? Look for another woman?"

"*NO.*" I shake my head as I stare at the carpet.

Jack frowns.

"Fine, yes. That's exactly what I was doing."

"The dinner story was a lie?"

"Yes... NO! I have dinner, and dessert, and even wine, but I didn't think you were here so I just came up to see if you were with—" I pause momentarily, knowing if I say it out loud I'm going to sound like a completely pathetic jealous girlfriend. Which basically is exactly what I am.

"You just came up here to see if I was with someone else. Got it. It's nice to know that even after two years of dating you still don't trust me at all?"

"I *do* trust you! But you never talk to me anymore." I can feel emotion welling up in my chest with my racing heart. This isn't going to end well.

"I'm busy, Ems, trying to make partner at the firm. We've talked about this. I'm basically at Andy's disposal until he decides I've earned it. Why can't you understand this?"

"Because I don't know why it means I'm last in your life," I cry. "It's not fair."

"It's also not fair that you're digging around in my apartment, is it?" I watch Jack roll his eyes at the bra I'm still holding and walk past me to sit on the edge of his bed. "Listen," he sets his hand on my thigh as I sit down next to him. "I think maybe we should take a break until I've done some thinking."

"What do you mean a break?" My voice cracks as I ask, knowing exactly what he means.

"Like, no more Jack and Emi until I've made partner and figured some things out. Clearly, this is stressing you out, and I can't worry about what you're up to next when I already have so much on my plate."

"You're breaking up with me?!" I squeal, flipping the bra in his direction.

"I think it's for the best right now." He picks the bra up off the floor and hands it back to me.

"You are such an ass! There *is* someone else, isn't there?" I yell, but he's already directing me towards the front door.

"Emi, just stop."

"I can't believe you would do this!"

"I could say the same." The front door is open and he's willing me out of it. "I'll call you, I promise. I just need some time. That's all."

"Fuck you! Don't call me, EVER!" I grab the doorknob and slam the door shut behind me, forcing myself not to allow the tears to take over until I'm safely down in front of the building. Lily at my side.

"Ems, I'm *so* sorry. I didn't think he was in town, had I known I'd have—"

"He dumped me! He said he couldn't worry about what I might be up to next while he's got so much on his plate at work."

"He what?!" Lily is as mad as I am.

"Yeah." A single tear rolls down my cheek before I wipe it away. "I'm going home."

"Do you want me to come with you?"

"No." Before she can object I'm in my car, doors locked, waving, and hoping she'll get the BFF ESP that I'll be fine, eventually.

*

"Emi, I know you're home, your mom let me in, please open the door." Jack's voice wakes me. I glance around the room and realize I'm still in the clothes I was wearing yesterday, food cartons are lying across my bed, and the bottle of wine on my nightstand is empty.

"Ems," he knocks again.

I crack the door open for him and disappear into my bathroom.

"Whoa... What happened in here?"

"I ate our dinner last night," I say, reluctantly walking back into my room, "*after* you broke up with me."

"*All* of it?" He lifts the half-eaten cake from the box, his eyes wide with surprise.

"Nearly."

"Listen..." He sighs as he walks towards me but I back away from him, holding my arms across my chest. "I didn't sleep at all last night."

"Good," I spit at him, with as much hate as I can muster at nine in the morning without coffee.

"You breaking into my apartment wasn't exactly the right thing to do, but I can kind of see why you did it."

"You can?" I look over at him.

"Yeah. You're right, I've been putting you at the bottom of my list and that's not fair. I'm sorry for that. I do need you to understand, though, that this is a critical time in my career and I need you to be patient with me."

"Well, you dumped me, so I guess you don't have to worry about *that* anymore."

His deep sigh, frown, and hand through his hair make my heart pitter-patter in my chest hoping he's having second thoughts. "I don't *want* to break up with you, Emi. You just frustrated me."

"You frustrate me." I fight back and watch him laugh under his breath.

"I'm sorry for breaking up with you. I hope you'll forgive me and maybe take me back?" He disappears out of my bedroom door and into the hallway before reappearing with a giant bouquet of yellow roses. "The lady at the florist said that yellow roses signify innocence and apologies. I know I'm guilty of not putting you first but I hope you'll overlook it and give me another chance." He hands the roses to me.

"How am I supposed to say no to this?" I ask him quietly, a little ashamed of myself.

"You're not."

"You promise there is no one else?"

"There will never be anyone else, Ems. You should know that by now."

"And why aren't you at work now? Aren't you going to get in trouble for this and lose your possible partnership?"

"Come with me, I want to show you something." He holds out his hand for mine. "Please?"

I set the flowers down on my bed and follow him to his car, not realizing he's taking me somewhere outside the house. The route he takes tells me he's bringing me to the office with him. Considering what I look like right now (red puffy eyes, still wearing yesterday's clothes, and with the added bonus of a cheesecake stain on my shirt), I hope he's not bringing me in to see anyone important.

"That." He points to the sign advertising his practice on the front of the building.

"*Morgan, Steller, & Cabot?*" I say out loud with a grin.

"I made partner, and this was Andy's surprise to me. I guess they updated the sign while we were out of town yesterday." I look at him and his smile says everything. He's elated that his hard work has finally paid off.

"I'm sorry, Jack. I acted like a crazy, jealous girlfriend and I didn't mean to do that. I just…" I bite my lip looking for the right words. "I've never loved someone the way I love you, and I was scared I was losing you." I glance down at my own hands. "Seeing that sign last night might have also saved us both a lot of trouble…" I force a laugh as he wraps his arms around me.

"You'll never lose me. OK?"

I nod, tears filling my eyes. When he kisses me, the tears spill out on their own.

"Why are you crying?"

"That was the worst night of my life," I sob, as he pulls me as close to him as he can in the front seat of his car.

"I know, babe, and I'm sorry. But… at least you got a great dinner?"

When he laughs, I can't help but laugh with him. It's not every day you get to scoff down two entrées, an entire bottle of wine and half a cake, all by yourself.

Fifteen

The Great Escape

Present Day

Northwest Portland, Oregon/Northeast Portland, Oregon

As I wake up the morning after the wedding, something catches my eye near the table by the window.

"JACK?" I squeal when he moves, scaring the crap out of me. "*What* are you doing here?" He's sitting in the corner wearing jeans and a t-shirt, arms crossed, a somber look on his face as he stares out into the sliver of light the partially opened curtains are allowing in.

"I didn't mean to scare you. I came over early to talk to Evan, he thought maybe you'd be up too but," he stands from the chair he's sitting in. "I can go, this was probably a bad idea."

"So, you didn't just sit there all creepy and watch me sleep all night?"

"No," he shakes his head.

I sit up, turning the switch to the bedside lamp and pulling the blankets up to my neck as if he's never seen me in my pajamas before.

"You said you didn't want to talk last night, and I was OK with that. I needed the same thing, to just hold you."

I feel myself sigh. The same sigh I've had a hundred times since the entire ordeal last night. I'm sure Evan and Hannah set that Maid of Honor and Best Man dance thing up after Amelia filled them in on exactly what was happening. I wanted to be mad but I couldn't.

"I need to talk now, though," he says walking over to sit on the edge of the bed.

"OK..." I glance at my phone on the nightstand next to me. "At seven in the morning?"

"Yeah..." He nods, leaning his elbows on his knees, causing his hair to fall onto his forehead.

"For the last year I've felt like someone I don't even know. I've had to live with the guilt that you were hurt by something I didn't even understand until last night. What you saw that day, wasn't me. I think you know that." He glances over at me before looking back down at his hands.

"I get why you didn't want to talk to me because my excuse, even though it was the truth, didn't sound very believable. That and you're incredibly stubborn when you want to be."

I force a smile, I can't say he's wrong.

"I never have and I never would cheat on you, Emi. Ever. Canceling the wedding was the second worst day of my life."

"The second?" I ask, wondering what could be worse than that?

"Realizing I'd lost you was the first."

"Ah..."

We both sit silently staring anywhere but at each other.

"Can I ask you something?" I finally break the awkward silence.

"Anything."

"I can understand the Madison thing being a set up but I can't understand the Greta thing. You let her into our apartment, and then as soon as I land here this week, I'm told you're actually dating her. Why?"

Jack nods with a frown and sits up, resting his hand on my foot.

"I couldn't have you see me alone and miserable this week so when Greta asked me out for the thousandth time, I accepted. To make sure you didn't find out she was just a decoy, I told my mom and sister that she was my girlfriend. For the last month I've made it seem like we were indeed dating so it would be believable. It was a bad idea, I know, but I needed to see if you had any feelings left for me and I thought this would be a way to do that. I didn't realize that she would take the whole situation and run with it."

I nod. If it didn't sound so plausible, I probably wouldn't believe it.

"I was devastated when you moved with Lily and Josh but I respected that you needed a change. I wanted you to be happy. Even if it wasn't with me."

I bite my lip as I stare down at my hands, chipping away the nail polish to keep me from letting even a single tear escape.

"Over the last month, Greta and I have spent time together. I wouldn't say it was romantic in any way but she filled the time when I didn't want to be alone. Having her believe we were a couple helped everyone else believe it too." Jack looks at me, tears shining in his eyes. "I'd convinced myself she was all I'd ever deserve, but I could have never become serious with her. I had no romantic feelings for Greta. She wasn't you."

"I hated you." I finally say in a whisper.

"I know," he stands and starts pacing the room before turning back to me. "I hated you too."

"For what?"

"For what?!" his voice gets a little louder. "We dated for five years, Em. Did you actually think I wouldn't do anything for you? Did you actually think I would cheat a couple days before our wedding?"

"I don't know..." I shrug my shoulders. "Everything was so perfect and when I walked into the office and saw you both, I realized it was too perfect, that brought me back to reality. I mean, come on, I was given away by my birth parents and my real parents died while I was in my twenties, I was fired from a job I loved, and a once nude model was so insistent that my boyfriend was better suited for her than for me that she constantly found ways to force her way into his life. That's a lot of heartbreak for one person. A lot of bad luck. I kind of hoped after all that, life would at least give me a break with *us*. And after everything we've been through..." I swallow away the tears "I thought it was just the streak of bad luck that seemed to be my life. I never thought *you'd* be the one who hurt me the way you did. So I just... I couldn't see past that. Running away was easier than admitting to myself that maybe my life would never be easy. I thought maybe it was time to admit that possibly I was never meant to have a real family of my own."

Jack rubs his forehead before wiping away a few escaped tears, making me tear up all over again.

He walks over and kneels down in front of me, taking both of my hands in his, and looking up at me through tears he's better at controlling. "You *have* a real family Emi... I'm *so* sorry I hurt you. If I could take it back, you have to know that I would. Never in a million years would I ever want to be the person who did this to you and to know that I am, kills me inside. I'll do anything for a chance to show you how much you still mean to me. How much you've *always* meant to me."

I nod, carefully pulling a hand from his to wipe away the tears now sliding down my cheek. If I knew what to say, I'd say something.

"I'm not asking for you to forget everything and take me back. All I want is for you to know how important you are to me and how incredibly sorry I am."

"I forgive you, Jack. I don't hate you anymore. I don't know what I feel, actually," I shrug my shoulders.

I might not know exactly what I feel, but it's not what I felt yesterday, last month, or even the day I walked away. I didn't think a face-to-face heartfelt apology would stir up all the feelings I've ever had for him, but it did. It's clouding up my head and my heart, so much that I can hardly see through it enough to even consider how I feel, let alone tell him.

"I get it," he says with a half defeated frown. "I'll always listen when you're ready to talk about it, if you ever are."

I nod again, forcing a small smile as a thank you. He squeezes my hand still in his and returns my smile, as he stands. "You know what hurt the most last night?" he asks as he walks back to the windows.

"Her wearing my engagement ring?" I ask without even thinking.

Jack turns to me with a smile, "That was quite the shock. How exactly did she plan to break the news to me? Was that her announcement plan? To make a toast to the whole room, me included, that we were suddenly engaged?" a nervous laugh escapes him.

"It's Greta..." I remind him. "She's capable of anything."

"Yeah," he nods. "Thing is, my mom knew the Madison story and she kept it quiet. Why? She could have cleared all this up before the wedding and she didn't. Why not?"

"I don't know... Maybe she didn't really put it all together until last night?" I love Amelia like my own mother but I know how secretive and vindictive she can be when she wants. Not to me, or her own children, but to someone like Greta. I wouldn't be surprised if she had put it all together and was just waiting for the right moment, pouncing when Greta would least expect it.

He starts pacing again, stopping near the wall of windows still shaded by the curtains. "Can I ask *you* something now?" he asks without turning to face me.

"Sure."

"You and the bartender, is it romantic?"

"Romantic?" I ask, knowing full well it's not. "No," I shake my head, almost ashamed that I even tried to trick him. If I didn't already know that he did the exact same thing, this might be harder to explain.

"Why'd you bring him?"

I throw my hands out, "The same reason why you told Hannah that Greta was your girlfriend... Because I'm single in couple land and even my ex had supposedly gotten over me. *With* my arch-enemy, I might add. I mean, come on, how pathetic was I, still clinging on to someone who tore out my heart, so badly that I relocated thousands of miles from him so I could try and get on with my life. Then, when I finally see him again, I see parts of the guy I knew but parts of a guy I didn't. A guy who'd clearly moved on without me."

Jacks face drops from irritation to shame and he makes his way back to the side of the bed.

"That's the furthest thing from the truth," he hesitantly lays his hand on mine.

"Then what is the truth, Jack?"

"I've never moved on from you. I think about you every day, but I didn't want to crowd you. I don't own you, and if you don't want to be with me, I wasn't going to force that. I wanted you to have space and discover who you were and how you felt without me constantly reminding you of the past. I didn't want to chance hurting you again." His chin quivers slightly before he pulls himself together. "When I saw that guy kiss you the other night," He shakes his head, obviously a bit distraught by the memory. "I knew exactly what you must have felt when you found me with Madison that day. No matter *what* it was, I'm sorry you had to see that."

"I don't know if we can go back to the way things were. I don't know if I can ever get that moment out of my head. There is too much..." I motion between us and he nods. "I've made a life for myself in Dallas. I'm happy."

Am I, though? I've been suppressing my real feelings for a year, eating them away, hiding them from my best friends and family. I've been so nervous about even just the possibility of this exact conversation that I've stressed myself out for weeks in preparation. All the secrets that have come out and his apology has me rethinking everything.

Jack nods, forcing a smile as he stands from the bed. "That's all I ever wanted for you."

He makes his way to the bedroom door slowly before stopping and turning back to me. The light now trying to shine through the curtains reflects on his face, reminding me how good looking he is even when he hasn't slept all night.

"I know I've got no place in your life right now. And I get why you needed to leave. Please just remember that if there is *any* chance for me to fix what's been done, I will."

A tear slides down my cheek, again. I literally have no words but I can feel the emotion quickly surfacing again and I'd rather he didn't witness it because I don't know what I feel at this point. I don't know if I'm crying because I lost him, I miss him, or just the overwhelming knowledge of finding out all the truths at once.

"I mean it, Ems, I'll do anything. I know you're not ready right now, and maybe you never will be, but if you are, one day, I'll do my best to make sure you know how perfect it could be, again. Just please don't push me away anymore."

"He, Ems... wanna go get—" Lily walks into my room, still in her pajamas, stopping midway through the door just a few inches from Jack. "Oh... I didn't mean to interrupt." She flashes a hopeful smile my way, "I'll just come back later."

We both watch her back out of the room, closing the door behind her.

"I don't know what to say." I shrug my shoulders. I can't tell him the feelings racing through me right now because there are so many that I can't sort them through.

He nods, forcing a small smile. "I'll always be around for you," he reaches down pulling my hand to his lips as I nod.

When he turns to walk away I catch a hesitant and sad forced smile that screams how much pain he's in. A real one that stabs me right in the chest.

"Jack?" I stand from the bed, taking a step towards him.

He turns, his hand still on the doorknob.

"For what it's worth, I'm sorry I've shut you out. I'm sorry I'm so stubborn. I'm sorry I didn't believe you. I'm sorry I've pushed you away for an entire year. And I'm sorry I'm always so suspicious of things, you know, like the time I broke into your apartment..." I roll my eyes at myself. That was so pathetically immature of me.

He laughs under his breath.

"I don't mean to be like that, I just..." I walk towards him. "I've lost *so* much in my life and I never wanted to lose you, to lose *us*."

The growing smile on his face finally reaches all the way to his eyes as he walks in my direction. He slides an arm around my waist, pulling me against him without hesitation, pressing his lips to mine in a kiss that starts out almost innocent before it turns desperate. Let's just say, I don't fight it. Is there a better way to work out feelings than physically? Apparently in my case the answer is no.

*

"You *slept* with him?" Lily spurts out coffee across the table, her voice high and weird, gaining the attention of the entire Starbucks.

"In my defense, it wasn't my fault."

"How is that a defense?"

"I don't know." I sip my coffee, hoping she'll end the interview about my drama.

"So, what does it mean? Are you getting back together?"

"I don't think so... I don't know what I feel yet. I need to think about things."

"And...?"

"It's only been two hours!"

"You. Slept. With. Him." Lily jabs it out like strokes on a typewriter. "I think you gave him your answer."

"No... That was just..." What was it? "Old feelings working themselves out, like unfinished business."

"Unfinished screwing?" She laughs, rolling her eyes. "You're crazy. You know you just made this whole thing worse?"

"How? We're both adults. He's as guilty as I am. It's not like when we were finished I allowed him to slip the engagement ring back on my finger. We have an unspoken understanding. I just need some time to work out my feelings."

"Do you *want* to get back with Jack?"

"I don't know. Maybe…?"

It feels good to say it out loud. Now that I know the truth about everything that happened that day, it's easier for me to imagine myself with Jack again. It's a lot easier not to hate him too. But at the same time, I now live in Dallas. And I like it there. I've built my own life, my own success. Which is something I didn't have much of here.

"You're seriously considering this?" she asks.

"Who wouldn't? Jack and I have history, we were nearly married. I owe it to myself to at least consider how I feel."

"What about Liam?"

"Liam was a distraction and kind of a decoy. Plus, we only just met and like I've told you a thousand times before, it was just a favor, that's all. I don't even know what's going to happen with Jack and me. I might not know for a while."

Lily grins. "I know someone who would know, Aunt Maggie."

"No, we're not going to visit Maggie and her crystal ball. You promised me the last time was senior prom, when she predicted that I would be voted prom queen, and that didn't exactly work out like I thought it would. It's so weird."

"Worked out for me... she was only one person off." Lily winks, obviously thinking back to her short prom queen reign. "So it's a little weird, everyone needs a little weird in their life now and then. And you know she's always right. Remember at the engagement party, when she predicted that you and Jack would overcome a trial? Maybe this is it. Come on..." Lily begs. "We used to love visiting Maggie for insights into our futures when we were young! One more reading won't kill us and I'm sure she'd be thrilled to see you. Maybe it will even help with your decision."

I tap my nails on the table while I bite my lip nervously. When you're twelve, a supposed psychic in the family is a fun party game. When you're thirty, it loses its sparkle.

"Fine, but you have to promise you won't let this get out of hand."

"Cross my heart and hope to die," Lily says as she does the actual movement with a giggle.

The drive across town takes a lot less time than I remember it taking, and when we pull up at Aunt Maggie's old run down Sears kit craftsman home, she's in the front yard clipping flowers.

"Oh! She squeals as we get to the gate. "Emi! You came to visit, you darling girl you, and you brought Lily! Wasn't the wedding just beautiful?"

"It was," I nod.

She motions us through the gate and up the porch stairs. "Wow! I haven't seen you girls together on my porch in years."

"Aunt Maggie," Lily says as she wraps an arm around Maggie's shoulders, "we need some advice."

"We?" I ask her, unaware that this would be a double reading.

"Of course, we," Maggie says, patting Lily's hand. "I have lots of advice as you girls well know. Come on in and I'll get us some coffee, cookies, and advice."

We follow Maggie into her cluttered living room that hasn't changed since I was ten years old. An entire wall is full of books of every age and color of binding. Old toys from her childhood line the shelves in front of the books. Photos both in color and monochrome adorn the walls from floor to ceiling.

One of my favorite things about coming here was hearing the stories behind the photos. Not knowing my own birth family always had me so interested to know about everyone else's. Such adventure silently sits in a photograph. One shelf, in particular, holds photos of her with her childhood friend, Relia, and my mother. She always told me that Relia stood out in the photo because her name meant gold, so she shimmered in the light as if she was made from it. The crystal ball she treasures is in the center of the shelf, glimmering in the sunlight just like it's made of gold.

"I have your favorites, *srdieckas* made with raspberry jam. You still love those, right?"

I glance down at the heart shaped cookies with their gooey centers, and for a moment I'm a child again. I always felt like a trip to Maggie's was a trip to another world. It was like walking into a storybook and I never left disappointed.

"I do." I reach down for one, hoping they are as good as I remember.

"Aunt Maggie, Emi is wondering what you see for her and Jack in the future?"

"Listen, sweet girl. First, you have a question for yourself."

I turn towards the couch they're sitting on, suddenly interested in the reading not even meant for me.

"So, it is a double reading..." I laugh. "And what exactly are you wanting to be enlightened on?"

Lily grins nervously before finally letting out a sigh surrounded by a giggle.

"OK, so, you know how I always have insisted I do not want children?"

"Yup."

"Josh and I may have changed our minds. We've been trying but nothing has been happening so we have an appointment next week with a fertility doctor."

My mouth drops open. "And when were you planning on telling me? In the delivery room?"

She shrugs her shoulders, "I don't know, we hadn't really nailed down all the details yet."

"You won't need the specialty doctor..." Maggie pats Lily's thigh. "Sometimes things happen when we least expect them and I see that for you and Josh. You're about to enter a new phase of life and it's going to be just beautiful."

Lily tears up as she hugs Maggie. If there was ever a way to make my own question seem less than important this is it. Here's my best friend, the one girl who once applauded a restaurant implementing a no children policy and her heart is set on having her own baby.

"Congratulations, early, I guess," I say, when Lily finally stops crying.

"Thanks," she smiles.

"Now for you," Maggie stands, walking me across the room to the windows facing the backyard. "Jack is an amazing man. You know this. But, you've built a life you love and it would be wrong to give it all up for a man. He's about to get some news, maybe truthful, maybe not, that could complicate things further but I want you to stand strong in exploring your feelings and what you want. If it's meant to be, it will be." She walks back across the room and takes a cup of coffee from the tray she carried in earlier, taking a sip.

"What does that even mean?"

"You will know when the time is right. Patience is a virtue, Emi, and sometimes surprises aren't bad things."

I look over at Lily with a half glare. "You know in high school when we'd get these vague messages it was exciting to find the clues leading up to the so called events. But now... it's really just kind of pissing me off." I take three more cookies off the tray.

"Don't stress over this, Emi. You need to do nothing to find the ways of your heart. It will come to you this time." Maggie smiles before wrapping her arms around me in a huge hug. "Your mother is so proud of you. She just can't wait."

"Wait for what?"

"Your future."

"Which is?"

"For your heart to decide." Maggie winks, knowing I hate this game. There is a reason I don't spend a lot of time with Aunt Maggie. I adore her, but I don't adore the cryptic messages she finds such fun to give out.

"You remember," Maggie says as we walk to the car. "You call me with anything, understood?"

"Understood," I nod.

*

"Who is here?" I ask, noticing a few extra cars in the driveway as we pull into Evan's.

"I don't know, maybe they're having a honeymoon going away party." Lily laughs. "I wouldn't put it past Hannah. You know how she loves the spotlight all the time."

"Isn't that the truth?" I sigh.

We walk in the front door to Evan, Josh, and Hannah all sitting on the stairs together, heads cocked, and quietly listening to the commotion coming from a floor above them.

"What's going on?" As soon as the words leave my mouth, I hear screeching from a room upstairs.

"Greta..." they say in unison.

"She's *here*?"

"For the last hour. She brought Amelia and her father."

"Why? Are they going to tie Jack down and make him date her?" I laugh, but honestly can kind of picture it.

"Um..." Hannah's nervous smile through clenched teeth tells me that whatever it is, it's bad. "I'm not sure yet." She cranes her neck, trying to hear the voices upstairs better.

"You guys are sitting here to eavesdrop?" Lily asks.

"Obviously," Hannah rolls her eyes.

"Well... spill it."

"I... uh..." Hannah shrugs her shoulders. "I'm not quite sure yet. I've heard 'Greta isn't the person she once was, she truly loves Jack and that Jack owes it to her as a man', and—"

"That's all so far." Evan butts in, squeezing Hannah's hand.

I can tell that's not all.

"Josh... You should help me in the kitchen," Lily says, winking at me, before wandering off towards the kitchen. Clearly, she wants to let him in on Maggie's big revelation.

"You guys are all weird." I start up the stairs to drop my bag in my bedroom, but only get a few steps from the top, when the door down the landing swings open violently, hitting the wall behind it and causing something inside to crash to the floor.

"If that's the kind of father you want to be, then we'll see you in court!" Greta's father storms out, glaring at me as he walks past. Greta follows him out, a blank stare on her face. I'm not sure she's even seen me; even though she's walked right past me, her head is clearly somewhere else.

"For God's sake, Jack, this is a disaster. I can't believe you didn't tell me yesterday."

"I didn't know yesterday, Mom; how could I have told you when I didn't even know myself? Besides, this changes everything."

I stand still, listening to them talk. They obviously don't know they're being overheard by the whole house.

"Well, you know now. Today changes everything, Daddy." As Amelia walks out, she looks in my direction and forces a less than thrilled smile. "Emi," she acknowledges me by name and continues past me towards the stairs, causing Hannah and Evan to jump up and pretend they've not been straining to hear from midway down them.

"Daddy? No, he said it wasn't serious with Greta..." I say under my breath; my stomach is swirling and my heart is racing. I know I haven't really stopped to even think about how I feel about Jack yet but I'm not ready for the decision to be made for me again by a girl who is pure evil.

I inch towards the door, making it just in time for Jack to spot me before nearly closing it on me.

"Emi. Did you uh – H-how long have you been here?" he stutters.

"Why did your mom just call you Daddy?" I ask, my voice shaking, already knowing exactly what it means but desperately hoping I've heard it wrong.

"Shit." Jack drops his gaze to the ground before looking back at me with pain in his eyes. "She's pregnant."

"What?" My heart sinks to my stomach so hard it almost makes me physically sick. "She's pregnant with —"

"Apparently it happened on a night where I wasn't having my finest moment. I was trying to decide whether to go see you and get everything out there before the wedding. It was a bad night and I had a few drinks, which you know I never do so it kind of laid me out. When she showed up I knew her being there was a bad idea, but I wasn't exactly in a state of mind to stop whatever happened either. I don't remember sleeping with her, but she swears we did and as drunk as I was she could be right. I'm sorry." He shakes his head and runs a hand through his hair.

The heaviness in my chest can't just be the disappointment of hearing this, it's more. It's even more crushing than the day I walked away from him. I know what my feelings are for Jack, I just don't want to admit them, and this feeling is exactly why.

"And she just told you today?" I fight back the tears. This can't be happening. Why does it seem like he and I are the only ones being hurt in all this?

"Apparently today was the perfect day to announce it and fuck me over once again."

"I..." I stand stunned. Any decision I wanted or needed to make has been changed in this instance.

"I'm sorry, Em. I gotta go."

"Go where?" I ask, following him down the landing.

He turns to me, pulling me against him, wrapping his arms around me in a way that tells me he doesn't really want to leave. "I'm so proud of you, babe and I'm *so* sorry, for everything" He kisses my forehead and holds me for a minute before making his way down the stairs.

I follow behind him, nearly in a run, passing my friends and family in a blur. "Jack! Please don't run away. Please..."

"I just need some time," he says to me before disappearing out of the door, leaving me staring into the room wondering how everything could go so wrong so suddenly.

Sixteen

The Getaway

Five years, six months ago.

Portland, Oregon/Malibu, California

"He asked you to go away with him? *Already?*" Lily almost drops her fork into her lasagne when I say it. Like it's such a shock that a man could ask me to go away with him. Even though it *has* never actually happened.

"Yeah. I guess his parents own a house in Malibu, California."

"Out of state?"

"Yes, Malibu... Like where Barbie lives." I wink at her.

"What did you say?"

"I said yes, duh."

I've actually been waiting for this day for the last few months. We've had such fun dating but I think an overnight trip will really show me if Jack is who I think he is.

"I hope you're planning on having sex with him, because guys don't take women to fancy Malibu beach houses for long weekends and not expect to get laid. Not to mention that you've been dating for a few months now and you still haven't given it up." She scrunches her face as if talking about it is the ickiest thing ever.

"I wanted to be sure!" I glance around the restaurant to see who now knows just what a prude I am since she's talking about my celibacy so loudly. No one appears to be listening in, but who knows?

"Sure of what?"

"That he wasn't just one of those guys who would screw me and then move on to the next." I shrug my shoulders. So, call me old-fashioned. "Apparently, he's not."

"I've told you the whole time, Ems, he's a good guy. You should stop holding him at arm's length like you're scared of him. This is a big step in your relationship."

"I know it is. And I'm so freaking nervous! I have no idea what this is going to be like."

"Don't even pack clothes, you won't need them." She takes a bite of her lasagne before nearly choking on it when she looks up at my horrified face. "I'm kidding! If I know Jack, and I think that I do, it'll be all romance and rainbows and he'll set the tone for your entire relationship."

"A good tone?"

"A romantic tone…. Maybe we should go shopping?"

"For what?" I pick at my salad, almost too nervous to eat.

"Uh, hello, have you not been listening? For lingerie ya weirdo. You do want to make him want you on your first time, right?"

"Yeah."

"Then you need good lingerie. Have any?"

I think about my underwear drawer for a minute. Which I'm pretty sure putting nice lingerie in a plain old underwear drawer pretty much proves that I've got none. "I have a pair of bra and panties that match?"

"You are so sad."

"I know, seriously, you have to help me."

"Don't worry, Lily to the rescue." She grabs her phone and starts tapping away, planning goodness knows what, in order to get me ready to consummate my relationship.

*

When we walk into the shop I'm almost a little scared. This is no *Victoria's Secret*. Lily's friend Merri used this shop when she was shopping for her wedding night. They make private appointments and do fittings to suit your body type.

"I don't know about this..." The room is filled with racks of swanky lingerie, expensive underwear, and floor to ceiling mirrors. "I feel like I'm in a secret sex shop."

I glance through some of the racks, peeking at the prices and knowing full well that I shouldn't be here. I'm a college student, there is no way I can afford over forty dollars for a single bra.

"Ladies!" A middle aged woman in a dress far too tight and short comes walking in from the back part of the shop, carrying an armload of what looks like hot pink lace string bikinis.

"Are you Esther?" Lily asks.

"I am!" Esther has a sing-song type voice. "You must be Lily! I'm thrilled to meet you!" When she speaks, every single sentence ends with either a question mark or an exclamation point. Lingerie obviously excites her.

"And you must be Emi!" She grins over at me. "Lily told me a bit about you and based on what she said I pulled out a few items for you to try on. They're waiting in here..." She leads me to a giant dressing room with three way mirrors and a plush couch. People actually watch others try on lingerie? Is that why the couch is in the dressing room? "Try them on and come out for our opinions."

"You want me to model?"

"Well..." She glances over at Lily. "You don't *have* to come out, but we're here to help you make the best decision for this special occasion. You're in a safe place and there is no one here but us."

"No cameras?" I ask.

Esther bursts out a laugh, then quickly stifles it away. "No! No. No cameras; that would make the news, dear. Now go, try and model."

I make my way into the dressing room, glad there is a locking door as opposed to a curtain. I glance through a few things hanging on the rack. Obviously, Lily didn't tell her I'm a business major, not an X-rated dance major. Everything she's chosen is skimpy, lacy, some crotchless, and wild colors that would definitely make me feel like the center of attention when all I normally want to do is blend in.

I pull one set out of the line up, the only one I'm even halfway willing to try on and that's only because it's got the most material. Of course, it's see through, but it counts, I think.

"Yeah... I don't think these will work," I say, struggling to pull the panties of the lavender baby doll set past my hips.

"Why?" Lily calls back.

"Because I don't wear a size stripper and I'm not trying out for an X-rated movie." I grab the robe and the... I dunno... outfits and open the door. "Can't *I* pick something? I feel like these all say I'm trying too hard. Jack is gonna know something is up."

"Something *is* up, you're losing your Jackinity." Lily and Esther both laugh at Lily's dumb joke.

"Stop. I'm serious, don't you have anything like... just normal, but sexy?" I glance over at Esther who is sitting at a desk with a hot pink fluorescent light around the top.

"Normal?" She hops off her stool and heads to a far section of the store and is out of sight for a moment, returning with a few hangers in her hands. "Like these?"

When she holds them out I know I've found my normal. Light gray lace, girly bra and matching panties, without any frills. "YES!"

"Ems... Those are *so*, boring!"

"I like boring." I pull my actual double digit size from her hand and head back into the dressing room. "Jack likes boring, too!" I yell through the door.

I glance into the mirror and breathe a sigh of relief. Finally, I look like a normal, twenty something woman who is having sex and not trying to look like she's the lead in *Emi Does Malibu*.

"Let's see it," Lily yells back at me.

I hesitantly open the dressing room door and step out of the room, checking first for eyes of people that weren't here earlier or the flashing red lights of hidden cameras that Esther insists don't exist.

"Well?" I ask, but both Lily and Esther have on their poker faces. "Not good?"

"It looks lovely, dear, but for your first time don't you want to *wow* him?" She holds up a bright red negligee and swings it back and forth as if trying to entice me with it.

"No. If he's not wowed by me being me, then he's not the guy I want."

"Oh..." Esther lays the red nightie on her desk. "You're a sweet girl. I have this set in a couple of other colors if you'd like more than one?"

"Load me up." I look over at Lily whose face is not so approving.

"This is it?"

"Yup... I'm not as flashy as you. Or as easy." I smile before disappearing into the dressing room before she can throw something at me.

"I'm not easy, I just want to test drive my men to see if I should go on a cross country trip with them."

"Whatever," I laugh at her ridiculous comparison. I like to play it safe. That's just me, though. From me, there will be no sleeping with a guy on the first date to see if I'd like there to be a second. That's Lily's game and she is good at it.

I'll admit, though, Josh is the first one for a while to pass the cross country test for Lily. Her last few boyfriends barely made it to the two week mark, but there is something different about Josh. I don't know him very well yet, but I feel like he's the exact guy she's looking for. She's so happy when he's around, relaxed even. He could very well be her lobster. Maybe she's onto something with the whole testing out a guy to see if they pass the test physically, because I'm hoping that Jack's my lobster too. I guess I'll know soon enough.

*

Today is the day I go to Malibu with Jack. I've never been on an overnight trip with a boyfriend before and now I'm exiting a plane in southern California.

"You'll get to meet my sister, Hannah. She's really excited to meet the girl who's stolen my heart." Jack squeezes my hand in his.

"Aw... I stole your heart?" Mine races in my chest as we walk through the airport. I get more and more nervous with each step. "Wait, your sister will be there?"

"Yeah," he nods with a smile. "My whole family, they're excited to meet you."

"Jack! Oh, my God, you didn't tell me I was meeting your family. I'm not ready."

I stop walking and try to stop myself from hyperventilating. Why would he surprise me with this? He knows I hate surprises and meeting a guy's parents for the first time is a big deal as a surprise. Finding out your meeting them when you've prepared for a weekend of no clothes is an even bigger deal.

"Don't be nervous, babe. They're gonna love you." He runs his hand down my arm before once again squeezing my hand reassuringly.

"Really? 'Cause this is important."

"I know," he nods his head.

"I mean like... this is *we're-in-a-serious-relationship* kind of important."

"I know," he says again with a smile.

How is he not worried about this? We've never even talked about how serious we are or where this relationship is going. Yet he felt arranging a meeting with his parents without telling me is where we are.

"So, what you're saying is, that we've reached that point, the serious relationship point, even though we've never... you know?"

I watch him laugh as I nervously glance about at the people heading to their destinations around us.

"Yes, I'm ready to hit that serious relationship mark. I actually wanted to... uh... talk to you about something this weekend." He runs a hand through his hair, something I've noticed he does when he's nervous or frustrated.

Oh my God, he's going to propose. This is way too soon; we haven't even slept together yet! In this case, I probably should have gone for the racy lingerie. Please don't hyperventilate Ems, this is not the time or the place.

"Talk about something?" I repeat, it comes out all squeaky and weird. Definitely not the cool card I'd planned to use right there.

"It's nothing bad. I promise." He takes my hand in his. "Ready?"

No.

"Sure."

I'm anything but ready, but I'm not telling him. He cannot know how freaked out I am about meeting his family.

*

The house is nothing short of spectacular. Even Barbie couldn't compete. It's a modern style house sitting on a rock bluff overlooking the ocean. The deck surrounds an infinity pool and there's a path from the back patio all the way to the beach. This I did not expect. I mean, I kind of figured the house would be nice considering it's in Malibu but mansion on the beach never even entered my mind. Why does it make me even more nervous to be here?

"Hello Jack, and you must be Emi?" We're greeted by an older woman with dark hair pulled up into a perfect bun at the top of her head. The chic kind, not the librarian kind. Her face is pulled unnaturally tight and made up like she just walked off Broadway. "Isn't she just darling?" she asks Jack as if I'm not standing right in front of her. "I'm Jack's mother, Amelia, and this…" She motions towards the next room at a man who's sitting so still on the couch that I didn't even notice him. "This is Robert," she says, somewhat unimpressed. "Jack's father."

Robert glances in my direction with nothing more than a nod before going back to the paper sitting on the table in front of him.

"It's nice to meet you both," I say, not knowing whether I should shake their hands, bow, curtsy, or run.

"How nice that you could join us. I'm sure Jack has spoken to you about the sleeping arrangements?"

"Sleeping arrangements?" I ask, looking at Jack nervously.

"Mom, we just walked in."

"You will be sharing a room with Hannah, Jack's sister. She's out by the pool."

I glance through the room that looks out onto a pool, the figure of a perfect body is lounging at the far end.

Why in the hell did I go to the trouble of buying lingerie in preparation for our big night if I won't even be sharing a room with Jack?

"You may bring your bag up. Jack will show you the way."

Jack rolls his eyes at his mother's demands but grabs my bag as she suggested and heads off up the stairs. I follow him into a room so pink that I feel like I've just walked into a bottle of Pepto Bismol.

"How old is Hannah?"

"Too old for pink," he laughs. "She doesn't come out here often so the room hasn't been updated since she was about fourteen."

He sets my bag on the floor near the door. "Listen, I normally sleep out in the pool house so…" He glances towards the door to the balcony off the bedroom. "I don't expect you to stay in here. My parents never go out there, and they're very rarely home anyway so they'll never even know you're out there with me."

"What about your sister?" I whisper.

"She's cool. She'll cover."

"What if she doesn't like me?" I ask, worried his whole family will think I'm a complete whore if they find out I'm sneaking into Jack's room at night.

"She doesn't like anyone. But I'll make sure she does. If you'd be more comfortable I can get a hotel room, it's no problem."

"I don't want to cause trouble..."

"You're not any trouble at all, Em." He pulls me by the hand to the edge of one of the twin beds. "I wasn't going to say this right now, but I know this isn't going exactly how you expected, so now is as good a time as any."

I shake my head, "Jack, I can't have sex with you on your sister's single bed. It's wrong." I scrunch my face up in disgust.

"God," he jumps off the bed. "No. I'm glad you feel that way," he laughs. "That wasn't what I was going to say. I actually asked you to come here so you could meet my family because I wanted to take things to the next step in our relationship."

Oh, my God. This is it. He's going to propose in a hot pink fourteen year old girl's bedroom. Not exactly how I pictured it, but oh well.

"OK," I say, through the butterflies suddenly swirling in my chest.

"We've been together now for three months and it's been the best three months ever."

"Really?"

"Of course." He stops and takes a deep breath. "I am falling in love with you, Emi, and from here on I don't want to see anyone but you. I think you could be the one."

Has he been seeing other people until now?

No, Emi, stop. That's not what he's saying. He just said he loves you.

Why did I think he was proposing?

"Did you hear me?" he asks nervously.

"Yes, yes. Me too." My heart flutters in my chest. I wish I had more of a way with words and could maybe impress him just a tad more, though.

"You too?"

"I mean... I think you're the one too. I fell in love with you before I even officially met you."

"You did?"

"Yeah. I'm sorry, I know this is *so* romantic but I'm really nervous about being here with your family and I don't want to ruin it."

"You're not going to ruin it." He leads me back out into the hallway, away from the blinding pink bedroom. "Come on, you can meet Hannah and then we'll go relax. I have a surprise for you later."

Ugh... another surprise. I hope it's not a wife and kids.

I follow him out to the pool and see the tall blonde wearing a tiny pink bikini lying next to the pool exactly where she was a few moments ago. She's perfect: her hair, her skin, her designer swimsuit that will put my

Target one to shame. She's completely the opposite of me.

"Hannah... I want you to meet someone."

We both watch her turn her head in our direction, propping herself up on her elbows, looking me over through her mirrored lenses.

"*You* must be the infamous Emi?" She lifts her sunglasses and lies her magazine on the chair next to her. The way she says it I can already tell she's not impressed. I've been here less than thirty minutes and so far, this is the worst trip of my life, even though the man of my dreams just basically told me he's falling for me.

"I am. It's nice to meet you too, Hannah."

"I'm sure it is." She pats the chair next to her and flashes a million dollar smile at me. "Come sit, I can't wait to get to know you."

I look at Jack, who honestly looks as nervous as I am about me having a private chat with Hannah. She has a quality about her that screams *I'm going to chew you up and spit you out.* I'm a little scared, but I follow her command and sit on the lounger.

"So..." She starts talking but stops and looks over at Jack who is still standing off to the side of the patio watching us. She lifts her glasses with a sigh. "We're fine, Jack. Go do whatever it is that you do." She rolls her eyes, slides her glasses back on and turns to me.

I chew on my lip nervously. She's intimidating, and I wasn't expecting it. I feel like I'm on trial to see if I could hold my own in the family, which is seeming quite unlikely.

Jack and I haven't talked much about Hannah, other than that he has a younger sister whose dream is to be a southern California socialite. I'd say she's a definite contender, she's gorgeous. She doesn't have a single blemish on her skin. Her makeup is flawless, even in the sun. Her long blonde hair is perfect, even in the wind. She seems practically supernatural.

"So..." She pauses dramatically. "Tell me what you love the most about my brother?"

I didn't realize there was going to be an entrance interview and I'm not exactly prepared. "He's uh..." I pause, not the way she did, but to pick out just one thing that I love about him that I think might impress her. Even though it's only been three months, I'm more in love than I ever thought possible.

"Rich?" She interrupts my train of thought.

"What?"

"He's rich," she repeats herself.

The Jack I know doesn't live like this house suggests. Until thirty minutes ago I didn't even know this side of him existed. I just thought he was a normal guy, a law student who wasn't considered poor, or something like that. Rich isn't a word I'd ever used before now to describe Jack. He's so... modest.

"OK..."

"So, you're with him for the money?"

"No. No, I didn't even know he had money until I got here. This isn't *his* money, though, it's your parents."

"They gotta die someday," she laughs. "So, that's a technicality. OK, I'll bite, if not the money, then what?" She removes her glasses altogether and sits up in her chair. "What's so special about Jack?" The way she says his name makes me cringe a little. I know brothers and sisters are often pretty mean to one another, but I could never say Evan's name implying that I was better than him.

"He's amazing, he's a gentleman, he's kind, he's humble, he's caring, he's…"

"Ugh… I get it. You think you're in love with him. They all do." She rolls her eyes at me before lying down again, adjusting her suit so not to disturb her growing tan lines.

If eye-rolling was a sport I have a feeling Hannah would be the champion. "You're just one of the many women he's brought out here to meet us. You've reached the meet the family level. He always thinks he's found the one and then a few weeks later they're gone."

"Gone?" He has relationship levels? Like a video game?

"Not dead, but you know, dumped."

"Oh." I bite my lip so hard I can taste the blood. "That sucks."

"Not really."

"So, you don't like *any* of Jack's girlfriends?"

"I wouldn't say *any*... but few. Jack is... Well, he's too easy to fall in love."

"He falls in love a lot?"

Crap. Not good for me at all.

"Well, I don't know if *love* is the right word, but he's been with some girls if you know what I mean." She sighs, lifting her bikini bottom to check her tan line. "I guess if you make it out here more than once we'll know that he's more serious about you than the others."

I don't really have anything to say to that. How can a conversation like this one follow the one I just had with Jack?

"Quit the crap, Hannah. You're not scaring this one off." Jack suddenly reappears on the patio, obviously having been listening from somewhere he couldn't be seen. "Either you're nice to this one, or you'll never meet another. Stop acting like you're Queen Bee of Nothing."

"JACK!" She screams at him, like a dramatic younger sister with a hot pink bedroom would, and throws her sunglasses across the patio before disappearing into the house.

"Ignore her. She tries to act important a lot."

"Do you really bring a lot of girls here?"

"No. I think you're the second. Like I said... She's a bit much, especially for the truth. The less you listen to her the better off you'll be." He reassures me with a kiss on the lips before lying down in the chair Hannah had been using. "She's a bully, Ems. I meant what I said earlier. I love you."

"You love me?" I can't help the smile that's now taken over my face. He didn't exactly say that earlier, he said he was falling in love with me. This is a whole new level.

"I do."

"I love you too. I even bought something for you especially for this trip, before I knew your family would be joining us."

"You did?"

"Yeah, but it's not exactly, uh, family friendly, if you know what I mean." His eyes get as big as saucers and his smile is contagious. "Hopefully, I'll be able to show it to you later."

He lets out a small nervous cough, "Luckily, I made reservations at a very romantic restaurant in town so we can sneak into my room later and see what all the fuss is about," he winks.

Seventeen

Leaving on A Jet Plane

Present Day

Portland, Oregon

I decided last night that this was all too much for me to process, so as soon as Evan and Hannah leave for their honeymoon, I'm catching the next flight out to Dallas. I know it seems selfish but this week has been a rollercoaster ride of emotions which I still feel it isn't over.

There is only one thing I need to do first and that's thank Liam for being there during a very weird moment in my life.

"Someone has to find him," Hannah pleads with Evan as he carries their bags out to their car. The two of them were supposed to be at the airport an hour ago, but it's been a rather sleepless night. After Jack stormed out last night no one has heard from him and Hannah is more than worried. If I didn't know any better I'd think he was four years old and hiking down the train tracks with a hankie on a stick over his shoulder, full of peanut butter and jelly sandwiches.

"Hannah, Jack is a grown man. When he's ready to talk, he'll talk. Until then he can take care of himself." Evan is getting irritated, rightfully so.

"I know, but how horrible to relive the whole him and Emi thing and then end up trapped in a pregnancy by that terrible Greta! It's like a bad Disney movie where the villain actually wins. That's not fair, Evan!"

I roll my eyes, overhearing them from my room upstairs. I opened the window so I could overhear them but now it's just kind of pissing me off.

"Maybe Emi could look for him?" she suggests.

"Jack is not Emi's problem. Can you just stop worrying about your brother and focus on the fact that we're going on our honeymoon? White sandy beaches, warm breezes, and food to die for, and just the two of us for a whole week."

"Right," she sniffles up her worries. "It's going to be so romantic," she cries, making it sound anything but romantic.

"Where exactly are *you* going?" Lily asks as she walks into my halfway packed room.

"Home."

"Our flight doesn't leave until tomorrow."

"I sweet talked an agent into getting me on one this afternoon." It was no easy task either. I had to promise to bring him and his crew members Starbucks, and lunch.

Lily purses her lips together. "So, you're just going to avoid this whole mess and go right back to pretending that Jack doesn't exist?"

I shrug my shoulders. "I dunno. I think spending some time where I feel good about myself, until I can sort out how I feel, is never a bad thing."

She nods. "True. And if he contacts you?"

"Then I guess we'll go from there. But, I'd say Jack has much bigger things to deal with than an old girlfriend."

"You think that's all you are to him, an old girlfriend?"

"I don't know what I am, Lily. All I know is that everything that's happened over the last twenty-four hours is too much for me to handle. Do you have any idea how many times my heart has been broken over and over again since yesterday? I just want to go home."

"OK, I get that. Are you at least going to say goodbye to Liam? I mean he *did* do you a favor."

"Yes, as soon as I'm done here I'm headed straight there."

I've been thinking about what to say to Liam but I've got no idea. I feel a little bit like a loser if I'm honest. Not only did my big plan of making Jack jealous, and swoon over me and my lucky dress not work but now

I'm once again running away from a situation that scares me.

I pull my bags towards the stairs to make my way to the car out front where Evan and Hannah are preparing to leave on their tropical honeymoon. I feel like the conversations I've had up here in the last twelve hours are echoing off the walls as I walk away. Spinning in confusion in my head. And I don't know what to do with any of them.

"Congratulations, again, you guys. The whole thing was beautiful." I say to Evan as he hugs me goodbye.

"I can't believe you're not going to follow him. You two are so perfect for each other," Hannah pulls me from Evan, crying into my hair. "Don't you love him?"

I swallow down the lump in my throat when she says it. There are so many more things to consider now that I don't know if I can wade through them fast enough to grab the fleeting feelings before it's too late.

"You should find him," Hannah finally says, holding me at arm's length.

"No. If I follow him I'm just some girl who forced herself on a guy who ran from us because he now has bigger issues. He didn't do that to me. I don't know what I want, but I know it's not being the girl someone settles for. I want to be *the one*. The one you don't even think about, you just know that you can't go on without them. I don't know if I'm that girl anymore for Jack."

Hannah nods with a forced smile. "I guess I can see that."

"OK, now no more tears! Honeymoons are not supposed to start with crying." Evan opens Hannah's door, coaxing her into the car so they can finally start their vacation.

Josh, Lily, and I wave from the curb until their car is no longer visible. Right on time, a blue car pulls up to the curb with a honk.

"That'd be my Uber." I pull a bag to the door, Josh, and Lily pulling the rest of them.

"I guess we'll see you back at home later, then."

I nod, glancing back at Evan's glorious house, a little sad this week went the way it did.

"I just have one more opportunity to make a fool of myself," I laugh. "Wish me luck."

"You don't need luck, you're a pro!" Josh waves over at me with a laugh.

*

When I walk into the bar, Liam is standing behind the counter wiping out cups. A smile spreads across his face, which makes my heart sink the tiniest bit more.

"Hey there. How's my favorite unlucky bridesmaid?"

"Liam... I wanted to talk to you."

"Uh-oh. Sounds like we're breaking up," he winks as he walks around the counter, taking a seat on one of the barstools. "I think you should do it."

"What?" I ask, a little confused.

"I saw the way he looked at you at the wedding. And in my experience when a man looks at a woman that way, especially after everything you two have been through, you belong together."

I smile and look down at the counter. "It's a little more complicated than that now."

"What happened?"

I shake my head, not really wanting to relive it. "I know a year doesn't seem like a long time to be apart but in this case, it's turned into a lifetime and I'm not sure it's salvageable at this point."

I sigh, hoping to get through my speech of thanking him without pouring my feelings out onto the bar like I did the day we met.

"I just wanted to stop by and say thank you. I've been really stubborn, and I might have led you on a little. I never do that, and I wanted to apologize before I left."

"Don't worry about a thing." Liam smiles. "Actually, I should be thanking you."

"You should?"

"Yes. I asked for a favor in exchange for our deal, and without even knowing it you gave me one." He pauses with a small smile. "I've been playing it safe for far too long, and seeing what you and Jack went through this weekend, reminded me why I shouldn't do that. I want that love worth fighting for like I have a feeling you two have." He's now nodding through an almost frown. "Despite what happened after I left, I'm sure Jack loves you."

I shrug my shoulders because I'm honestly not sure.

"Do you love him?" He asks.

"I don't know, there is a lot to consider. Maybe?" I sigh.

"There is something I didn't tell you before I left the wedding the other night..." He starts.

"What?"

"I didn't realize it until the middle of the blow-up, but, I've met Jack before. He came in a few weeks ago, by himself. He sat right there," He points at a stool up the bar, "and he drank, alone."

"Really?" I ask, only surprised because I know how little Jack drinks, especially in public, alone.

"Yup. He looked like he was struggling with something, so I got him talking for a few minutes, and I felt for him. I wish I'd realized it was him sooner."

"What did he say?"

"He was nervous about seeing the only woman he'd truly loved again. The woman whose heart he broke, even though things weren't quite as they seemed. He felt like it was his fault that you were both miserable, possibly forever. He said it was no longer his place to get involved in your life even though it's all he wanted to do."

"I'll tell ya, I'll never forget the way he talked about you. He misses you, and if I'm reading him right, he truly loves you."

I nod, forcing a smile, not wanting to say that he's now linked to Greta for life because she took advantage of his vulnerability.

"Thank you, for telling me."

"My pleasure. You're a great woman, and he's a lucky man. I promise I'm only a little bit jealous of him." He laughs. "I've no doubt that whatever has come up that you two will somehow make things work out."

I hop off my barstool and wrap my arms around Liam. "Thank you."

"You have my number…"

"I do, so if you're ever in Dallas, let me know."

He nods, a smile on his face that is so sincere it makes me a little sad. Liam is a great guy, and in any other situation, I'd have jumped at the opportunity to date him. But, right now, my world is a mess and I can't pull someone else into that. I don't doubt that he will have no problem finding some lucky woman to woo. I think half the bridesmaids were dreaming of him as their date. He deserves his very own happy ending and I'm sure he'll get one worthy of a romance novel. It's just not meant to be with me.

Without his help this week, though, I'm not sure I'd be any closer to figuring out what I feel for Jack. Because of Liam, the truth came out and while it was a little, or rather very, hard to hear, he kind of saved me from anymore heartache. I don't think I could be more thankful for that if I tried.

*

I settle further into my window seat, my headphones plugged into my ears as I stare out of the window at the world below me. I have no idea where Jack is but I hope he's able to figure out what he needs so he can be happy. He deserves at least that. If for nothing else then for the sake of his child.

His child. Even just thinking it makes me miserable. It shouldn't be Greta having his baby. She doesn't deserve him. If I'm honest she doesn't deserve anyone. She's just a master of manipulation. Those types do seem to always walk away with what they want.

I pull up the last email I got from Jack, the one that only asks if we can talk this week. I stare at it, wishing it could have been that simple and then hit delete. If I can't see it, I can't dwell on it, and I definitely can't respond to it.

As the wheels skid to a stop my phone vibrates in my pocket.

"You already miss me?" I ask Lily with a laugh.

"Did Amelia call you?"

"No?" I say a little worried. "Why? Is everything OK?"

"You should probably sit down."

"I can't sit down, Lily, I'm getting off my plane. Just say it, what is going on?"

"I don't know what's going on but something big is happening and when she came over earlier to talk to you, she wasn't thrilled you weren't here. I think she's on her way to Dallas."

"On her way to Dallas?!" I yell, startling the people also pulling their bags from the overhead bins around me. "Why would Amelia come to Dallas? Shouldn't she be looking for Jack and trying to help with his problem?"

"You know Amelia, always meddling in something. This time, Jack and your lives."

"You're making me nervous."

"I'm sure it's nothing, she loves you! You know that."

"Right. I'm sure everything is fine and I highly doubt that she is headed here for whatever reason. I mean, I've been living here for a year and she hasn't shown up yet. I'm just going to go home, get in the bath and get ready for work tomorrow."

"Sounds like a plan, we'll see you then."

I drop my bags at my front door, pulling a few things from one of them and heading to my bathroom. I hang my robe on the back of the door and start the water. When I turn back towards the door I see a hand towel lying on the floor. A towel that for years I've used to dry my face after I've washed it. I reach down and pick it up, the words Lewis & Clark Law Student – Jack Cabot stitched into the seam stare up at me. I forgot I had this. It must have gotten mixed in with my robe when I washed it last.

It was a ridiculous gift of a set of towels from Jack's parents when he was accepted into law school. The kind of gift you give a newly married couple. Embroidered towels. Like a reminder that he actually did become a lawyer at an actual law school. I run my finger along the stitching as a tear slides down my face. Why can't things be as simple as they were before all this happened? We were so happy until Greta. Now, despite the fact that I know deep inside I do have feelings for Jack, feelings that I'm not sure ever went away after all, I don't know if it'll ever be the same if we tried it again.

<u>Eighteen</u>

The One

Five years, seven months ago.

PSU, Portland, Oregon

The first week of my senior year of college and my mind has wandered through every single class. What can I say, I'm in love. It's actually my first time truly being in love and I must say it's a little overwhelming.

Tonight though, despite my plans to lie around and dream about Jack, I have to study for an exam being held on Friday. If I don't, I'll fall behind, and I won't graduate from University at the end of the year and if there was ever a reason for my parents to kill me, that would be it.

Who can study when they're starving though? I glance over at my room mate, Hilda, wrapped up like a mummy with some weird puddy crap smeared on her face, asleep at midnight. It's gonna be a long boring year.

Maybe Lily will bring me something? I can't possibly sneak out because if I wake Hilda, she'll probably report me to my guidance counselor for disturbing her studies and I'll end up with an even weirder roommate.

I tap Lily's number into my phone, thankful that I turned off the screen sounds earlier in the week.

"Lily," I whisper into the phone, huddled in the corner of my dorm room. "What are you doing?"

"Uh, sleeping. What the hell are you doing?"

"I'm so hungry!"

"You're always hungry. Go get something to eat."

"Can't. Or Sleeping Beauty will wake up and have my head or turn me in for harassing her again or being too loud during 'quiet time'."

"You do end up with the weirdos, don't you?"

"Yup," I stifle a laugh. Says the weirdest girl of them all. "Will you bring me something?"

"No! I'm in bed..."

"Alone?"

"That's not important," she laughs. "Why don't you just call Jack?"

"Because we've only been dating a couple of months and it might look weird."

"Giving you a black eye on your first date is a little weird too, but it didn't seem to turn you off."

"Fine! I'll text him." I jab 'end call' irritated that whatever boytoy she's got with her is more important than me and pull up Jack's contact.

I know we're dating and things are slowly moving towards a *little* more serious but I've never called him in the middle of the night to ask him to come clear across town and bring me a cheeseburger. It seems a little selfish and I'm pretty sure it's as far from romantic as one could ask.

Here goes nothing.

> Hey! I know it's late, and I'm sorry but I just wondered if you were up for some dinner? A late dinner, but I haven't really eaten yet and only just realized how starving I am... anyway, let me know...

I sit in the corner, re-reading my ridiculous text wondering if he'll even respond. How old am I, ten? Of course, he won't reply, he's asleep. And he's clear across the city at his own college. Ugh, if only there was a way to take back a text after it's been sent. The beep of an incoming one causes me to jump nearly out of my skin.

> You think I'd say no to sneaking you out in the middle of the night so you don't starve to death? Meet me in thirty minutes at the Ira Keller Fountain downtown. Take a cab! I don't really want you murdered!

The giggle wells up inside me, and it's nearly impossible to stifle away as I quickly pull on a pair of pants, shoes, t-shirt, and jacket. Cheeseburgers in the middle of the night might not be romantic but a midnight city walk with the person who I think about the most is.

The Ira Keller Fountain is a water feature dedicated to a man by the same name who pushed ahead with controversial and sometimes successful, but often unpopular, urban renewal plans. After he died it became apparent that, despite some of the Portland population not loving what he brought to the city, he was instrumental in revitalizing the business districts. So, both the Ira Keller fountain and the Keller Auditorium were named in his honor.

The fountain is beautiful during the day, but at night, it's illuminated from underneath and is really quite romantic.

I step out of my cab about thirty minutes later and make my way up the sidewalk towards the fountain. In the water below the fountain are large overlapping dry square concrete slabs that the water pools just under. Jack stands on one, a white hand towel, embroidered with his name slung over one arm like he's a waiter, a blanket sits on a dry concrete slab in the fountain pool, with bags of food, a single rose and lit tealight candles around it.

"You ordered dinner?" he asks with a laugh.

"You're crazy…"

"I am a little bit." He laughs. "Ready to hear what's on the menu?"

"Sure," I take a step over the still water and onto the slab where he's standing.

"I have a delicious all cheese pizza, because the pizza place didn't listen I had to eat all the olives and pepperoni off it on my way here. When I discovered from a not so impressed passer-by that that might gross you out, I also grabbed a bag of the best burgers in town for a hangover, just in case, so I'm told. And... a box of chocolate chip cookies that are still warm. I also grabbed two bottles of wine, whatever was closest to the door, so it's probably not that great but... anything stand out to you?"

I take a step towards him, stand on my tippy toes and kiss his lips. "You are perfect. Thank you."

"You're welcome," he kisses me back. "Shall we... before we get caught and arrested?"

"Let's do it."

If I didn't know it before this second, this is proof that Jack is exactly the guy I'm going to spend the rest of my life with.

Nineteen

A Surprise From Amelia

Present Day

Dallas, Texas

The pounding on my front door can only mean one thing. Amelia did indeed fly to Dallas last night and she's not waiting around to tell me whatever it is that needs saying.

I glance at my phone. 6 a.m. I was going to go down to the shop this morning, but after Lily warned me that Amelia was on her way here for some reason, I texted Alisha to let her know I would be back tomorrow. After the drama of whatever this is settles down.

"Emi! It's Amelia! Open this door!"

I pull the chain from the slot and crack the door open to her perfectly made up smiling face.

"Good morning," I say with a smile as she storms her way past me into an apartment she's never been in or even invited to. "*What* are you doing here?" I ask her, confused even though Lily warned me.

"I should ask the same."

"I *live* here, why should you ask the same?"

"Do you want to know about Jack, or not?"

"Did your plan not go as you thought it would?" I laugh, knowing there was a plan. There is always a plan.

She forces an unimpressed smile.

"If you're talking about Jack and Greta being pregnant then not really. I'm trying to forget it ever happened." I open one of my kitchen cabinets to brew a pot of coffee. "Tea?" I ask her, knowing she doesn't drink coffee.

"Emi, please sit down."

I give up the playing it cool act and hop up onto one of the bar stools facing the living room where she's still standing.

"Jack and Greta are *not* having a baby. They were *never* having a baby."

I stare across the counter at her speechless. But I heard them. And they are. Aren't they? A mix of emotions race through my chest. Giddiness, hopefulness, anxiousness, and something that feels a little bit like relief.

"But, even Aron was there? You're saying her own father was lying?"

"Yes, yes, it was a part of the so called plan," she uses air quotes around the word plan with a roll of her eyes.

"But you got anxious and disappeared before I could work out phase two."

"You were *playing* me?"

"Well, not in a cynical kind of way like you're making it sound, but sometimes you have to create a situation so that the right outcome will prevail. Especially, when your two players are so stubborn that they'll never figure it out on their own."

"And why would Greta lie to Jack about being pregnant? He was devastated."

"Because I told her to. Greta knew what she did to you two was wrong and she also knew that I could and *would* cut her out of my circle if she didn't make this right. She did more damage to your relationship than I ever could have imagined myself. And as you know I can be pretty devious. That girl is pure evil."

I nod. She's not wrong about that. "Where is pure evil at now?"

Amelia waves a hand my way as she strolls through my apartment. "She's on her way to a spa in Berlin with her father to discover herself." She laughs with a roll of her eyes. "I have a feeling she's going to be there for a while. Anyway, it's not important. She owed me a favor and she delivered. What matters now is that she's out of your life for good. Jack's as well."

"Amelia, you had her lie to your son about being pregnant. That's not a little thing. That's life altering."

"I'm well aware, and not only altering his life but yours as well."

I shake my head. "How's that?"

"Before the pregnancy announcement, you were considering your feelings for Jack? Yes?"

"OK," I'll give her that. It would make a good excuse as to why I suddenly slept with him without much thought.

"And when you heard she was expecting, what were your feelings then?"

I sigh heavily, "I was devastated, not only because she won but because he even slept with her after telling me they weren't that serious."

"Because you love him." Amelia says simply.

I stare at Amelia trying to figure out if she's right. "She's *really* not pregnant?"

Amelia shakes her head. "I'm not sure the two of them ever even slept together. She showed up at his apartment on a night that wasn't his finest and convinced him they had or took advantage of the situation, I don't have all the details there, nor do I want them. But I know Jack, and I'm not sure he could have or would have gone there with anyone but you."

"Does Jack know that she's not—"

"Of course he does, do you really think I could lie to my own son?"

"Yes... you did!" I laugh.

"Plans may not always go the way I'd like, Emi, but I would never *intentionally* hurt my children. By now you should know I think of you like my own daughter. And I know as well as anyone else that life can come with complications. Sometimes we have the strength to pull ourselves out of them and sometimes we don't. I've watched Jack fall down a hole that I didn't ever think he'd be able to pull himself out of. I wanted to help, but Lord knows he did not want my help. He thought he'd lost you forever. He had somehow convinced himself that giving you space was what you needed. I couldn't have forced him to chase after you for anything in the world."

"Actually, he's been trying to contact me for while..."

"He has?"

I nod, "He sent me an email last week, asking to talk."

"For Christ's sake, Emi." Amelia shakes her head.

"I just wish he told me all this in the email."

"If you had known you would have what? Taken him back on the spot?"

I shrug my shoulders. "Well, no..."

"Exactly, you weren't ready until now."

"And how do you know that?"

"At the wedding, I watched the two of you on the dance floor and I knew. I think everyone knew. Things would be a lot easier if the two of you weren't so damn stubborn, you know?" She sighs, pulling a pamphlet from her bag and sitting it on the counter next to me.

"Over the last year when Jack got overwhelmed he'd disappear to a place that he said reminded him so much of you that he could breathe again. He's there now, suffering in silence. Worried that he's lost you forever."

I open the pamphlet, inside is a single plane ticket to Cancun San Lucas. The number 233 is written on the envelope in black ink. My heart drops in my chest. It's the hotel where Lily got married. The same place we agreed would be the perfect place for a private wedding. He's even staying in the same room.

I laugh through an almost cry that's bubbled up in my chest.

"He's there. Trying to escape life and wishing you were right there by his side. When I told him what I did, which he was not happy about, he was ready to pack his bags and come straight here himself, but I've convinced him to let you be and work out your feelings. I hope you'll go there, and if nothing else, make your peace so you can both finally move on."

"You chasing me down is how you let me work out my feelings?" I ask as I stare down at the ticket. A lot has happened in the last week. Heck, a lot has happened in the last few months. I know I feel something for Jack but will all this other stuff get in the way? I pick up the ticket, emotions stirring in me even thinking about going back there to the place where things were simple.

"I would assume that since the two of you slept together yesterday, that you had already been in the process of working out your feelings…"

"How do you know about that?"

"When I called Jack to confess he told me that my interference wasn't necessary after all. He thought that the two of you were headed down a path that might lead you back together. He asked me to simply call, confess what I'd done and let the two of you work things out on your own."

I chew on my lip as I stare at Amelia, now looking slightly embarrassed.

"Why are you here then?" I ask.

"Because I was already on the plane when I learned of all this." She sighs as she sits on the bar stool next to me. "Robert and I have never had the kind of relationship that the movies portray. I sometimes regret falling into a routine that our normal is well... pacifying at best. You and Jack have that cinematic love that people root for, me included. Never did I see myself so wrapped up in my child's relationship that I would lie, manipulate, and fly half away across the country on a red-eye flight to convince you that you're made for one another. It's not up to me whether you two get back together." She takes my hand in hers with a shy smile. "I do hope you can forgive me for being too involved and just know that it's out of love. I just want to see my children happy. I had already bought the ticket so feel free to use it if you wish, but no pressure from me from this moment on."

I hop from the chair and wrap my arms around Amelia's neck, feeling her slowly slide her arms around my back. "Thank you." I cry.

I knew last night when I found the ridiculous law school towel that I was still in love with Jack. I don't know if I ever really wasn't. Amelia may have a strange way of doing things but it's a way that gets things done and despite the fact that her plan was unnecessary, it's only proved what I was afraid to admit to myself.

"What about this?" I motion to my apartment.

"I'm sure the building will still be standing when you get back, dear."

"That's not what I mean, I live here, I own a business here and Jack... doesn't. Isn't that only going to complicate things more?"

Amelia shakes her head in frustration. "Love prevails over all my dear, if you and Jack choose each other, you'll make something work so you're both happy. I have no doubt about that."

"Is he expecting me?"

"Of course he isn't. Right now, he's probably trying to figure out a new plan, one where he can get you back despite what happened. It's what he's been doing since you left."

I nod, a tear sliding down my cheek. "I'm gonna go." I say with a nervous laugh. "I knew I still loved Jack the second I saw him this week. I was just so afraid to admit it and every time I thought I was ready, something else would happen and I'd convince myself I was wrong."

Amelia grins, "I knew it."

I grab my still packed suitcase and pull it through my apartment and into my room. I can't bring dirty clothes with me. I toss in new clothes as quickly as possible.

"Let's bring this..." Amelia hands me the dress bag containing my lucky dress. "I don't think you'll need the extra luck but it certainly can't hurt."

"Right. I'll take all the luck I can get," I say. "When does the flight leave?"

"We're boarding in two hours."

"Wait, we? You're coming with me?"

"Don't worry, I'll wait in the wings, as they say in show business," she laughs. "The ticket is bought and paid for. I'll just be there for moral support, and on my best behaviour, I promise."

I'd be nervous about her being there when I tell Jack everything that needs to be said but I've pretty much had my entire life announced to anyone who wants to listen this week. One more time can't hurt, I suppose. I just hope nothing else goes wrong.

Twenty

The Meet-Cute

Five years, nine months ago.

Waterfront Park, Portland, Oregon

"Oh my God, I am so sorry."

Even though I have my hands over my face, I know his voice. Never in a million years did I picture actually meeting him at the exact moment I'm assaulted by a rogue Frisbee.

When I peer through my fingers he's kneeling in front of me, with ten other guys behind him, reaching for my hands.

"Let me see it," he says, wrapping his hands around mine. "Go get her some ice!" He yells at someone near him who doesn't waste time taking orders. "Is anything broken?"

When he pulls my hands from my face he lets out a little gasp. "Is it bad?" I ask him, worried about what he's seeing. Is my eyeball hanging from its socket? Is there a gaping wound? Is my brain (or lack of brain) visible?

He laughs. "Nah, you're going to have a black eye, but I think your skull is still intact. I'm really sorry."

"Oh." I wave my hand at him trying to play it cool. "It's no problem. It's actually why I came down here. I haven't had enough black eyes in my lifetime, and I was needing a memorable Fourth of July story to tell my grandkids one day."

"Well... I don't think you have a concussion. Your wit seems to be still intact." He laughs, sitting next to me, inspecting my face closely. "It didn't break the skin but it is starting to swell. I feel like a real ass."

"You should, you ruined my face." I try to joke through the pain.

"It's a very pretty face too." He smiles sympathetically. "I feel like maybe I know you from somewhere."

"You do, I'm the girl who makes great coffee."

He comes to my coffee window nearly every day. His passenger seat is always piled high with books, and every day he orders the same thing: an Americano with room for cream, with two sugars. I never talk to him, apart from taking his order. How can I? He's beautiful. Probably easily the most gorgeous guy I've ever not formally met. His handsome face melts my heart every time he smiles at me as I hand him his coffee.

"Right! You *are* the coffee girl. I thought I knew you. How weird is this?"

"Weird that I don't spend every waking moment at the coffee shop?"

"No." His friend returns with the ice. He gently raises it to my eye which is feeling puffier by the second. "Weird because I always want to talk to you but, you know... In the drive through, there isn't a lot of time for conversation."

"You *wanted* to talk to me?" I'm a little surprised by this because he's always so nonchalant at the drive through. Like he's avoiding chit-chat with random coffee gurus.

"Of course. You're gorgeous, and you do make a heck of a coffee." He pulls away the ice pack to see its progress. He grits his teeth and scrunches up his face, obviously not impressed with my slow healing during the past sixty seconds. "How about I make this up to you today?"

I glance over at my friends, who are all anxiously nodding their heads. They act as if I've never met a random gorgeous man before.

"I'm kind of not looking my best today. Are you sure you want to be seen with me?"

"It is gonna be risky, but I think I can take the challenge. My dad actually owns one of the yachts in the pier but I feel like that's too much considering I just injured you." Jack laughs nervously. "I know the perfect spot where you won't be visible enough to scare children or anything?"

I laugh to myself. It probably is exactly that bad.

"The fireworks look great from there too. And... we can double dip into the jazz show coming from the restaurant up the block."

"What about your friends?" I glance around with my one good eye at the group of guys standing around watching my pathetic attempt at pretending I'm not jumping for joy on the inside. Which I totally am.

"These guys don't mind. Right?"

They all mumble something at us before grabbing the Frisbee and going back to their game.

I sigh, trying desperately to force away the overly excited smile creeping up on me. "I'll go, but only on one condition."

"Anything."

"Tell me your name?"

"Right. God, I'm sorry. I'm Jack Cabot. And you are?"

"Emi Harrison."

"It's nice to meet you, Emi. Ready?" He stands, holding a hand out to me, that I waste no time accepting. He hesitates to pull his hand from mine once we've done the formal introduction handshake thing. "Let's go."

It's not exactly easy to follow someone through a crowd when you're holding an ice pack over one eye.

Especially when you're not exactly coordinated to begin with. Jack is holding my hand, and that alone has my heart racing. Even my brain feels as if it might be overheating. I just don't normally have luck like this, so my heart and head are having a hard time connecting the dots here.

"Here we are..." we're standing in front of a patch of grass that no one else has claimed for the evening just yet, in front of a popular restaurant. Other couples and families surround us on the grass planning to picnic, watch the fireworks, and listen to the show. Hyped up children yell as they play with each other everywhere you look. "What do you think?"

"I may still scare the children?" I point to my eye with a smile.

"I have the perfect plan, I'll be right back. Sit." Jack races up the sidewalk and into a small store.

As he disappears I pull a compact mirror and some concealer out of my bag.

"Oh!" I say to myself when I see my eye. That's pretty gruesome. I'm not sure I even have enough makeup to help even a little bit, but I'm gonna do my best, dabbing, and smearing, and dabbing a little more softly and I now have an eye that resembles more of a slight bruise than direct impact with a frisbee.

Jack reappears a short time later with a couple of paper bags in each hand.

"I've got everything, dinner, dessert, snacks and... these." He pulls out an oversized pair of sunglasses that only a Kardashian could pull off. "Although it's looking better already, we don't want to risk those around us having nightmares." He slides them on my face with a smile, tossing an impressed hand in the air. "See... didn't even notice it."

"Perfect," I smile. "You're quite the charmer, aren't you?"

"I have my moments. Luckily, you're making it easy for me."

"Do you come down here every year? You know, to hit girls with frisbees and set up romantic evenings under the stars?"

"Not *every* year. But I knew the moment I saw you sitting there that I had to meet you and my friends, well they were all up for help—" he stops mid-sentence, his eyes growing big.

"You set this up?" I ask with a small laugh.

"Not the way it went, no. All I asked was for someone to throw the frisbee near you, not through you. Again, I'm really sorry about that."

I shrug. "I guess it'll make a good story one day."

He nods, a shy grin on his face. "Let's see it?"

I lift the sunglasses.

"UGH..." he covers my face dramatically, then breaks out into a laugh. "I'm kidding. Still just as beautiful as before."

"Do you eat seafood?" He asks, as he pulls some boxes from the bags in front of him.

I shake my head. "Yuk."

"Allergic?"

"Nope, just hate it."

He smiles, "me too."

"Really? Most people look at me like I'm crazy when I say that."

"I totally get it, it's the fishy flavor and the texture, and don't even get me started on the whole raw fish sushi trend. Yuk!"

That's it, we're soulmates. We both spontaneously hate seafood and he can practically read my mind. I'm convinced he's the one.

"Tell me about you, I feel like I know nothing but your name and your coffee order."

"I'm a law student at Lewis & Clark, hence the passenger seat full of books all the time."

"Oh yeah, is that what you always wanted to do?"

"Um... My dad's a lawyer so it's always been on the back of my mind, yeah. How about you?"

I roll my eyes. "I'm about the most indecisive person on the planet. I'm in business school at PSU because I can't pick just one thing I want to do."

"You're good at the coffee thing."

"Yeah... maybe it'll somehow turn into a career?"

The darker the night gets the more romantic things become with the lights shining off the pier near us and the band playing in the restaurant behind us.

"I'm gonna go grab some wine and glasses from the boat... my mom practically has an entire wine cellar out there. And it'll seem a lot more romantic if we aren't drinking it out of dixie cups..."

I laugh with a nod.

I swear I've dreamed of this day. Not the details exactly, but the dream of being swept off my feet in a single evening by a man mesmerizingly perfect.

"Are you cold?" he asks after about thirty minutes of us sitting and talking about anything we can think of.

"A little." He drapes his jacket around my shoulders as he pulls me to my feet to watch the fireworks show.

"You know, when I was a kid, my mom forced me to take dance lessons."

"Is that right?"

"Yup, I'm pretty sure I could give Fred Astaire a run for his money," he laughs.

"You might have to prove that..." I say at the exact moment that *The Way You Look Tonight* plays from the restaurant behind us.

He slides an arm around my waist, holding my free hand in his and swaying to the music exactly like he's been taking lessons his whole life.

"Impressed yet?"

"I am, actually."

"I really am sorry about earlier. I mean I'm not at all sorry I got to meet you, and have dinner with you, but for, you know, injuring you."

I put the glasses on top of my head. "It feels a lot better, actually."

He runs a thumb just under my eye. "It looks better too. Just as beautiful as the non-injured one."

It's in that second that he surprises me by pressing his lips against mine, and basically stopping my heart, right there in the middle of a crowd of people as we dance like lunatics to a song playing around us.

Be still my heart...

Over the next hour, Jack and I learn everything one could learn about each other on three dates. He's got a sister, parents who adore him, a father who's made being a lawyer look so great that he's in law school, he's got a terrible frisbee aim, he's only ever had one somewhat serious relationship that lasted a year, and he believes in fate. He appears to be a truly good guy, which after dating the guys I've dated over the last couple years, I know is a rare find.

I also learn that I'm completely smitten with him even though we've only just officially met. If I believed in love at first sight, I might think that's what this is, but my luck just doesn't go that way normally. I love the way he raises his right eyebrow when I say something questionable or unladylike. When I tell him, hesitantly, that I've never been in a serious relationship, he seems relieved instead of scared.

"I'll drive you home," he volunteers as we pack up the picnic after the fireworks.

"It's clear across town; I don't mind calling a cab."

"I want to, Ems," he says.

He started calling me Ems about midway through dinner. Normally only the people closest to me use that name. It's another sign from fate that we are meant to be. "It'll give me a bit more time with you."

He takes my hand in his and leads me to a black SUV parked in the lot of the pier.

"I'd like that."

*

Even though I've just had the best, most unexpected date of my entire life, the car ride to my house is quiet and awkward. There isn't much left to talk about, and the sexual tension is far too much for me.

"It's the house on the right."

His eyebrow rises again when he looks over at me with a smile. "So, you have my number?"

"Yes." I'd pull it from my purse to prove it but I don't want to look like that obsessed girl. "You have mine?"

He nods. "And I'm not going to wait forty-eight hours either, so be prepared for that."

"I hope you don't." My words are playing cool and I hope my face is playing along, because my brain is struggling with me just getting out of the car and playing my last card at hard to get, or waiting for him to kiss me, or me just mauling him and doing him right here in the car in my driveway, which I promised myself I wouldn't do.

Luckily, I don't have to wait long and he kisses me. "I'm really glad I met you, officially," he says, as he pulls away a moment later.

"Me too."

"I'll wait until I know you got in safe."

"OK." I open the car door and slowly walk towards my front door and the porch light flips on as I'm halfway there. I glance back at Jack who is still watching me and give him a small wave.

"Where've you been?" Evan asks, the second I walk through the door.

"Out."

"Who drove you home?"

"My future husband, if you must know."

"Poor guy…" He rolls his eyes and walks away from me, unwilling to hear every detail of the best night of my entire life.

Twenty-one

The Clues

Present Day

Cancun, Mexico

A flight with Jack's mother is anything but normal. As if the entire situation wasn't awkward enough, now she's as nonchalant as I've ever seen her. Me on the other hand, I've never been as nervous as I am right now. I wasn't expecting a week away ending in me telling Jack I am still in love with him. I've written and rewritten a speech at least a dozen times and nothing seems to come out the way I want it to.

I have a headache and my emotions feel raw, which makes them hard to sort out because every memory I have sends me into a fit of tears. Which Amelia is more than annoyed by. She thinks I should just tell him I love him and let that be that but there is just so much more to say.

The plane lurches towards earth, slowing up for a landing at the airport below us. Even just from the plane, it looks exactly the way it did when I was here the first time.

"Now... my hotel is across the way..."

"You mean you're not staying *with* me, too?"

"It could be arranged, if need be..." she says in a motherly tone.

"No, no. I'm sure I'll be fine. I hope."

I have a dress bag thrown over my shoulder and my suitcase rolling behind me as I walk into the hotel I stayed at so long ago.

"May I help you?" A woman at the front desk smiles warmly.

"Yes, I'm looking for Jack Cabot, he should be staying here?"

The woman types as she scans the screen in front of her.

"And you are?"

"Emi Harrison? A friend of his, I need to—"

"He's here," she nods. "Staying in room 233." She slides a key card across the counter at me.

"You're giving me a key to his room?" I ask, remembering Amelia saying that he didn't know I was coming.

"Yes," She looks at the computer again. "It says here that he's expecting you?"

"Oh... right, I forgot. Of course, he's expecting me." Another moment where I've no doubt never ending finances have played well for Amelia and her *plans*. If I was any other woman, I think she'd have scared me off a long time ago.

"I hope you enjoy your stay," she smiles.

I nod, a nervous smile plastered on my face. I'm suddenly more than nervous. Obviously, I've had some time to consider what I want and what I want to say but the moment of panic over the whole pregnancy thing is still somewhere in the back of my head. I don't know that I'll totally believe it's not true until I hear it from Jack.

Stepping into the elevator is like finalizing the decision to tell Jack exactly how I feel. I feel like I'm in that episode of *Friends* where Rachel is waiting for Ross at the airport with flowers, only to see that she's too late and he's moved on without her and come home with a random woman. I just hope I'm not too late in telling him how I feel. Being stubborn never seems to pay off, when will I ever learn this?

The ding of the elevator reaching the right floor happens far too soon, thoughts are still swirling in my head and my heart, neither are quite ready to throw up the white flag of negotiation.

I slowly roll my suitcase down the hall towards room 233. I stop, facing the door, the key card in my hand.

"Maybe I should just knock? It's not like we're all of a sudden a couple with nothing to work out? I don't want to surprise him if he's not feeling what I might be feeling?" I mumble to myself.

"But then again, she did give me a key and said he was expecting me. For all I know he's staring at me through the peephole just waiting for me to let myself in."

I stand on my toes trying to peer into the lookout hole but obviously, seeing nothing.

I knock as I swipe the card, the door popping open.

"Hello?" I say in an almost whisper. "Jack?" I leave my bag in the front sitting room and walk through the suite, peeking in each room but not seeing Jack anywhere. Only his bag on the bed in the bedroom we stayed in.

A knock on the door makes me jump nearly out of my skin. Why am I so nervous?

"Jack?" I answer the door, but it's not him. A man in a suit and tie is standing outside the door holding an envelope with my name written across the front.

"This was left for you at the front desk, Miss Harrison."

I take the envelope from his hand, "Thank you." I say, acting as if I was expecting it and closing the door, tearing open the envelope.

Ems,

I know you're shocked to be here, and probably by whatever my mom has filled you in on. I don't blame you one bit. I never imagined how things would turn out for us, but I always hoped I'd be able to give you everything we wanted in life. I may have failed at that for a while, and I hope you'll forgive me.

Please, follow the clues I've left. I can't wait to see you.

Jack

"Follow the clues?" I say aloud, looking around the room for anything that stands out to me as a clue. "If I was Nancy Drew I'd have figured out the whole Greta thing a long time ago..."

"Miss Harrison?" Another knock at the door I didn't quite get closed behind me startles me yet again, causing me to drop the card in my hand.

"Yes?" I walk towards the door, almost afraid to find out who stands on the other side, but he's harmless, just another man dressed in a suit, holding a small bag and the garment bag that I must've left on the counter downstairs. "You left this downstairs."

"Thank you," I take the items from him nervously wondering what exactly all this is?

'*Open me first*, is written across a card pinned to the bag. I know that wasn't there when I got here. I pull the card off and set the dress bag on the table next to me.

You gave me the best five years of my life, then a year long nightmare I couldn't wake from each night.

You once revealed to me a secret as I slept on the beach. Wear this dress and the next clue will be within your reach.

"Sweet Mother of Moses." I unzip the bag, revealing my lucky blue dress. I knew it was in there but knowing that he wants me to wear it for whatever he is planning is making my heart do flip-flops in my chest.

Inside the bag are also the sparkly heels he bought me to go with the dress that I don't remember packing. I assume Amelia is behind it since she was in my apartment.

I wonder if I should have some kind of speech planned? And I would if I could have actually put down a few thoughtful sentences on the plane, without deciding they weren't at all right.

I pull the dress over my head, something poking me in the face as I do. Another note card marked *Clue Two* is pinned to the inside of the dress, invisible from the outside. Thank God it was just the corner of an envelope poking me and not a needle to the eye. That might have tainted the mood a little.

Tossing the envelope onto the counter I get dressed as fast as physically possible so I can tear it open and see what's next.

In loungers, we slept under the moon, because when I walked I tripped into the dunes.

In that spot, you will find clue number three.
Try not to fall, but if you do, fall for me?

Fall for him... The way my heart is suddenly galloping in my chest reminds me that I fell for Jack a long time ago and I've never truly gotten over him. I may be more than stubborn over the last few months but things are now starting to make sense. I make my way down to the lobby, and past the front desk with a wave. Pulling my shoes off when I reach the beach, so I can walk across to the loungers we laid in the night that I had to babysit Jack, during his first and only drinking binge that I witnessed.

I remember it like it was yesterday, and it makes my heart hurt the tiniest bit. Back then things were so innocent between us; there was no fighting, no supposed cheating, no crazy mean girls, no official wedding plans, and just the two of us in love. It was simple.

As I get closer I spot the flickering light of torches stuck in the sand ahead of me. If I wasn't afraid he might be watching from somewhere I'd run there.

But I need to keep my cool. Or at least try and not blurt out some offensive word in the middle of something that might be terribly romantic.

I'm now walking down a path in the sand created by the glowing torches, making the whole thing incredibly romantic. There are random people walking along the beach in the moonlight but it's not packed with people as it would be during the daytime. As I get towards the end I see another envelope sticking out of the sand.

Clue Three is written across the front. This must be the last clue because the torches block me from walking any further than this. I tear open the envelope.

Turn Around.

"Turn around?" I say, hesitantly looking past the flames in front of me. I turn as I hear someone shuffle behind me and see Jack standing just a few feet away. He's no longer looking distraught as he was just the other day. He is once again the gorgeous Jack I know.

"Jack..."

"Boy, am I glad to see you," he laughs nervously, as he makes his way towards me. "I was so worried you wouldn't show. But, you told me something once, a long time ago and I couldn't think of a better place to tell you what I need to say."

"That Greta isn't pregnant?"

He lets out a relieved sigh and nods his head. "I'm as relieved as you are about that. I didn't think it was true, but I guess when you're desperate you'll try anything. My mom shouldn't have gotten involved, but since she did, we're standing here, so she means well. She also didn't expect you to still have a mind of your own and throw her plans into the wind." He laughs.

"You don't have to do all this..." I say feeling a little guilty that he thinks the only way to fix things is to go over the top.

He takes a step forward and hesitantly takes my hand in is. "I do. There is something you don't know. I sent you an email just before you left for Portland asking if we could talk. I actually sent that email from just outside your coffee shop."

"What?"

He nods, "I was so nervous about seeing you during the wedding that I wanted to just get the whole thing over with before so I could relax. Your shop was busy and you were off to the side in an office, Lily was with you. You were discussing the email."

I look down at the ground, knowing exactly what he heard that day.

"You sounded happy as you told Lily that you were over me. You weren't a bit worried about seeing me and right then I assumed my chance was gone. I couldn't say what I came to say, so I left."

"Jack... what you heard wasn't exactly the truth."

"No?"

I shake my head, hoping the tears trying to force their way out will hold off for just a few more minutes.

"If I didn't say those things out loud, I could have never gotten on that plane to even go to the wedding. I needed to say it so that maybe somewhere, deep inside, I'd believe it. I used to actually repeat it over and over to myself whenever I was having a bad day. But the moment I saw you at Evan's, I knew it wasn't true. Then the whole Greta thing, my heart and my head have never had such a war as they did this week."

I force myself to breathe through the emotions inside me trying to take over. "I wish I'd known you were there."

He shakes his head, "It wasn't the right time. I should have never gone."

"What about now?" I ask, wondering if this is the right time?

"Now…" he nods his head. "I've loved you for almost six years and I'd like to add sixty more to that." He reaches into his inside jacket pocket, pulling out a tiny white box. "I knew the day I met you that my life would never be the same again. I knew when you spilled that beer on me the other day that I'd never gotten over you." He kneels on one knee, in the sand, taking my left hand into his. "I also know that every single person who loves you thinks we belong together, me included. And they wouldn't let me do this without being here to see your face when it finally happened." He nods behind him, a silly grin on his face.

When I look behind him, I can't help but laugh. His parents, our siblings, even Josh and Lily are all standing in the sand, not far from us, with looks of anticipation across each of their faces.

"Your mother is a little invasive…" I laugh, looking back to Jack.

"Yes, she is. We could always leave the country, but she'd still show up without warning." He laughs nervously.

"I want to marry you, Emi, right here, right now, just like you wanted to all those years ago if you'll still have me..." he opens the ring box displaying a ring that is NOT the one I recently saw sitting on Greta's finger.

"Holy shi-" I blurt it out before quickly covering my mouth with my free hand. I, of course, would have to curse at this exact moment.

"Em... If you say no..." The look on his face breaks my heart in a split second. "I will walk away and I promise I'll never look back. I just want you to be happy."

I wasn't exactly prepared for a proposal today, but the sudden fluttering in my chest is the same recent fluttering of my brain. I know exactly what my answer is.

"And if I say yes?" I ask, before biting my lip to hold back whatever my face is trying to do that might not match with the excitement I feel within.

"If you say yes," his voice cracks, "If you say yes, I promise that every day will be the best day of your life."

"Our lives," I correct him, watching the smile spread across his face.

"WELL??!!" Hannah yells from the sidelines. "IS THAT A YES? 'Cause we found a preacher!" she pulls a small suited up man from behind her, pointing down at him.

"Of course, she found a preacher..." I cry out. I pull Jack up off the ground, stand on my tiptoes and kiss his lips, the tears sliding down my cheek. "How is it even possible that this time was more perfect than the first?"

"Is that a yes?" He takes a step back, momentarily staring at me, his face as tense as I've ever seen it.

"Definitely, yes." I hold my left hand out, watching him sliding the ring onto my finger.

"Finally." A smile that reaches all the way to his eyes spreads across his gorgeous face. That's what was missing from him this last week: sincere happiness. He sighs a huge sigh of relief as he pulls me against him, kissing my forehead.

That's when it hits me. I pull away, worried.

"I can't get married in this dress…" I glance down, knowing that it's been so lucky thus far but him seeing the bride in the dress before the wedding is bad luck.

"Why not? I love it."

"I know you do, and that's why. You've seen me in this dress dozens of times and it's bad luck when the groom sees the dress before the wedding. I don't want to risk it. We don't need anymore bad luck."

He kisses my lips softly, wrapping his arms around me again.

"Well, it is your lucky dress, right? No crazy superstitions or bad luck. It was meant to be. You in your lucky dress and me in my lucky suit on our wedding day. Together, maybe it'll just equal a lucky life…"

A Note to Liam

Dear Liam,

You, my friend, have made many book boyfriend lists since I created you. I wrote you into this book as a much needed distraction for Emi, but you seem to have wooed your way right into the hearts of just about every person who's read the book (obviously, mine included).

I can't count how many emails I get requesting that I please, *please* write Liam's story. 'He needs a happy ending' they say. And... I agree. Your story is being written and I have the perfect woman for you. Get ready, 'cause I'm going to need your charm, romantic ways, and witty sense of humor at full capacity for this one.

Summer of 2019 is your year, Liam!
Aimee, your first love & your creator.

Acknowledgements

There are SO many people who deserve credit for helping in the creation of this book (twice!). It was first published with the title of *Little Gray Dress* and did so well that as a first time author I was a little (read that as a *lot*) shocked at its success. So many fabulous reviews (and a few bad ones...) were left by the most amazing book bloggers, readers, and complete strangers. I can't thank you enough for taking a chance on a new author the way all you fabulous readers did and helping promote my first book baby.

To my little family, Corey, Brentan, Hallie, and Rylen; they've had cereal for dinner more times than I can count as I've been busy writing, rewriting, marketing, and working tirelessly on these books. Well, that and the fact that I hate to cook... I can't thank you enough for supporting me through this. Once you've read the book and turned in your report, I'll hand out your prizes...

I'd also like to thank my extended family, including my parents, grandparents, siblings, aunts, uncles, cousins, nieces, nephews, friends from high school, ex co-workers, and people I've met while we moved around the country. You guys have been *so* supportive and *so* excited for my journey. I'm so thankful you were put on my path in life and love having you on my journey.

Whether I saw you yesterday or twenty years ago, it means so much to me to have your support as I release pieces of my heart for the whole world to judge. Even if you don't love what I write, you've been supportive and I thank you *SO* much for that. My agent, Sarah Hershman, and her entire team, took a chance on a debut author and has done wonderful things for me. Not only is she always on my side, but she knows everything I don't and truly has my best interest at heart. Without her I don't think I'd be where I am now. Thank you, Sarah, from the bottom of my heart. I'm overjoyed that you are on this journey with me.

Aria Fiction, my publisher, and more specifically, Melanie Price, my editor, has had the excitement about my writing that I didn't even know was possible by anyone but myself. She's helped make this book 100 per cent more than it previously was and at times has literally read my mind. I seriously can't thank you enough for being the publisher I've never had, but dreamed of. We make an amazing team. Thank you to everyone at Aria Fiction & Head of Zeus that have helped make this book what it is today. I'm *so* excited to be working with you all.

The following people have been there for me through this process and at times listened to me when I just needed someone to hear me. They've cheered me on, given advice, overlooked my nonstop cursing, and have been the best support team a person could ask for. I am SO glad that the interwebs exist and that despite the ocean between some of us, that we're able to connect whenever we need a friend, an ear, a laugh, or even advice. Thank you, Brook McCoy, Kate Armitage, Sheryl Babin, Sarah Smith, Meredith Schorr, Cat Lavoie, Joy Norstrom, and Joanne Mallory. You guys are amazing friends! Most of these ladies have their own fabulous books out that you should all really go buy and read.

A Note From The Author

Thank you so much for reading this book! I honestly hope you loved reading it as much as I loved writing it.

If you enjoyed this book, I'd like to ask you to please leave a review on Amazon. Amazon book reviews are almost as important as book sales themselves. Reviews are SO important to authors and how Amazon decides if our books make the bestseller lists or not. Each review helps Amazon show my book to other potential readers and helps rank me up the charts. And well, selling this book is how I pay my bills, feed my kids, and all the fun things that being an adult requires. Thank you so much for reviewing the book for me! I appreciate it more than words could say.

Want to say hello? I'd love that! I'm all over social media (my phone and I are in an intimate relationship at this point...) and would love to hear from you! Follow, friend, or subscribe to keep in touch and not miss a single update from me about events, giveaways, and upcoming publications. You can find me at the links below.

HELLO FROM ARIA

We hope you enjoyed this book! Let us know, we'd love to hear from you.

We are Aria, a dynamic digital-first fiction imprint from award-winning independent publishers Head of Zeus. At heart, we're avid readers committed to publishing exactly the kind of books we love to read — from romance and sagas to crime, thrillers and historical adventures. Visit us online and discover a community of like-minded fiction fans!

We're also on the look out for tomorrow's superstar authors. So, if you're a budding writer looking for a publisher, we'd love to hear from you. You can submit your book online at ariafiction.com/we-want-read-your-book

You can find us at:
Email: aria@headofzeus.com
Website: www.ariafiction.com
Submissions: www.ariafiction.com/we-want-read-your-book
Facebook: @ariafiction
Twitter: @Aria_Fiction
Instagram: @ariafiction

Printed by Amazon Italia Logistica S.r.l.
Torrazza Piemonte (TO), Italy